# GROUNDS *for* RETURN

## A YADKIN VALLEY NOVEL

MELISSA COLLINS HARRELL

 FriesenPress

One Printers Way
Altona, MB R0G 0B0
Canada

www.friesenpress.com

ISBN
978-1-03-832044-5 (Hardcover)
978-1-03-832043-8 (Paperback)
978-1-03-832045-2 (eBook)

*1. FICTION, FRIENDSHIP*

Distributed to the trade by The Ingram Book Company

# GROUNDS *for* RETURN

## A YADKIN VALLEY NOVEL

"But why had he always felt so strongly the magnetic pull of home, why had he thought so much about it and remembered it with such blazing accuracy, if it did not matter, and if this little town, and the immortal hills around it, was not the only home he had on earth? He did not know. All that he knew was that the years flow by like water, and that one day men come home again."

—Thomas Wolfe, *You Can't Go Home Again*

# DEDICATION

This book is dedicated to all military, first responders, and their families. We honor with heartfelt thanks the gifts of freedom, safety, and compassion that you so willingly bestow on others. Your service is the invisible backbone of our communities, and the necessity of these critical services would only be truly recognized if suddenly they ceased to exist.

Dear Reader,

As I began to work on this novel, I came to realize that winemaking is a beautiful analogy for life. Much like the harvested grapes, our lives go through a variety of seasons along with multiple cycles of clarifications and refinements that mold and shape us. Some seasons we have a great harvest with triumph and joy, while other years, disasters threaten to take our entire crop. At times, the pressing can be unbearable, but if we hold tight, the end product, while often much different than expected, may be more than we ever anticipated. In the end, life gives us two choices: we can harbor sour grapes over loss and disappointments, or we can take the grapes we're given and create our own unique signature blend. So grab your favorite wine or sparkling grape juice and get ready to go on a journey to Chatham!

Cheers to many hours of happy reading!
Melissa

# Table of Contents

# Prologue

May 1965

The nurse wraps the pink, wrinkly newborn in a blanket and places the baby in the exhausted mother's arms. The indescribable pain and temporary feelings of violation are still fresh, and from the sound of things, she's not alone. The baby lets out a high-pitched scream to announce the displeasure of the recent eviction from the safe cocoon into a strange world of chaos.

Her eyes are heavy, but the weary mom knows she has very little time. Her lips kiss the smooth head as the baby's fuzzy hair tickles her nose. Her finger traces each line on the warm face as she attempts to memorize every tiny detail of her baby. Her finger stops short as the child grabs her pinky, almost as if to say, "Hello, Mommy, I am here." Her eyes lock with her child, and she feels a rush of joy that she has never known.

A knock at the door abruptly interrupts this silent conversation. Ms. Dodds, the hospital social worker, enters the room. Glancing back at her baby, a sense of panic sets in, and she knows that she needs to undo this situation. The young mother opens her mouth to speak, but no sound comes. She wants to say, *"You can go. I'm keeping my baby.*" Resigning herself to the fact that she has no choice, she reaches down and her lips find that warm, soft space for one final kiss. Her silent tears flow like a steady rain that washes over her babe with a baptism of love. Reluctantly she transfers the tiny infant to Ms. Dodds and watches her baby exit not only the room, but her life.

The distraught mother looks through tears that have now shifted from love to anger at her own mother. She knows that for the rest of her life, a piece of her heart will be lost. A piece that even now, at the tender age of 16, she knows can never be replaced by a husband, career, or more children. She fears that she is permanently damaged. How can she not be when a piece of her heart will always be away from her? Exhaustion takes over, and as her body surrenders to sleep, she soothes herself with a promise. Whatever it takes, one day she will find her child and they will be together again, even for just a moment.

# THE HARVEST

September, 2009

# Chapter One: Michelle

I mages of green, rolling hills whiz by Michelle Richardson like flickers on a movie screen. If she could project her thoughts through her Bluetooth, it would say: DETECTING ERROR, WRONG WAY, MAKE A U TURN IF POSSIBLE. Her brain GPS was correct. This was most definitely not the route she intended. Instead of these winding country roads speckled with cows and pastoral scenery leading her to a new life in Germany, she was rewinding her way back in time to her hometown of Chatham, North Carolina. She shook her head in disbelief. *I can't believe I'm actually doing this.*

When she boarded her first flight from Germany, she just pretended she was on another work assignment. Yes, just a few short months back in North Carolina and then on to the next chapters in her life. However, this mind game didn't work for long. As her plane landed in Raleigh, reality set in, and she was hit with a barrage of emotions. Sure, she'd been home to visit over the last 20 years, but actually living here day in and day out left her with a mixture of fear and dread. Yet every mile west she drove, like a magnet, she felt the pull of home. This pull led to a shift from dread to anticipation of seeing those she loved. What kept her from Chatham was most definitely not the people here. She was blessed with a wonderful family and had more than a pocket full of happy childhood memories. Crossing the county line, she notices a new and rather large sign that proudly boasts: "Welcome to Chatham." There's no turning back now.

The quirky yet charming town of Chatham is nestled in the foothills of western North Carolina. These foothills serve as the gateway to the Blue Ridge Mountains. Every fall, the Blue Ridge Parkway, which runs well over 400 miles through 29 Virginia and North Carolina counties, hosts millions in search of nature's latest masterpiece. These wide-eyed leaf gazers drive about with their heads hung out windows like hound dogs as they "oooh" and "ahhh" at the vibrant display of colors that can only be produced in nature. Today these infinite winding roads lead to vast stretches of mostly family-owned farmland turned into vineyards. The Yadkin Valley is home to some of North Carolina's most beautiful vineyards and skilled winemakers.

Chatham is the place where every crop you can think of has its own festival and queen. The bright fall leaves bring the Pumpkin Festival, and as the spring blossoms emerge on the dogwood trees, you know the Strawberry Festival is near. It doesn't matter that each festival hosts the same itinerary: the church-lady crafts booths, costumed characters making balloon animals, funnel cakes, and more items dipped in chocolate than can ever be imagined. These festivals, while traditions for locals, help create much of the allure that now draws so many tourists.

Like many other small Southern towns, this town is steeped in sweet tea and strong faith roots. While religion continues to be an integral part of the community, as a child, church wove its way into every part of the fabric of life. Here you will find a denomination for everyone and a church on every corner. Michelle recalls when, as a child, summers brought extra opportunities for worship by way of tent revivals. Large tents popped up in random fields, and hours of singing and preaching were meant to bring the lost sheep back into the fold. Ironically, these seemed to be held on sweltering July nights, possibly a strategic move to remind people that hell would indeed be hot. Many preachers were astounded at the moving of the Holy Spirit as one by one sinners ran to the altar to be baptized—likely not so much to "be saved" by Jesus for fear of burning in hell, but everyone knew that the quicker you repented, the faster the preacher would let you go home.

As twilight set in, the sweet voices of children could be heard counting backwards from ten and then the scurrying of feet as hours of hide and seek began. Each kid raced with confidence to the one spot they believed no one would ever think to look for them. They would peer out from their victorious hiding spot, breathing as quietly as possible and hoping the iridescent glow from lightning bugs wouldn't give up their secret location.

Back in those less hectic days, porches weren't for curbside appeal but for sitting and sharing the latest family and community news. Front porches were where you learned who was getting married, who was sick, how someone was your distant cousin, and where everyone pondered whatever in the world ever happened to Old Man Pete. To this day, no one knows, but many theories were speculated on the front porch about Old Man Pete. While chatting about these events and the weather, parents would take turns hand-cranking homemade ice cream while drinking glasses of fresh-squeezed lemonade. Although this is the wine country now, alcohol was frowned on and most areas around were dry counties. However, Michelle still wonders if there was a bit of adult liquid added to that lemonade. No judgment here. Who can blame them? This adulting is hard for sure, and she didn't even have the stress of raising children yet.

Even with all its quirks and at times backwoods ways, Michelle loved this place, and up until the summer of 1989, she never dreamed she would live anywhere else. She tried to recall how she felt at 18 before her entire world fell apart. She was sure that she once felt excitement and anticipation for what adventure lay ahead. Like many of her friends, as she prepared to graduate from high school, she had dreams of starting a career and then building a life in Chatham. Her imaginary vision board had always included raising kids near family and, of course, Allie, her best friend. She and Allie were more like sisters than friends. Their moms used to joke that they shared joint custody of each girl because they were always together. Their houses were within walking distance, and they attended the same school and church. One would think that this much closeness would eventually lead to disagreements, but she couldn't think of one harsh word that had ever been shared between the two. They passed their summer days playing outside until the last light of day. On holidays, they somehow managed to rope all the neighborhood kids into their parades and front-porch shows. Legend holds that there was some bribery involved; thankfully their moms kept the freezer stocked with popsicles and rarely took inventory. Michelle started dating Benjamin first, and then it wasn't long before Allie met Dave. The two couples became inseparable, lulling them into a belief that their late-night preteen chats of raising families together could really become a reality.

In a modern-day world of online dating and global abilities, some people may find it hard to believe that you can find and know such deep love so young. But even at 38, Michelle has never experienced those feelings since her days here—a secret she keeps tightly tucked in her heart, especially from her current love. Now here she is, twenty years later, coming back to the place she had loved so dearly and never dreamed she would leave.

From her years in the US Air Force, watching people come and go, she noted that there seemed to be two things that drew people back home after moving away. For some, it was a deep desire to return to their roots, while others returned because of circumstances beyond their control. Today, Michelle fell into the second group. Her sister, Katie, would never want to inconvenience anyone, even her annoying little sister. Rounds of chemo and radiation had ravaged her sister's body, leaving her with aplastic anemia. She was now transfusion-dependent and had reached a point where a stem cell transplant was her only hope. Since siblings are the most likely match, Michelle had been tested in Germany, but sadly she was not a match.

On their last video chat, Michelle's heart had been pierced by Katie's sudden decline in health. From behind her exhausted eyes and pale face, Katie's heart seemed to whisper the words that she would never say to her sister: "I need you." In addition to raising three kids, Katie and her mom were partners in running The Dogwood Inn and Bakery. With the expansion of tourism in Chatham and the popularity of Airbnb apps, their business had exploded over the last five years. As summer ended, the tourism wave would head from the beaches of Eastern North Carolina westward. From late September through December, the inn would be booked up and the bakery running full blast. The aroma of batches of apple and pumpkin pies would permeate in fall, followed by an array of holiday cookies and cakes that would rival the North Pole.

Michelle is an expert in tasting these delicious family recipes, but she's absolutely clueless about this business. Nevertheless, she has a feeling that she's about to trade in her rifle and combat boots for an apron and a spatula. Yes, this is definitely going to be interesting, since her idea of homemade is serving the takeout order on the fine china. Baking? Please, she left that to the professionals in Europe.

Yet none of that matters because in a crisis, especially in the South, families rally around each other. Grudges go on hold and temporary truces are declared, and that includes your entire community of neighbors. This was one of the things that she had missed so much about Chatham and the small-town life. While big cities offered her fine dining and entertainment, she often longed for the deep connections she had growing up. It was one of the parts that made her feel so much guilt for leaving. She knew she would have the support of so many to heal if she remained here. In the end, she just couldn't stay. Cities had offered her an escape and refuge and allowed her to spend the last twenty years avoiding this place. Michelle knew that for her family, moving back home was the right thing to do, even though it meant putting the next phase of her life on hold. At this juncture, her desires had to take a back seat to the needs of her family.

Hopefully soon a donor match would be found. It seemed that everyone in town was getting tested. And thanks to Barbie Jo Settle, the local queen of social media, there was surely no one across the globe who didn't know that Katie Mercer needed a bone marrow transplant. Once she got the inn and bakery through the seasonal rush and Katie was stronger, she could move on to the next chapter of her life in Germany with Alex.

Germany had captured her heart on her first deployment there years ago. When the chance to return had surfaced, she jumped at it. The history and beauty drew her back, as did the proximity to so many other European towns. She could travel to France, Belgium, Switzerland, and Italy on a whim. She had met Alexander while on her second tour in Germany. He worked as a contractor in IT, and with her work in meteorology, their paths often crossed. She'd been a bit hesitant at first, given that he was recently divorced and came with a 15-year-old son. His persistence paid off, and they had now been dating for a little over three years. It had taken her years of therapy to build up the nerve to even imagine building a life forever again with one person, and she was not going to screw up this chance to plant some roots and finally have a family. At 38, her biological clock was far from ticking, but it was blinking down the last ten seconds to destruction.

Leo is now 18 and off taking a gap year backpacking Europe before starting his art studies at the university. He's quite the opposite of his father and takes after his mother. Michelle secretly blames Leo for her growing desire for children. Moving in, she had feared the dreaded teenage "monster," as they're described, but that wasn't what she found at all. Leo had such a kind and gentle spirit, and in addition to some spirited Mario Kart matches, they shared some deep intellectual conversations. She and Alex talked often about getting married, and lately she has a feeling that he might pop the question any day.

*Oh crap,* she thinks, *I totally spaced and forgot to call Alex when I landed.* She glances at her phone and sees six unread messages. *Great, this long-distance thing is off to a stellar start!* She picks up the phone to call, but the glowing orange light on the dash grabs her attention and takes priority. He'll just have to wait, as she needs to scoot in for gas or she'll be walking the rest of the way.

She misses her Honda; this new, fancy rental car is definitely not for her. She likes her cars well broken in and without all the bells and whistles. It's late August and hot enough to scorch a lizard, as her mama would say. She spent the first half of her trip with the windows rolled down, since it had taken her over 100 miles to figure out how to work the new-fangled air conditioner. While it might be hot here, these westerners don't experience heat like eastern NC. During her time stationed at Seymour Johnson AFB in Goldsboro, NC, she was pretty sure that those training grounds were literally built on top of the gates of hell.

Some days she felt they might as well be in the desert. Of course, without fail she often had to hear her first sergeant say, "Richardson, you know it's not the heat down here that makes it so hot."

"Yes sir, I know, it's the humidity."

"That's right, we need an assignment to Vegas so we can get us some of that dry heat."

She didn't care if it was the heat or the humidity—it was brutal, especially in full basic duty uniform.

She slows down and makes her way to the gas pump. Great, now to spend ten minutes looking for the hidden gas lever.

Even though her trips home had been few, every time she half expected it to be just as she'd left it in 1989. It was so chaotic after the accident. Everything happened so fast, she just felt that time should have frozen, like hitting pause on a movie, and when she returned, she could just pick up where she'd left off. Sadly, that's not how life works. Buildings and the people she loved had aged, including herself. She would have never admitted it then, but at 18 when she left Chatham, she was still very much a young girl. She looks in the mirror while adjusting her ponytail and acknowledging her crow's feet, noting that a hair color appointment will be one of her first calls.

One thing is right where she left it—the old Hendrick's store. Still in the same place, right next to the old Benham School, but she could certainly say it was no longer stuck in the 1980s. By the looks of it, it had been bought out by a large convenience store chain. They had updated the country store appearance by replacing the rustic wood with industrial siding. Honestly, it looks like a bad facelift. Some things should just be left to age gracefully. She fears that as the world attempts to modernize the hillbillies, much of what made Chatham will be lost forever.

She never considered herself a hillbilly until she was branded that nickname in basic training. While in basic training, a southern accent combined with growing up in the hills of NC earns you that term of endearment. Still, it's better than some names awarded to her other comrades. Since WWII, it's been common practice to give pilots a call sign, but that tradition became common practice for many branches. A career in the military—yet another thing Michelle could have never predicted in her life. She had skillfully avoided eye contact with every local recruiter during career day and evaded every follow up phone call. She wished she could erase the event that sent her to the air force, but since it couldn't be undone, it had turned out to offer her some incredible opportunities. A fresh start, discipline, and drive had been just what she needed to awaken her inner strength and confidence that she'd feared would never return.

After basic training, she'd headed to Keesler Air Force Base in Mississippi to train as a weather tech. In her eight months there, she learned the basics of weather forecasting and meteorology. Following her time there, she was assigned to the 4th operations weather squadron as a weather apprentice. She spent two years there working with her fellow airmen to ensure that pilots, command, and support crew had the most precise forecasts. After a brief return to Keesler AFB for the weather observer course, she had been assigned to the 21st Operational Weather Squadron at Kapaun Air Station in Germany. Yes, this career had been a much different path than she'd envisioned, but it had exposed her to many new experiences. She was grateful for all her experiences and that it had led her to Alex and Germany—a place that she had grown to love as much as home.

Her eyes register the sliding glass doors as they gently glide open, but her ears still hear the hinges of a creaky country door opening. The memory of that sound sets off a memory sequence like a chain of dominoes. Anytime her dad grabbed his keys to head to the store, Katie and Michelle would be like two bird dogs off for the hunt. When he'd arrive at his truck, he'd be met by two precocious daughters begging with their best little puppy faces to take them with him to the store. It would always start the same: "Not today; maybe next time." But eventually it would end with "All right, hop in the truck." Once they had successfully secured their spots, Katie and Michelle would smile at each other with intense sister satisfaction. War could resume later, but the temporary truce was worth the sweet promise of ice cream or a candy bar.

One of the gifts of childhood was completely living in the moment and believing that life would always be happy and good. Nana Lucy used to warn her of this growing up. "Michelle, don't wish your life away. Just you wait, time speeds up every year you live. One day you wake up and see an old lady staring back at you, and you wonder where your life went." But when you're young, time seems to be something to speed up to get to the good stuff. It felt that time was this villain making you slowly wait for all the good things in life. She wished that she had taken Nana Lucy's advice to heart, to truly savor each moment, because she had no idea that those days were days she would long for as an adult.

As she approaches the counter to pay, she's temporarily blinded by the "LOTTERY TICKETS SOLD HERE" sign flashing behind the clerk's head. She pauses and chuckles to herself. Oh, the prayers that must be lifted up by the Ladies World Prayer group for the sinful gamblers who buy these tickets. She could only imagine what Cathy Hedge had to say about this.

Cathy Hedge had taught third grade at the local elementary school for what seemed like 100 years. Either the water in Chatham is from the fountain of youth or she's preserved by the gallons of Rose Milk lotion. Whatever the case, she never seemed to age. In addition to being a dedicated teacher, she was and still is a cornerstone of Calvary Baptist Church. She had made it her personal charge to shepherd every single child in Chatham to their salvation—that is, with the exception of Declan Carlyle, who could never sit still long enough to get through the sinner's prayer of confession. Today he would likely be diagnosed with ADHD, but back then his only diagnosis was a severe case of ants in his pants, which many parents felt could be remedied with a good swatting of his behind with a fly flapper. Of course, only to kill the ants.

Michelle can just imagine all the ladies circling around and holding hands in Cathy Hedge's parlor: "Lord, we just pray for those who struggle with gambling. Release them from their bondage and bring them back to the fold." She also speculates that after prayer, there are more "prayerful conversations" about who had seen who buying tickets the day before, and how next time they will pray specifically for them by name. She silently snickers as she wonders how many in that parlor have snuck across county lines to secretly buy a few tickets of their own. Without a doubt, if they're ever caught, they'll profess that the winnings will be used to do the Lord's work.

As her car slowly rolls towards the railroad tracks, Michelle, out of instinct, reaches down to turn the radio off and cracks her window. Her dad, Steve Richardson, had been with the fire department and responded to almost every crash here since way before she was born. She had been drilled in safety habits from a young age and can still hear her dad now: "Young lady, watch your speed. An accident is just around every corner. Half of accidents occur just a few miles from your own home. You see all those crosses along the road? They are a trail to follow to the local church all right … straight to the cemetery!" He sure doesn't need to know that she coasted into town on fumes and had broken the never-go-below-a-quarter-of-a-tank rule. She feels an involuntary smile spread on her face. No matter how old she gets or the miles that separate them, she's a Daddy's girl and is ready to see him.

She had missed her friends and other family, but leaving him had been one of the toughest. She had always known that any man in her life would have to measure up to him. His calming presence helped soothe her on many occasions. Between her and Katie, the Richardson girls had their fair share of stitches and casts in their day, but her dad always seemed to make it all okay. She knows that underneath that calm exterior, her dad carries tough memories from some of the more difficult calls he responded to.

She also knows that even though he will never admit it, he carries a huge scar from that summer of 1989. Truth be told, so does the whole town.

# Chapter Two: Drew

Like clockwork, Drew Jones rolls up to the doors of Calvary Baptist Church at 10:59 a.m. and gently slides into the pew by his Grandma Rose. She gives him a disapproving look followed by a smile. Try as she might, she can't stay mad with that boy. Drew holds a special place in her heart, and he knows it. Every Sunday, just like he promised her, he attends church with her. Even years after the death of his papa, he still doesn't feel entitled to sit in his spot on the pew.

Silas Johnson had been one of the most respected men in this community. If ever there was a man who lived what he believed, it was Silas. Drew knows that with his tumultuous past, he will never be that man, but these days he's trying to be at least a fraction of that man. Working through his twelve-step program has helped to quieten his self-pity and awaken a side of him he thought was beyond resurrection.

He does believe in a higher power, but his spirituality is very different from that of his grandparents. Organized religion is not the place where he's working out his goodness. He may have believed all this when he was a child, but he has seen enough evil in this world to have very little faith these days. He doesn't understand how in these teachings, a God could sit back and watch children be beaten, innocent lives cut short, or medics have to make the decision to save one life over another. Even with this jaded view, he still considers himself a spiritual man. Over the last few years, he's found other ways to connect with God, and most of that occurred outside while he worked or stood in a stream fishing.

It would break his grandma's heart and send her straight to Jesus if she knew how he truly felt. He hopes to never cause her pain or disappoint her again. She didn't deserve all the hell she had suffered, and he still carries some guilt for the part he played. She doesn't need to know that he's just going through the motions to please her. So he bows his head and prays, says "Amen" when it seems appropriate, and drops money in the offering plate.

Thelma Smith holds the last chords on the organ and makes her way over to the piano. God must give church workers exceptional immune systems, because as far back as Drew can remember, she's been here every Sunday to play. She's such a fixture of the church that when he was a young child, he assumed that she lived at the church. He imagined that she must live in a room off in some secret, unexplored corner of the church building. He presumed that she would pass the time in her room reading the Bible and cross stitching until it was time for her to work. One day he walked into the Northwestern Bank and Savings with his mother, and there was Thelma Smith, with her perfectly pinned-up hair, working behind the teller stand. That was the day he had two revelations: one, Thelma Smith didn't actually live at the church, and two, church pianists need day jobs.

Mark Terry rises and buttons his navy-blue suit jacket. "Please stand and turn to hymn number 87, 'Amazing Grace.'" Even though Mark has been the pastor here for almost ten years, it's hard for Drew not to imagine him in his football pads and getting ready to give him the beating of a lifetime at practice. Drew was a scrawny freshman, and Mark a bulked-up senior. No matter the bruises, Drew loved every moment of the challenge. Football was one of the only healthy ways he got his rage out back then. Few in Mark's class were shocked to see him go off to Campbell University and become a pastor. He really was a good kid. He didn't drink, smoke, or cuss, and he was always running all the community projects.

Drew looks over and sees Mark's wife, Elizabeth, trying to quietly wrestle their two wild boys. Now marrying Elizabeth Bedford—that was a shock. She was the complete opposite of a pastor's wife in high school. A true ditsy blonde and boy crazy didn't even begin to describe her. Drew remembers a few instances of fending her off at parties, where she was three sheets in the wind. But, like most, she outgrew her wild streak and now owns Cuticles and Curls, a very successful hair salon in town.

As the hymn winds down, she looks over at Drew with a sense of exasperation. Drew considers helping her out by grabbing some rope from his truck to hog tie those boys, but he decides that a smile of encouragement will probably be best. He feels a little twinge that he has felt more often recently, and he knows it has to do with kids. He went back and forth in his mind on the kid thing. Part of him wanted the legacy and joys, but he also wasn't sure he was cut out for the daily grind and hassles like he just witnessed. No need to fret over that when he not only didn't have a steady girl but not even a prospect in sight. He and Suzanne had been over for years. She grew tired of his inability to commit to a future, so she moved on and is now married with kids of her own.

Drew could recite the history of this church probably quicker than he could the Pledge of Allegiance. His gaze shifts from the boys down to the pine hardwood floors. The floors date back to 1896, but the church membership dates back to the early 1800s. After moving in with his grandparents in middle school, he spent many hours following Papa Silas all over this church and helping him make repairs. These handyman skills that he learned at his papa's side have served him well. He rubs his hands together, noting each callus and scar. Some people are made to learn inside a building, but he needs to learn with his hands. Another reason he doesn't mind sitting here for an hour each Sunday is that he feels closest to his papa here. He remembers them climbing the wobbly ladder to change light bulbs, and sweating on hands and knees waxing the floors, but the best part is remembering his voice. Though he was a tough farmer, he had a gentle voice and spirit, which was a shocking contrast to Drew's father. There was nothing gentle about Papa Silas' former son-in-law—maybe even nothing human about him.

Grandma Rose taps Drew on the leg and discreetly hands him a small candy encased in yellow cellophane. Apparently, his engagement with his memories was more noticeable than he thought. Drew reaches into his coat pocket and deposits the butterscotch candy in with the rest of his collection. He never cared for them, but he knows he can unload them quickly onto some of the kids after church.

"Please be seated," Mark says as he takes a sip of water and opens his Bible. Drew wonders what topic he will dwell on today: love, forgiveness, service, or maybe it's time for the yearly reminder on tithing. He glances at the bulletin. The title of the sermon: "So you want to follow Jesus?" *No offense, Mark. I'm going to zone this one out.* Drew begins to calculate some numbers in his head and make a running to-do list once he gets to the Taproom. He isn't looking forward to facing the latest pile of past due bills. One thing he has in common with his late grandfather is that his paycheck is ultimately signed by Mother Nature. With several fires and above normal rains, there have been a few rough years. But last year produced a stellar crop of grapes, and he thinks that the holiday sales will put him back in the black. Times like these he longs to talk with his papa because he lived through the ups and downs of farm life.

In the 1970s and 80s, two things powered the town of Chatham: farming and textiles. Most had a relative employed at Chatham Manufacturing, the local textile mill, or who grew tobacco. It was a different era, when although it was becoming controversial, smoking was still an accepted part of everyday life. Emptying ashtrays and replenishing cigarettes into fancy holders was as much a part of a child's chore as making their bed. The soil and climate in this area, along with its high market value, made tobacco a staple for many farmers. The demand for blankets, pillows, and other textile products was so high that Chatham Manufacturing ran three shifts every day of the year except for religious holidays and the week of July 4th. Tobacco and textiles allowed many to make a good living with nothing more than a high school diploma. Unlike today, years ago it was hard to find someone who wasn't born here, and transplants were extremely rare. One quick way to see if someone is a true local is to ask, "Did your parents prime tobacco in the 110-degree heat when they were growing up?" If they say no or, worse yet, have no idea what you're talking about, they're definitely not from around here.

Dark days came to Chatham with hits to both the tobacco and textile industry. Rounds and rounds of layoffs came as the textile jobs began to be outsourced for cheaper labor overseas. Then with tobacco buyout programs, farmers were challenged to find new crops to grow or get out of the business altogether. In a once thriving economy, many people for the first time had nowhere to turn for jobs. A few programs were offered for the unemployed to go to school and train in a new skill, but the jobs for these skills came with a long commute or required you to move. These were tough times for Papa Silas, but he always managed to find a way to make it through. Drew glances up in hopes that some of luck will come his way. He knows if Papa were here, he'd tell him that there's no such thing as luck. You have to work hard and then put your faith in God

Thelma makes her way back to the piano and begins to peck out "Just as I Am." Within the first few lines, one by one people make their way down to Pastor Mark for prayers of comfort or absolution of this week's sins. Drew watches as Mary and Charlie Long make their way up to Mark. Grandma Rose leans in to whisper, "Just breaks my heart for them." She's referring to the recent death of their daughter Samantha from a drug overdose. She had finally managed to get away from her loser boyfriend, Mike Jones, and it looked like she was on a good path to recovery. She'd only been out of rehab for a few weeks when her eight-year-old daughter found her lifeless body when she arrived home from school. Mary and Charlie have had no time to grieve, because they're now the parents of Samantha's two girls.

Addiction is a demon that impacts more than the addict, and Drew knows that better than anyone. It's a battle that at times addicts themselves don't understand. It never ends; you have to get up and fight it every single day.

Mark wraps up the service with a reminder of the BBQ fundraiser next Saturday and a quick blessing. Drew steps out of the pew and motions for Grandma Rose to make her way out. He reaches down and gives her a hug. "I'm heading to work. I'll call you later."

She grabs his hands. "Okay, I love you." Her eyes began to swell with tears as she touched her hand to his stubbly face. "Drew, I am so proud of you." Those words are why he fights his demons every day. No matter how hard the battle, he never wants to disappoint her or Papa Silas ever again. He will become the man they raised him to be and maintain the integrity of the Carter family name.

# Chapter Three: Allie

Allie smiles and holds the door open for the older gentleman as she walks out of the local convenience store. Smiles are free, and that's a price she can afford these days. As she slides into the car, she begins to open the cellophane package with a mixture of joy and guilt. She knows that smoking is bad for her, and certainly isn't the answer to her current problems. However, at this point she rationalizes that there are worse things she could be doing.

Glancing at the clock on her dash, she sees that she'll have just enough time to finish her cigarette before her shift begins. She puts the key into the ignition and closes her eyes, as if that will ensure that the car will start this time. *Come on, baby, you can do it.* As the car starts, she lets out a sigh of relief. With two kids in braces, and college looming around the corner, this is not the time for car repairs.

The sliding glass doors open, and the mingled smells hit her immediately. Most people don't like the smell of hospitals, and for good reasons. Besides being born in one, the other trips there are generally not pleasant memories. Her nose is accustomed to the scents of rubbing alcohol and disinfectants, and her ears immune to the repetitive sound of pages over the intercom. With a mom who's a pediatric nurse, and a dad who's a physical therapist, she always knew she was destined to walk these halls. For her, the hospital is like a second home; the things that freak most people out bring her an odd measure of comfort.

"Good morning, Chaplain Allie." Judy beams with way too much enthusiasm.

"Morning, Judy." Allie can see that Judy, the head of the sunshine volunteers, has definitely had her share of coffee this morning.

"Can't you feel that fall is just around the corner? I just love this time of year when summer slips into fall." She sets an arrangement of flowers on the desk

"Yes, ma'am. I can hardly wait. Those are lovely and should brighten someone's day for sure."

"They're for Bessie Weeks. If I had to make a guess, I'd say they're from that old playboy Howard Watts. You know he's had his eye on her ever since her husband died last winter. Of course I would never read the card," she says with a coy look.

"Isn't he forty years her senior?" Allie asks.

"Honey, the heart wants what it wants, and I guess he figures time is not on his side. You have a wonderful day!" Judy calls back over her shoulder.

Allie rolls her eyes and squeaks out, "You too!" while making a mental note to not be that cheery when she gets older. At least not so early in the morning; it's just downright annoying. She imagines, though, that once you get to that age and get rid of the stresses of raising kids, and most likely your husband has gone to be with Jesus, you probably do feel pretty dang happy. *Oh my Lord, what is wrong with me? These are horrible thoughts.*

Typically this time of the year does give her a burst of energy, but not this month. No amount of pumpkin spiced anything is going to get her out of this funk. The burnout is real. She can feel it in every inch of her body, and there's literally nothing left to give. Years of giving all she had to everyone has eroded away at her soul. She feels like a shell of herself. Her phone begins to vibrate, and she digs through her bag, reaching to the bottom

"Hey, Dave, is everything okay?"

"Yes, fine. I'm just going over my calendar for the week and wanted to make sure that you were going to be able to pick up Mia after dance practice tomorrow."

"No, Dave, I have that ecumenical prayer meeting and I'm the lead. I cannot miss." She places her bag down and digs through the contents in search of her office keys.

"Well, I have a meeting that I told you about last week, and I can't miss that either. You assured me that you had it figured out."

He's right. She remembers the conversation now, but just like everything else recently, it went in and out. She feels frustrated with herself but also resentful at her husband for not noticing how much she's struggling.

"Fine, Dave, I'll handle it." She hangs up and sighs. *Just like I handle everything else.* Heading up the parent teacher organization, remembering the supplies for school parties, and dragging herself out to the store at 8:59 p.m. to get glue for school projects. She wonders if any mother has ever handed in their letter of resignation. Honestly, she's just about there.

She really should have listened to her parents and gone into real estate or something with computers. Maybe that job would have been less mentally draining and definitely more lucrative. Like most people who wind up in ministry, very few had it on their dream career sheet. In fact, Allie is confident it wasn't even in the occupational pamphlet distributed in high school.

While this wasn't the path her parents had envisioned for her, they could only say so much. Prior to starting their medical careers, her parents had met while serving for several years in the Peace Corps in Sierra Leone. Her mom was a native of Chatham, but her dad grew up outside of Chicago. Years later after a long bout of infertility, they returned to Sierra Leone to adopt Allie from the orphanage where her mom had worked—a rare event in the 1970s in a nearly all-White community. While adoption wasn't unheard of here, matching children to homes that looked like the children in terms of race and ethnicity was more the standard.

Outwardly, her parents had received great love and support from their church and community. As her grandmother Agnes told her many times over the years, "Allie Louise Luffman, you are loved with a special kind of love. Adoption is one of the highest acts of Christian love, as it mirrors the love of Christ as he adopts us into his eternal family." That may in fact be true, but as an adult, Allie knows that many disapproving conversations had been held behind closed doors.

As a young child, Allie never felt like she didn't belong. She had close friends and was invited to her share of birthday parties and sleepovers. The feelings of being an outsider didn't creep in until around middle school. While all her friends were questioning who they were and rebelling against parental standards, her search for her identity was more complex. She began to search for answers about her origins. What would life have been like in Sierra Leone? She spent hours in the library learning about her birth nation. She studied the geography, learning that Sierra Leone was located on the west coast of Africa, bordered by Guinea, Liberia, and the Atlantic Ocean. She was particularly captivated by the story of the capital and largest city, Freetown, which sits on the country's western coast. Initially, British philanthropists and abolitionists sought to create a settlement in West Africa to provide a safe place for freed slaves and to serve as a base for efforts to suppress the slave trade. She was intrigued at how Freetown grew to be a center for missionary and education activities as well as hosted a diverse population of people who sought refuge for various reasons. These facts made her ponder her ancestors and lineage. What about her parents? Were they refugees? Were they still alive? Did her parents die or were they just unable to take care of her? Would she even want to know the answers to these questions?

By her senior year, she was fully committed to finding her birth parents. As a graduation gift, she had asked her parents for a trip to Sierra Leone. Her initial request was met with resistance, but she persisted, and in time, she wore them down. As adoptive parents, they knew this day would come, but it was still difficult. Her mom had remained in contact with Beatrice Guilaume, who ran the orphanage. She had graciously agreed to host Allie for the summer, giving her a taste of her birthplace and helping her unravel the mystery of her birth parents.

Her quest to find her parents came to an abrupt halt right after high school graduation. After the accident and with Michelle reeling from the loss of Benjamin, Allie felt that she couldn't leave her best friend. Even with Michelle leaving and rarely returning home, they had maintained a close friendship. In the early years, it was letters exchanged through the mail on pretty stationery and matching envelopes. Then slowly emails and texts replaced these letters. Allie still had a box in her closet with each letter she had received.

They had been through everything together. As soon as they'd started getting crushes on boys, they'd made a pact. Boys would come and go, but this friendship was for life through thick and thin. To this day that has held true. What was intended as a brief delay of her trip became a series of delays. Her trip became a series of "afters": after she finished college, after graduate school, after she got married, but then kids came and, well, here she was. This was no longer a delayed flight; this flight seemed to be canceled.

Her desire to help her best friend through her grief and to make sense of all that happened led Allie to dive deeper into her faith. She felt such confusion and anger over Benjamins's death. She needed this to make sense, so as a young college student at

Appalachian State, she spent hours in the library researching and reading. She desperately wanted to find the answer to the burning question of all humans: Why do bad things happen to good people? She read C.S. Lewis' *The Problem of Pain* several times. Maybe she held out hope that he would have a revelation and change God's views on this from heaven. No, every time the conclusion was the same. According to Lewis, human suffering was not sufficient reason to reject belief in a good and powerful God. Okay, next book. Then she went on to read his later work, *A Grief Observed*, reflections on his journey after his wife's death. It was here where she felt the connection. Every page resonated with the rawness of grief and gave her relief from her own guilt over questioning God. She discovered that indeed even Christians don't avoid pain and suffering. She eagerly shared all of her knowledge each week as she wrote to Michelle.

She wasn't sure if any of it helped Michelle, but for Allie, this initial search stirred something within. She decided that if she couldn't stop people from suffering, she wanted to be there to help them through. She graduated from App State with a double major in religious studies and psychology. A few years later, she obtained her Master's from Wake Forest University and did her clinical pastoral education residency at Baptist Hospital in Winston Salem. No small feats for a woman in the late 1990s but also a woman of color in a White-male-dominated denomination.

Allie reaches into her mailbox and then juggles her mail, coffee, and bag as she turns the key to enter her office. A knock at the door reveals Julie Frederick. How the girl who cheated her way through high school biology class became a registered nurse still blew her mind.

"Chaplain Allie, we have a patient's family in the ICU that needs to meet with you. Can you see them now?"

"Sure, send them down."

And so it begins, she thinks, another day. She runs her hand along the top of her couch and pauses for a moment in the stillness. She reflects on the many people who have sat on this couch while she attempts to share in their unthinkable decisions and pain. The blinking red light on her phone along with the messages in her mail demand her attention. She flips through the stack of referrals in her box, and her phone vibrates with a text alert.

Michelle: The eagle has landed. Back to the motherland!

Allie texted back: Well, I hope it wasn't a crash landing. I'll call you after work and we'll make plans. Can't wait to see you; so much to catch up on!

She opens her email and searches for *Beatrice Guillame.*

Allie has remained in touch with Beatrice over the years and has led fundraisers in church to support the work of the orphanage there. It's still hard to wrap her mind around how many children are forced to live without parents not just in Africa but all over the world. The work Beatrice and her staff do is remarkable. They've given so much love and transformed so many lives.

Subject: Possible Visit

Hello Beatrice,

I hope this email finds you and your staff in good health and doing well. I have decided that it's time for me to make the trip to visit you all. I still have to talk with my husband and get approval from my work, but I was hoping to come after the first of the year. Would this timeframe work for you? I look forward to hearing from you.

In peace, Allie

With a knock at her door, she gives herself a pep talk. *I can do all things through Christ.* She walks to the door and welcomes the family into her office.

"Hello, I'm Chaplain Allie. Please come in and have a seat," she says with a compassionate smile that she hopes is enough to hide the true lack of light she feels in her soul.

# Chapter Four: The Inn

The afternoon rain splatters off the roof like hot grease popping out of a skillet. Linda Richardson surveys the ceiling and skillfully moves buckets to catch the rain in the laundry room. Miss Victoria, her nickname for the inn, is quickly approaching a hundred years old and is really showing her wrinkles today.

Linda reflects back to when she first fell in love with Miss Victoria. She was around ten years old and riding in the car with her mom when she spotted this beauty on North Bridge Street. She smiles as she recalls that she and her sister Judy used to call it the Pink Princess Palace. Today, she looks more like she drew a social security check, but this Victorian beauty was definitely fit for a queen or princess in her heyday. Her pale pink hues popped against the intricate white trim work. She was the epitome of beauty, featuring both height and curves. Her high-pitched roof and spiral turrets soared alongside the treetops, while her spacious wrap-around porch gave her just the right flow and curves. With all her beauty, it had always been the wrap-around porch that drew Linda to this house. Large, inviting steps nestled between detailed white columns just seemed to call for visitors. The porch was spacious enough to offer many sitting areas, including a corner porch swing that had become her favorite spot. While she didn't get to do it as often as she'd like, when the opportunity arose, she'd sneak away to sit and swing. For her, swinging was a soothing movement that took her back to childhood. She didn't know if there was any science to it, but she knew that she felt a lot more relaxed as a kid after a long swinging session at recess. She would close her eyes, and the only sounds she heard were the squeaking of the chains and the occasional car driving by. Sometimes she'd grab a book, but most often she just enjoyed the peace and quiet while it lasted.

Before Linda purchased the house, Victoria was lovingly cared for by the Johnson family. Bill Johnson had inherited the home that his grandparents had built in the early 1900s. While new homes are fine for some, she preferred the ones that came with stories. So much life and death has filled this home, and she loves to imagine all the events that have transpired here. Birthdays, holidays, and social events—and this house has hosted many. Linda finds a sense of comfort in the fact that many children were born in this house. Babies were born in the beds they were conceived in, and loved ones transitioned through death from the safe space of their home and slipped gently into heaven.

She thinks about how hard society has worked to sanitize death. In Victoria's early days, it was common for bodies to be laid in the parlor while people came to pay their respects. As time moved on, it became increasingly rare to birth a child at home, and now funeral homes host the viewings.

While Mrs. Johnson was living, she ensured that even if you didn't own a calendar, you would know the month by her decor. The door and porch were always adorned with festive holiday decor. Easter tulips and cute bunnies paraded in the spring, while large pots filled with bright petunias and trailing ivy graced the steps in the summer. A cornucopia of fall gourds and stacks of hay bales hugged the porch in fall. But nothing compared to Christmas, when Mrs. Johnson turned her into a life-size gingerbread house. From Thanksgiving to New Year's Day, if you were in a hurry at night, you knew not to take North Bridge Street. The cars would come to a crawl to allow time to take in all the sights. Her shutters were adorned with large wooden candy canes, which accented each window's fresh evergreen wreath suspended by scarlet ribbon. At night her twinkling lights outlined her beautiful frame, and the flickering candles gave off a welcoming glow. For many years, Bill and Sue hosted an open house for the kids and they were Santa and Mrs. Claus.

The home was always kept immaculately until Bill and Sue died. Their children had moved away from Chatham, and for years the house just sat in disarray. At times, Linda couldn't bear to drive by, as each week she seemed to decline more and more. Poor Victoria. Linda identifies with Miss Victoria, as she feels the wear and tear on her own body with menopause. For years she fantasized about buying Victoria and opening a bed and breakfast. As her retirement from teaching approached, the desire to do something bold in this new stage of her life felt like perfect timing. She had truly enjoyed teaching, but it was time to try new things. After all, when she went to college, women had two choices: teacher or nurse. For her it had to be teaching, because if she saw blood, she'd begin to vomit immediately. A terrible trait that at times had made motherhood very challenging but also made it convenient to be married to a first responder.

One day she baked Steve his favorite lasagna and worked up the nerve to share her plan with him. His reaction was exactly what she'd expected: "Linda, are you crazy? That house is a money pit, and here we are trying to plan for retirement. Plus, honey, you're great at many things, but you don't know the first thing about running a business."

Well, Katie and Michelle got their headstrong ways honestly, so Linda took the challenge. Over the next year, she took classes at Surry Community College and began to connect with other Airbnb owners across NC. The final brick that would allow Steve to give her the greenlight was that she received a significant business startup grant for women. Running a small business certainly had its challenges, but she never regretted her decision. Restoring the inn and sharing in the day-to-day business in the bakery with her Katie had brought a sweet new season to her life.

The chimes of the front door ring now for a second time. She wipes her hands on her apron and makes her way downstairs.

"Good afternoon, or maybe I should say good wet afternoon. Forgive the delay; I was upstairs and didn't hear the door. Please, come in out of that rain and let me take your umbrella and coat."

The tall man gives off a distinguished vibe that hints to Linda that he's likely more acquainted with larger cities. She hangs his coat on the mahogany coat rack and places his dripping umbrella into the base of the rack, one of her marvelous recent finds while on an antiquing trip with her sister Judy. They had spent many days rummaging through antique stores all over the state to bring Miss Victoria to life. She steps behind the hand-carved Victorian period reception desk, one of her favorite finds. Lucky for Linda, Judy has a real eye not only for finding antiques but possesses the bargaining skills to boot.

"Now, do you have a reservation with us?"

"Yes. Matthews, Phillip Matthews." He wipes his hands over his face to remove the rain. "It's definitely a mess out there."

Linda types in the name and hopes she remembers how to use this new system. Katie said they needed to get with the times, but she still prefers a good old paper reservation book.

"Oh yes, I see a single room for … hmmmm. Bear with me; I'm learning a new system. I don't see a checkout date, Mr. Matthews. How long were you planning on staying?"

"No, that's correct." He reaches down to silence a call on his phone. "I don't have a checkout date because I'm not sure how long I'll be here. The lady I spoke with said I could stay on and just give you 48-hours notice. Will that still be okay?"

"You must have spoken to my daughter Katie. That's not a problem at all." Linda opens a folder and begins to place brochures inside with information on hiking trails, wineries, restaurants, and other local attractions.

"Are you with us for business or pleasure?"

"Well, I hope to have time for a little of both, but mostly business." He reaches down again to silence another call.

"Looks like you're in high demand today. Welcome to Chatham and The Dogwood Inn and Bakery. I do hope you get a little downtime to enjoy the town. Where are you coming to us from?"

"Boston."

"Boston? Oh wow, how did you hear about us?"

"My grandfather grew up here in Chatham."

"Really? Who's your grandfather?" Linda looks up from the desk

"John Matthews. Did you know him?"

"The John Matthews I know is a physician. Is that the one?"

"Yes, that's the one."

"He grew up across the street from my mother. They were classmates together."

"When they say small town, they really mean it. "

"Yes, this town would most certainly not make a great fit for a witness protection program. How's your grandfather doing these days?"

He glances down. "Sadly, he passed away this spring."

Linda stops typing and returns her gaze to him. "I'm so sorry to hear that. The last my mother knew of him he went to medical school at Bowman Gray School of Medicine at Wake Forest, but she never knew what happened after that. It's not like today, where with the click of a button you can get someone's life history."

"Yes, that's right. He met my grandmother, who was working as a nurse at Baptist Hospital while he was doing his residency. They married, and he took a position at Mass General. They relocated there and never left. He was an oncologist and spent the last part of his career leading cancer research at Harvard. He talked about moving back here for retirement, but he was so committed to his work, he actually never really retired."

"Oh mercy," she says, wiping the counter. "We could use his expertise now. My daughter Katie, whom you spoke with, is in need of transplant. Her treatment for breast cancer has led to aplastic anemia."

"I'm so sorry to hear this. Have you guys found a match?"

"Not yet; we were hoping that her sister would be, but she isn't. The word is out, and many people are getting tested. Her doctors are looking outside as well. Are you also a physician?"

"Oh goodness no. The sight of blood makes me faint. I'm a real estate investor. That's actually what brings me here. Assisting on a possible acquisition. This area is really attracting investors for tourism."

"Well, even as a business owner now, it's a double-edged sword. We're grateful that people enjoy our town, and the revenue has really revitalized us. We just fear losing all the peace and charm that used to be here. It's happened to many southern towns over the years. Seems the Yankees come to escape the rat race and then bring it all here. I certainly don't mean any offense."

"No offense taken. I'm sure it's a fine line to balance the tranquility that brings people along with the growing number of curious visitors." He places his phone in his pocket and retrieves his folder from the desk.

Linda walks out from behind the desk and heads to a cabinet that hangs on the wall. She reaches for a room key attached to a fabric swatch.

"We serve breakfast each morning from six to ten, or if you'd like, we can have it delivered up to your room. That, of course, is included in your stay. We also serve lunch daily until 2:00, or you're welcome to try many of our restaurants around town. You'll find a list of them in this folder, along with many activities to do while you're here in Chatham. Follow me and I'll show you to your room."

Phillip collects his things and begins to follow Linda up the stairs. He's struck by the attention to detail that has been executed to restore this home to its original grandeur. A brass chandelier hangs above the entryway, emitting a gentle light on the stairs. As Linda makes her way to the top of the stairs, Phillip pauses on the landing to study the striking grandfather clock that sits in the corner of the landing.

"My grandmother had this same clock in her house. This one is in beautiful condition."

"If you're interested, I can send you out antiquing with my sister. She has the knack for it."

"I'll certainly add that to my list of options while I'm here."

Linda places the key into the door and opens the room to reveal a four-poster king size mahogany bed. "Well, here you are. Your room is The Spinning Room."

Phillip takes the key from her and gives her a puzzled look. "I'm sorry, but did you say 'the spinning room'? Does this room rotate at night? Should I be concerned about vertigo while I'm here?"

Linda lets out a laugh. "My apologies. I see that you didn't read the history of our town and inn. Every room in our inn is named around the textile industry, and spinning is a part of the process of creating fabrics."

"Whew, now I feel much better. I will definitely read more about that while I'm in town. I'm a city boy, so it looks like I have a lot to learn. Do you have Wi-Fi here?"

"We do, but it's dial up. Look for the square outlet on the wall, used to be where we plugged the telephone in back in the day."

His raises his eyebrows, but before he can speak, Linda let out another laugh. "Relax, it's just a joke. We have excellent high-speed internet; the network and password will be on your desk."

He begins to sort through his bag but pauses to say, "I know it would be a long shot, but I will definitely get screened while I'm in town for your daughter. I hope that you find a match very soon."

"Thank you, that's very kind of you." Linda smiles and pauses to send up what feels like her millionth prayer just this month: *Please, Lord, find Katie a match.*

# Chapter 5: Ghosts

Gone. Even 20 years later, she still can't wrap her head around never seeing someone you love ever again. The problem with burying old wounds is that they don't stay buried forever. The memories, like seeds, lie dormant in the deep recess of the brain, tunneling their way back to the surface when least expected. Michelle can feel the swell begin to well up like waves. "Unfinished business." That's what her last therapist had called it. People say time heals, and they talk about closure, but this hole is a chasm that always seems too deep to ever be closed. She tried for twenty years to place something in that gaping hole—work, men, excessive running, alcohol—but nothing worked except to keep as much distance between this place and herself as possible.

She has a few minutes to spare, and as much as she dreads it, she knows where she needs to go. As she prepares to make her move home, she knows that she'll have to return to this place and finally face the pain she left behind. Most people would assume that the distance kept her from Benjamin's grave since his funeral, but even if she had stayed here in Chatham, the pain wouldn't have allowed her to return. Going to the cemetery and seeing his name etched in stone would make it real and final. It was so much better living far away, where she could pretend that he was still here in Chatham, living a happy life. Even after all these years, she feels like she should be able to drive to his house and find him in the back yard working with his dad. While no one is immune to tragedy, it seems to hit harder in small towns. That summer revealed just how fragile life can be—not just to Michelle but to so many.

Soon these quiet roads would be filled with tourists getting their fall fix of apple picking and leaf gazing. She has to admit that this spot, this view, make her pause and take it all in. It really is a peaceful place. These foothills are cradled by the rising mountains, like a mama bear protecting her cub. Until this moment, she had forgotten the sense of peace they brought her. Maybe when her time comes she'll want to be laid to rest here, but it has made the perfect spot for Benjamin.

The rain shower has ended, bringing a reprieve from the early September heat. She takes a deep inhale; the smell of rain evaporating from the hot pavement invokes pleasant memories of riding her bike following afternoon summer thunderstorms—a gully washer, as her nana would say. The rain left deep puddles of warm water that would splatter against her long legs as she raced back to the old mill to resume play. Her summer days were spent here in these very woods near Carter Falls, building forts and peeking under rocks in the stream for crawdads. She feels a twinge of sadness that today, technology stands in the way of many kids having these simple experiences in nature. The most high-tech devices they ever had in the woods were walkie talkies. The range was so poor that in order for them to work, you had to literally be standing beside each other—which, most can agree, defeated the point of these communication devices.

Approaching Benjamin's towering monument, she's reminded of another time not too far from this spot, just weeks before their high school graduation.

"Where are we going?" Michelle asked, climbing on the four-wheeler behind Benjamin.

"It's a surprise; just hold tight and enjoy the ride." Michelle recalls feeling annoyed. She had many things on her agenda to do, with upcoming finals and last-minute scholarship applications, bust she reluctantly agreed. Once they were in motion, she quickly forgot all her stresses and remembered one of the reasons why she loved Benjamin so much. She was always worrying about the future, and he made her feel that it all would work out. There was a feeling of safety and security that she didn't even know how to appreciate at the time. They made their way down by the old mill and raced along the creek, eventually making their way to a clearing.

As the four-wheeler came to a stop, Benjamin turned and said, "Well, what do you think?"

"Think of what?" Michelle looked around for something to comment on.

"This place?"

"Looks like an empty field to me."

He jumped off the four-wheeler and removed his helmet. Then, with an excitement she had rarely seen before, he mapped it all for her.

"I've worked out a deal with my parents to buy this land, and I'm going to build a house here. It will be small to start with, but then we can add on as our family grows."

"Our family?" Michelle's eyes widened with surprise.

"Yes, our family." Benjamin got down on one knee. "Michelle, I love you, and I want to spend the rest of my life with you. Will you marry me?"

Michelle began to laugh. "Benjamin Rodriguez, you can't be serious. We can't get married; we're barely 18!"

He slipped his grandmother's antique ring on her hand. "Of course not today, but until we do, I want every other guy to know that you're spoken for."

She notices the butterflies in her stomach as she savors the memory of that gentle kiss. In that moment, she could have never predicted that in only a few short weeks, her future would be so incredibly altered.

She reaches out and slowly allows her fingers to trace over the image of his face etched on his stone. She wonders what he'd look like today. Probably like his dad. He'd still be handsome, but a few lines would be creeping in around his eyes, and his hair would probably be thinning. Her fingers pause on the date: June 6, 1989. That date signifies a time that now defines all things in her life. Instead of a happy memory etched in her mind, or simply an ordinary day that one forgets, it became his date of death. Events in her life were always marked by either happening before or after that tragic day. Just weeks before, they'd been carefree, planning their future, and then suddenly she was helping his mom plan a funeral.

Her throat begins to tighten and she fights for each breath. Just as she feared, the pain is indeed right where she left it. She feels crushing sensations in her chest, and her legs tingle and beg her to run. After all, it's always been her natural inclination to leave as fast as possible. But today, she assures herself, she will fight this urge.

Rather than a rush of images, they unfold gently, like the petals of a rose slowly opening. It's as if her brain knows the speed at which to recall so as not to completely overwhelm her. She lowers herself down by his grave and allows the memories to come. She feels the first tear fall as she relives seeing him for the first time after he'd died. Her dad had begged her to let him go with her, but she wanted to go on her own. She didn't feel like he was dead, and surely she would have felt something different in her. So she entered the room with a tinge of hope that everyone was wrong and she would find him very much alive. She lifted his hand, which still held a sense of warmth, and placed it to her cheek. She stroked his tangled, wet hair with her fingers and settled it back into place. He was always particular about his hair. His lungs were absent of breath, but his face was still the same. Even in death his face somehow radiated a gentleness to her that gave her peace. The last time she saw him, it was much harder. Knowing after the casket was closed she would never on this earth see or touch him again was excruciating. He was then carried by his former baseball teammates to the spot where she sat today. They had a service, and it was over.

Then came the part no one warned her about. The silence. Everyone was gone. Sure, there was the random call or visit, but most had moved on with their lives. They were off to college, jobs, and families, while she was left broken and paralyzed. Most nights she would lie in bed, praying to wake up to find this all a nightmare, or to be taken away to where Benjamin had gone. On darker nights, she would pray to not wake up but be taken to be with him. A deep abyss of loss and pain that she wouldn't wish on anyone.

Life is so fleeting. How can twenty years be gone? At times it had gone by like a sloth, but now, standing in this moment, it seems like the blink of an eye. It suddenly occurs to her that she could have lived her entire childhood over in the amount of years that had passed. She remembers the first time she met Benjamin, and this thought brings a smile to her face. He and his family had just moved to Chatham the summer before they started high school. While it was a few weeks before the start of their freshman year, the temperature still registered the dog days of summer. Her T-shirt was clinging to her with sweat from early morning cheer practices. As they returned to school, every Thursday night she would cheer on her junior varsity football team. The sounds of coaches yelling, referee whistles blowing, and helmets clashing would be the soundtrack of her life all fall. She has no idea what had consumed her mind that day. She was likely thinking of how she was going to cram reading the last two novels on her summer reading list by the start of school. Whatever the dilemma to solve, she was brought quickly into reality by a hard knock with a football. She looked up to see Drew Jones laughing at her. Meanwhile, Benjamin came to her aid.

"Hey, sorry about that. Are you okay?"

She rubbed her arm. "Sure, just another bruise to go with my collection." She pointed to several on her legs.

"Man, didn't know cheerleading was so brutal. Maybe you guys should wear some pads as well."

"Well, you know what they say: If cheerleading were any easier, they'd call it football," she said victoriously.

He snickered. "Good one."

"Rodriguez," Coach Watson yelled sternly, "quit tom-catting around with that cheerleader and get over here."

He scooped up the ball and gave her a smile. That was the first time she noticed his eyes. There was something so gentle and kind about them that made her want to know him more. She loved reliving that moment over and over. She had fought hard over the years to try to focus on the good memories. Even with the pain, she will never regret loving Benjamin.

She begins to make her way back to the car and then she pauses. Her body is screaming that it has overstayed its welcome here, but her mind has one more thing it needs to see. She makes her way through the church cemetery, noting that even after all these years away, she still remembers the way. The cemetery is scattered with a mixture of new stones and those that time has eroded. Without a map, she quickly finds what she's looking for. The Carter family has a special area in the cemetery.

A fairly new stone of black granite reads :

*SILAS ABRAHAM JOHNSON*
*December 3, 1925–April 28, 2005*

She stops for a moment to pay her respects to Papa Silas. He had been such a wonderful man of the church and community. She always admired how kindly he treated Grandma Rose. He was known to walk into to the church handing her a rose from the garden, declaring that God had made his Rose just a little more beautiful than the others.

Her attention is drawn to the small heart-shaped stone to the left that reads:

*SHEILA JOHNSON JONES*
*July 14, 1952–October 27, 1983*
*BELOVED DAUGHTER AND MOTHER*
*WE WILL MEET ON THAT BEAUTIFUL SHORE*

Her heart sinks. While she never knew her all that well, as she stands here at age 38, she realizes how young this woman had actually been. She squats down to pick up the floral arrangement that has been displaced by the wind. In all the years following Sheila's death, this grave has been decorated for every holiday by Grandma Rose. She has no doubt that she's still as diligent to this day.

She is suddenly unsettled by memories of nights spent in this cemetery as a young teen that she hadn't recalled in years. It's as if this ground is conjuring up memories that she forgot were even there. These memories made her wonder. After all these years, did Sheila Jones' son still visit here late at night in hopes of seeing his mom just one more time.

# Chapter 6: Welcome Home

M ichelle exits her car, and her eyes are drawn to the vibrant pink Dogwood Inn & Bakery sign. She walks up the winding path, marveling at the beautiful array of flowers and well-manicured shrubs. Despite the heat, an array of bright petunias and greenery cascade from terracotta pots adorning the path leading to the steps. She pauses before opening the antique weathered door. *Here I go.*

The door lets out a subtle creak, and the doorbell jingles. "Hello, I'm looking for a room for one?"

"Michelle, oh honey, you made it!" Linda rushes from behind the counter to hug her. "You look tired. You must be exhausted. I bet you're already feeling the time difference." She studies her daughter's face and tucks a stray piece of hair behind her ear.

"I'm okay. It will really hit hard tomorrow."

"Come on, let's get you some coffee and find Katie."

Linda swings open the kitchen door. "Surprise! Look what the cat finally dragged in!"

Katie removes her oven mitts and jumps up to hug her sister. Despite the hot pink apron she's wearing, she is covered head to toe in flour. Michelle exhales as she finally feels the warmth of her sister's body as they embrace. Many nights she had dreamt that she didn't make it home in time. As she presses her hand on her back, her heart drops as she identifies each bone protruding from her sister's skeleton.

As they separate, Michelle reaches over and takes one of the oven mitts and attempts to dust her sister off.

"Don't bother," Katie says. "It's a hazard of the business."

"Hi, Nana." Michelle kisses her cheek.

"Well, aren't you a pretty thing? Are you married?" Nana Lucy grabs both of her hands and smiles at her.

"No, not yet, Nana." Michelle gives Nana's hands a gentle squeeze. She feels the gnarled joints of each hand that now carry arthritis from years of hard work.

"Well, honey, time is not on your side. You know you won't be getting any younger. What did you say your name was again?"

"Michelle, Nana. I'm your granddaughter. Steve's youngest daughter."

Nana looks confused and shakes her head back and forth.

Katie looks over at Michelle. "Some days are better than others, but dementia or not, she does have a point. I mean, you and Alex have been dating forever."

Ignoring her comment, Michelle lifts the dome off the cake stand and cuts a slice of red velvet cake. She carefully guides the slice of cake onto her plate and then licks the signature pecan cream cheese frosting from her fingers. The family recipe for red velvet cake is what led to the addition of the bakery to the inn. Katie started off just making cakes and treats for her coworkers, and before she knew it, she had a full-fledged business.

"Here, Nana, have a slice of cake and cup of coffee with me."

"Just a small sliver," Linda says. "We have to watch that blood sugar."

Michelle slides a piece of cake to Nana and pours two cups of coffee. Nana slowly picks up her fork and lifts the cake. Her mouth bobs as she searches to make the connection. "Ummmm, this is very good; it tastes like something I've had before. Where did you get it?"

"From here at the bakery, Nana. It's your recipe." Michelle smiles at her.

"Oh dear, I don't think so. I never was good at baking."

Michelle looks at Katie and then back at Nana, who, while oblivious to her past, seems to be enjoying her cake in the moment with the satisfaction of a young child.

Michelle cleans her fork of any last crumb and takes her plate over to the sink. "You guys didn't mention that you needed me to help out today. I thought you did all the Sunday cooking orders on Saturday. Let me get washed up and I'll help."

"No need, we're fine." Katie gently lowers a cake into the signature Dogwood Bakery box. I have to go in this week for a transfusion, so I'm just getting a jumpstart on some orders."

Michelle wants to inquire more about her sister's appointments, but they are interrupted. The back door flies open, and in like wild bulls fresh out of the pen come her two nephews and niece. Almost in unison they chant, "Aunt Michelle, Aunt Michelle." Karry, age six, and Joel, four, each take a leg and hug her tightly. Michelle loves her nephews and niece, even though much of their relationships had been developed by connecting over Skype and Facetime.

Brett holds out his hand. "Hello, Aunt Michelle. How have you been?"

Michelle looks over at Katie with a confused look.

"Don't ask. Mom signed him up for cotillion gentleman classes or something at Tina's dance school. She said this generation needed some better manners."

Michelle looks at Brett. "I am doing well. And you?"

"I am doing splendidly." Brett places his hands behind his back and walks away, smiling proudly at his Grandma Linda as she enters the room.

"Well done, Brett." Linda gives him an approving look.

The door opens again and Steve Richardson enters, panting and out of breath.

"Whew, these younguns have run me to death this morning."

"Hey, Daddy!" Michelle rushes to him. No matter how old she gets, in his embrace she will always feel forever like a four-year-old girl.

"Well, here she is in the flesh and blood. I do still have a daughter. I'm surprised you could find your way back home."

He reaches around her back and grabs a fresh cookie, quickly placing it in his mouth. He hands one to each kid. Linda takes the fly swatter and slaps his hand. "Steve Richardson, it's a wonder we turn a profit around here with you sneaking all those pecan sandies."

He winks at Michelle and smiles at Linda. "I'm a growing boy. I have to keep up my strength."

"Hmph. You're growing all right—growing right out of your pants is more like it."

"Michelle, do you see the abuse I've been putting up with for nearly 45 years? Of course your mama could start an argument in an empty house, so I've learned not to take it personal."

Linda waves the fly swatter in his face with a furrowed brow and then they both smile and kiss.

This has always been the connection between her parents. It was the type of relationship and love that Michelle had always desired. She can't imagine what it would be like to spend 45 years of your life with the same person, and at this rate she probably never will.

Steve grabs a set of keys out of a drawer and hands them to Michelle. "Here's the key to Nana's house. Now that door is a little cattywampus, so you may have to jiggle the doorknob a bit to get in."

"Boy, I can tell I'm back in Chatham. I haven't heard 'cattywampus' in years."

"Well, no matter how many fancy degrees or ranks you have, you need to remember where you were raised." He gives her another wink. "Oh, and also, that old house blows fuses like crazy; extra ones are on top of the fridge there in the kitchen along with a flashlight. You'll have to go down to the basement to replace those."

He gives her a hug and a peck on the cheek. "Good to have you home, sweetie. See you all later," Steve calls out. "I'm headed to check on things at the station. This rain today has put me on edge."

The room grew quiet, and if they're all honest, they'll admit that the rain has put them all on edge.

" If you guys are sure that you don't need me, I'm headed over to meet Allie at"—she reaches down to grab her phone—"The Tap Room Bar and Grill. I have the address, but where is it?"

"Oh, that's near Silas Johnson's place out near the old Carter Mill. You can't miss it; there are plenty of signs."

"I'll show you some mercy and give you tomorrow to get settled in," Linda says, "but I'll see you bright and early Tuesday morning. Hope you're ready for these 5:00 a.m. starts, and please give Allie my best. Tell her not to be such a stranger. I rarely see that girl, and she practically lived here in high school. "

"With a job and two kids, she's a pretty busy mom."

"I'll walk out with you," Katie says, removing her apron.

"Wow, Katie, I had no idea that Nana was that bad."

"Like I said, some days are better than others."

"And Katie, no offense, but sister to sister, you look like hell."

"Well, sister to sister, I feel like hell."

Michelle stops and gives her sister a loving but firm look. Now it's time for you to rest. I'm here to do whatever is needed."

Michelle heads to her car, and Katie returns inside. The screen doors let out a slam behind her as she ties her apron back on.

Linda doesn't look up from folding cookie boxes. "Do you think she knows about Drew Jones?"

Katie looks to her mom. "I doubt it. I've never told her."

"Me either. Looks like she's about to find out."

# Chapter 7: The Taproom

D rew throws Major's bone into his cage and closes the pin. "Don't look at me that way. If you stopped nosing through the trash every time I left the house, you could roam free. Until then, it's a lockdown for you, buddy." Drew rubs Major's head, who then sheepishly crawls into his cage, grabs his bone, and lies down.

Sliding into the cab of his truck, Drew smiles and shakes his head. Hard as it is to admit, he knows that old fleabag has been a huge part of his healing. The day Major wandered up to the cabin, that poor dog was as physically battered as Drew was mentally tortured. Apparently, some divine critter loving force must have temporarily taken over his body, causing him to bathe Major and take him to the vet. That was supposed to be the limit. He was most certainly not planning on allowing this mutt to take up permanent residence. Sue Jones at the vet's office gave him a scolding look over her bifocals when she asked for the dog's full name and he replied: "Major Pain." Well, what did she expect, Toto or Rin Tin Tin? After all, that's what he seemed like at the time: a real pain in the ass.

Days turned into weeks and then months as Drew searched for a home for Major. His cute face on the flyers around town made for many inquiries, but despite his gentle disposition, people were afraid to adopt a mutt with a pit bull and German shepherd mix. Eventually Drew came to terms that the two were destined to live together.

He had no idea how people raised kids; it was enough just to feed, water, and walk this beast. Not to mention this dog's insatiable need to be shown attention. And he thought his last girlfriend, Suzanne, had been needy. On Drew's darkest days, when he would have normally lay in the bed all day hungover from the cocktail of pills and booze he'd used the night before, he would be brought to life by Major. First a warm lick of his rough tongue on the palm of his hand, and then when that didn't encourage the action Major needed, he would gently grab the sleeve of his shirt and tug with a growl.

Morning after morning this routine continued until Major Pain simply became Major and was a part of his daily routine. Get up, let Major out, splash water on his face, let Major in, pour Major's food, make coffee, and sit and ponder how the hell he got into this place. His once chiseled Marine physique was far from combat ready. His shapely biceps and thighs were now half the size they used to be, and he had incurred a pretty noticeable gut from months of inactivity and heavy drinking. Most nights he would kill a six pack early on and then it was whiskey drinks until he passed out in his chair. Not to mention the cocktail of opioids that were already loaded into his system. Years of carrying heavy combat supplies, weighing at times more than 100 pounds, had destroyed his back and knees. After trying every OTC and physical therapy for his knee, he wound up with surgery. Post-op he was prescribed Percocet, and that was mistake number one. Not only did he feel less physical pain, but he finally felt some feelings other than depression. Unfortunately, to continue to feel good, he had to increase his doses, which also meant getting a hold of the drugs any way possible—even stealing from Grandma Rose's medicine cabinet, something he never thought he would do.

Having Major, something solely dependent upon him, forced him to do the basics things that he'd been neglecting. Major needed dog food, so while he was at the store, he picked up some food items that he placed inside his bare refrigerator. Up until that moment, it had only been used as a beer cooler. When he did eat, his diet consisted of takeout or beanie weenies. He had probably paid for Jon Wallace's college by now with all the tips for his pizza deliveries, and Mr. Huang at Noodles and More still sends him a Chinese New Year card each year, proclaiming Drew his number one customer.

Major had also made it necessary to clean up after himself. He had never owned a dog, but he was fairly certain they were descendants of goats. Nothing was off limits. If he didn't know better, there was some kind of dog dare social media group to see who could consume the most ridiculous items: paper, plastic, pizza, chocolate, socks, tennis balls, and probably barbed wire if he could have gotten a hold of some. The vet estimated that Major was about two years old upon his arrival, so he was still very much full of energy. Drew's attempts to put him on a leash and go for a walk became more like the dog walking him. One day, tired of the struggle, Drew let him off the leash to run, and Drew began to jog behind him. While he was certainly nowhere near his former pace, he had forgotten how freeing it was to run. In time, he created an obstacle course in the woods behind the cabin, similar to the O-course he had in boot camp on Parris Island. Every day, sometimes twice a day, he and Major completed the course: navigating low logs, high bars, clearing walls, and then sprinting to climb to the top of the 20-foot rope. The only things missing were drill sergeants yelling at him and the bell to ring at the top of the rope. Not only did his body begin to transform, unexpectedly so did his mind. He began to have confidence and dreams that he thought could never happen again. And as a side bonus, Major was knocked out so hard at night that he didn't wake up to play quite so early each day.

Drew rips off his tie and throws it in the back seat of his truck. As he opens the door to the Tap Room Bar and Grill, he untucks his shirt and rolls up his shirt cuffs.

"Hey, Billy, how's it going today?"

Billy looks up from wiping the counter. "Good. Just the busy after church lunch rush."

"How's that new baby of yours?"

"She's great, just no sleep, but we survived it with William, so I guess we'll make it again. "

"You're a better man than me. My dog gives me all the issues I can handle. If you need me, I'll be in the stock room."

Drew reaches up and grabs a box and brushes off the dust. Summer Crush, his first and last attempt at blackberry wine. He was glad he had experimented, but he learned that he should stick with the dry wines, like his bestselling Cabernet. When customers came in looking for sweet wines, he just sent them down the road to his buddy Walt. He had the touch for those wines that Drew just didn't.

A large crashing sound has him instinctively ducking for cover. His heart races and beads of sweat begin to form on his forehead as he crouches behind a stack of boxes. In the stillness of the quiet room, he can only hear his exaggerated breathing. The door slowly opens, and his hand is poised with a bottle in hand, ready to defend himself.

"Hey, Drew," Billy calls from the door, "everything all right in here? Sounds like a wild cat is loose up in here."

Drew stands up and lets out a quick exhale. "Yeah, man, everything is good. No wild cat, just a clumsy idiot. I knocked over that box of shipping materials. Will you take these out to the display rack? I'm getting ready to ride out to the vineyards."

Billy takes the boxes. "Still trying to unload these Summer Crush ones I see."

"You never know. That may be the perfect wine for someone. One of the mysteries of winemaking, you just never know how things will turn out until you try it."

"And even if you repeat it, it's not always the same."

"So, true my friend. See you in a bit."

Michelle can't believe that Chatham has stepped up to have a microbrewery. She's pleasantly surprised as she pushes open the doors to reveal an upscale bar. If she remembers correctly, this was an old storage space for a local trucking company. The inside has been updated while leaving some of the old nuances that gave the space a sense of timeless charm.

*Seriously, back in high school this was a dry county?* She walks up to the bar.

"What can I get for you?" Billy turns around.

"Any chance of a girl getting a glass of red wine, or is it strictly beer here?"

"You're in luck! We happen to have one of the finest Cabernets around." Billy slowly pours the wine.

Michelle swirls the wine and takes a sip. "Wow, perfect. Just start a tab for me please. I'm meeting a friend for dinner, but I don't know how long she'll be."

"Will do, ma'am."

"This is really good. Where's it from? Napa?

"Actually, no. It's called Driftwood, and it's a local wine made right here in Chatham by Rushing Streams Winery."

Michelle shakes her head. "Wow, I've drunk wine in Napa and Europe; this is pretty incredible."

"Well, thank you. We sure think so. Michelle Richardson, right?"

"Yes. How did you know that?"

"Hi, I'm Billy Anderson. Nice to put a face with a name. Your dad, Steve, is a regular here. Your daddy sure is proud of you; he brags on you every time he's in here."

"Oh boy, the curse of being the fire chief's daughter strikes again. You better believe my sister, Katie, and I couldn't get away with anything in this town. The news went straight on the radio and beat us home."

He chuckles. "I bet, my parents kept a pretty tight leash on me as well."

"Forgive me, Billy. I've been out of the loop here. Did we go to school together?"

"No, don't go wasting your time digging for me in any of your old yearbooks. I moved here from California a couple of years ago."

"California?" She says with a raised inflection. "What part?"

"Napa Valley."

Michelle nearly spits out her wine. "What in the world would make a person leave Napa Valley, California and come to podunk Chatham, NC. Have you been psychologically evaluated?"

"Not yet, but maybe I should be, since you're not the first person to suggest that. The short answer is that my wife, Kristen, and I were looking for a more quiet, laid back place to raise a family. We just recently had our second child. My parents own a vineyard in Cali, so it was very appealing to me to get into these local wineries from the ground up. I grew up running barefoot through a vineyard, and I get that same vibe here."

"Oh, congratulations on the baby. None for me yet, but hopefully soon. My boyfriend, Alex, is in Germany, and I'll be heading back there after I help Mom out at the inn and bakery for the holidays. That's as long as Katie is doing well."

"I'm sorry to hear about your sister. How is she doing?"

"I just saw her for the first time in person. She seems like she's doing okay, but she looks like hell. We're just hoping for a match soon."

"Man, she's really been through it. All those treatments and now this. We're doing all we can to encourage people to get tested." He points to a flyer on the wall with information on being a donor.

"I'll leave you to enjoy your wine, and let me know what else you need. Here's a menu. I have to brag—we make killer lasagna to go with that Cab."

Michelle takes her menu and seats herself at a small table by the window. She texts Allie to let her know she's there.

Through the cracked stockroom door, Drew glances out and catches a glimpse from behind of the brunette with long legs. She has a familiar look, but he's dated lots of women. He hopes this isn't one who will slap him for ghosting her and never calling back. He pushes open the door and walks out with wine bottles in hand, hoping to get a closer look.

"Drew?"

"Michelle?" He can't help but do a head-to-toe glance. Man, had the years been kind to her. "What are you doing here? The last I heard from Katie, I thought you were headed to Germany."

Michelle nervously shifts her weight. She knew she'd eventually run into Drew, but this is a little earlier than expected. "Well, I was, but I'm here through the tourism rush to help Mom and Katie with the inn and bakery." She looks around. "Do you work here?"

"Yep, it's honest work. I'm so sorry to hear about Katie. How's she doing?"

"Hanging in there. Billy just showed me the flyer. Please thank the owner for all you're doing to get the word out."

"I'll let him know. You know, Katie is like a sister to me, and I'll do whatever I can to help her out. I was tested, but no luck here." He glances down at the floor before returning to her gaze.

"I know, neither am I. It's so frustrating. I was so sure I would be, and I felt so much pressure, but it just didn't happen."

"Are you in a hurry?"

"Well, no, just waiting for Allie to get off work. We're having dinner together."

"Wow, I'm not sure that Chatham is ready for the wonder twins to be reunited."

"Haha, very funny."

"Follow me."

Michelle reluctantly grabs her purse and follows Drew as he opens a door that leads outside. Over the years, she had thought of him often and wondered what it would feel like to see him. Her information about him came in bits and pieces from Allie and Katie. She knew he had joined the Marine Corps and served in special operations in Desert Storm and again in Afghanistan post 911. He was medically discharged after Afghanistan and, like so many vets, got lost in a confusing system while trying to transition to civilian life. Michelle had seen it happen time and time again to her comrades. The incredible skills required to protect a nation and your fellow comrades often don't transfer into the civilian world. The last she knew of Drew Jones, he was deep into addiction. The thought of him becoming the one thing he never wanted to be, his father, was too much. So she'd asked Allie and Katie not to talk about him anymore. But clearly something had happened to change his path. If she had to place bets, she would say it was probably a woman.

Drew opens the door to a patio full of what she assumes are regular patrons. Quickly she realizes that many of them are her former classmates. Bodies, though aged, held smiles and laughs that were oddly comforting to be around. The questions started almost instantly, and soon it felt more like a CNN interview than a reunion.

How much combat did she see? *Much to their disappointment, none.*

What was her favorite place she ever visited? *Germany.*

Did she ever meet the President? *Yes, Bush 43.*

As she answers questions, occasionally she glances over at Drew to gauge his reactions.

"Sorry, I had no idea the wolves out here were so starved for news from the outside world."

Besides attending college, or the handful like Drew who joined the military, most of her classmates had built lives here in Chatham. Soon the group returns to conversations around kids, a topic to which neither Michelle nor Drew have anything to add.

Drew motions for Michelle, and they move to a small table inside.

"T-ball, braces, and teenage angst. Not a lot I can relate to, at least on a parent level," he says.

"Yeah, me neither. Feels like we're so behind, but I still don't feel like I'm old enough to be someone's parent."

"Can I get you another glass of wine?" Drew asks.

"No thanks, I am good for now." Michelle tucks her hair behind her ear.

They sit in an awkward silence, the kind that happens on a first date. A silence that years ago, Michelle never thought would exist between them.

She clears her throat. "How is your Grandma Rose?"

"Grandma Rose will probably outlive me, but Papa died a few years ago."

"I'm glad she's doing well. Please give her my best; she was always so kind to me. Mom told me about your Papa Silas, and I just left the cemetery and paid my respects. I know what he meant to you. I was so sorry to hear about his passing."

He pauses for a moment and leans in. "But you never contacted me."

Her heart starts to race and her cheeks become flush. Michelle can't believe all the feelings that are overtaking her. First the cemetery, now this. Nothing like just ripping the Band-Aid right off.

"I'm sorry, Drew. I just couldn't." She can feel the pressure of tears begin to press against the backs of her eyes. *Don't do it; don't cry in front of him.*

"I see that you're still wearing the ring Benjamin gave you."

Michelle manages to suppress the tears and glances down at her right hand, which carries her former engagement ring. She had tried to return it to Benjamin's mom, but she wouldn't accept it.

"What does your boyfriend think of you carrying a torch for a dead man?"

"That's none of your concern," she snaps back.

Her purse vibrates. Checking her phone, she's relieved to have an escape plan.

"I have to go. Allie is here. Good to see you."

As she walks away, she can't believe that at 38, Drew Jones is still the only person she knows who isn't afraid to call her bluff and can navigate his way through her otherwise safely locked internal doors.

Drew had always loved to drive to clear his mind. Something in the rhythm of the tires on the road and the distraction of all the scenery calmed him. These were times he really missed the feel of a Marlboro lit up in his hand, but he had left those behind with many of his other destructive habits. He drives past the entrance to the vineyard and instead turns down a gravel road.

Harvest time is drawing closer, and Drew needs to check on the grapes. Timing is everything in farming but especially for wine. The difference between good and great wine can literally be hours in the harvest. He's also glad for the excuse to leave because he had to get out of that space fast and get some air. The day had already been eventful with one unwelcomed memory from the past. Now with Michelle entering the picture, he still doesn't know how to react. It was no secret that Michelle was coming back to town; he had known for weeks, but he didn't want to let on to her that her return had consumed his thoughts. If you were looking to hide a secret or join the witness protection program, Chatham was not the place to be. Yet he had been foolish to believe that her return wouldn't impact him. Twenty years was a long time and a lot of water under the bridge for both. He hadn't expected these old feelings to resurface. Especially after all these years.

The truck rolls up to a locked gate blocking the rest of the drive. Two ducks are gliding in unison through the pond, offering a show to all who might enter their domain. He opens the glovebox and retrieves a key attached to an old shoelace. Once he's through the gate, he quickly locks it back and resumes the rest of the drive.

He parks the truck and sits for a moment with the window down. Since this morning, he's been feeling very out of sorts. Dr. Dan, his therapist, has fancier terms for it, but Drew can't remember those. He just knows he's out of his zone and needs to get back in.

*All right, let's see if this works. Focus on my five senses. What can I see, hear, smell, feel and taste? This better work or I'm firing him.* He first focuses intensely on the image before him. His eyes trace the outline of the mill, and he feels a sense of pride. The mill looks so different now compared to when he began the restoration project a few years ago. For Drew, returning to Chatham and owning this land and mill had been the goal that kept him focused and alive during multiple deployments. Most of his fellow Marines had a significant other or children as reasons to stay alive. His mind had a very direct list: stay alive, get back home, and own this place just for himself.

Purchasing the mill and the acres adjoining it had been a leap of faith financially and, to date, the ballsiest thing he had done in his life. He had poured his heart and soul into this mill. It had saved his life not only multiple times in combat but also from his most brutal and skilled enemy: addiction. Hours of manual labor not only brought this mill to life but served as a coping mechanism during his cravings.

Week by week, he held tight to the plan, working every free moment when he wasn't at the Taproom or winery. Once Billy came on board, it had really allowed him to focus more on the mill—sometimes working through the night and not realizing how much time had passed until the sun rose over the hill. The sunrise became his reward for a night of sobriety. One morning as he rinsed his raw and bloody hands in the cold water of the stream, he realized that for the first time in years, he felt things. He was finally free of the numbing substances and able to feel the discomfort and pain both physically and mentally that he had avoided for years.

The new metal roof glistens in the sun, having replaced the rusty tin pieces that were barely hanging on like the last sliver of the top of a tin can. One by one with meticulous detail he had replaced the missing and weathered boards. He runs his hand along the boards, noticing how smooth they are, the result of hours of sanding and then a high level stain to protect. Most people thought he was wasting his time on a huge money pit. In a digital technology age, who was going to come to a restored mill besides a few class field trips? Drew had blocked out the negative voices, something he had learned to do as an adult much better than as a young man. He no longer heard the voice of his father saying, "You're a piece of shit and will never amount to anything." He had replaced it with the voice of his Papa Silas: "Work hard and be honest. No matter what happens, your character is all you have." He saw a future and a vision for this old mill that few others could see. While most would see this rundown building as just a casualty of time, this mill represented his past and now his future. At times, he felt that he could identify with Noah as he built the ark. While he could do without a flood, he did hope his day would come when those who laughed would have to admit he was right.

A sweet fragrance lingers all around. He inches closer to the mill and picks a piece of the honeysuckle growing wildly all along the edge of the woods. Soon these abundant plants will begin to wither away as summer surrenders to fall. He inhales deeply to enjoy this scent. He opens his mouth and drops the delicious syrup onto his tongue. Closing his eyes, his body is no longer 38 but a 12-year-old boy. This mill holds so many memories. It was his sanctuary away from his cruel father, a swimming hole in the heat of summer, the place he and his friends tried their first taste of Jack Daniels, and the place where he first knew what it meant to be in love. A memory that still lingers in his mind to this day.

He may no longer be 12, and he can't get back the special people he's lost, but he can possess the place that holds the memories of some of the most important people and times of his life.

The sun is racing quickly behind the mill, and Drew heads back to his truck. As he's locking the gate, a large Suburban pulls in behind him, and Jeff and Robert Smith make their way out.

*Damn, not these idiots again. I am really not in the mood to deal with them today.*

"Evening, Drew," Robert says

"Robert, Jeff." Drew acknowledges them. "You boys have lived out here way too long to be lost, so what can I help you with tonight?"

"We came to make you one final offer on this property." Jeff says.

"You know it's a real shame that your parents paid for all that fancy education and you boys still can't understand one of the most basic words in the English language. For the last time, NO. I've told you, I am not selling this land to anyone, and most certainly not to you two."

"You're making a big mistake. We're making you a generous offer that could set you up for life. We only want the Carter Falls property; you can keep the vineyards and Taproom."

"This property has been in my family for hundreds of years, and that's exactly where it's going to stay."

Jeff takes a step closer. Drew feels the wave of heat flash through his body—a warning sign he learned to heed in his anger management training. Something he begrudgingly attended but is feeling very thankful for at this moment. *Stand your ground but don't engage. There is too much at stake.*

"Well, you might be able to tell us no, but good luck with the IRS. You aren't going to be able to get a free pass on your so-called integrity or your military honors. They'll want their money, and when you can't pay up, the land will be ours."

How dare this pompous ass who knew nothing of integrity or sacrifice bring up his military honors. There was no honor in not being able to bring home every Marine he'd led. A flash of faces and bodies scrolls through his mind, and then before he knows it, his body involuntarily lunges towards Jeff, and he grabs him by the neck.

Robert steps in and pushes Drew off. "Knock it off, Jones."

Drew releases his hold and steps back. He can feel the blood pounding in his head.

Jeff adjusts his shirt. "People say you've changed, but you're still the same hotheaded fool making stupid choices. I can't wait to see you crash and burn one more time."

"Well, for now this property is still mine, and you're trespassing. So get the hell off my property before I have to exercise my second amendment right."

The truck seems to drive itself as Drew is lost in his head. He knows that logically Jeff was right. He's taking a huge risk, and selling the property would be the safe bet, but he has yet to take the safe bet, and maybe—just maybe—this time it will pay off.

Michelle waves Allie over to her table as she jumps up to greet her. The two embrace and then settle into their seats.

"Sorry it's a little later than I expected. It was a hectic day." She takes off her blazer and hangs it on the back of the seat. "Oh, I don't know why I say that. It's always a hectic day. Feels like I'm always running around like a chicken with my head cut off."

"That's why you should move to Germany. The Europeans have a much different idea of what you should be busy doing."

"I wish. If I could, I would. Maybe once I get these kids raised."

"Have you tried this wine? It's amazing! Where is Rushing Streams Winery? We should totally take a girl trip there."

Allie smiles. "It's actually right here in Chatham. You don't know who owns that winery?"

"No. Who?" Michelle puts her glass down and gives an inquisitive look.

"Drew Jones," Allie says with a sense of satisfaction.

"Hush your mouth. Are you serious?"

"Dead serious. He inherited his grandfather's old tobacco farm and started a vineyard. He owns this place too. Pretty impressive."

Michelle watches Drew as he stocks bottles on the shelves. Yes, impressive, and he didn't even tell her.

"So he doesn't just work here?"

"No, silly. He's the owner. I heard he's also doing something up at Carter Falls, but apparently that's still in the works. Man, I miss those days; those were good times."

"They really were. Now you have kids at the age we were when hanging out there."

"Don't remind me. At least today I can spy on them way more than our parents were able to."

"I just had the oddest conversation with Drew before you arrived. I mean, I haven't seen him in all these years, and he starts drilling me about still wearing Benjamin's ring, wanting to know what Alex thinks of that."

"Well, what does he think?" Allie inquires.

"Et tu brute?" Michelle says with a look of disbelief.

"Sorry. Just wondering."

"You're a freaking chaplain. You should understand grief reactions and how I will never get over it."

"You're right, but something keeps you stuck. I'll leave that to you and your therapist."

Michelle doesn't feel like a therapy session. Not today. "Let's order. I'm starving. I'm getting lasagna and salad."

"You have to get the house dressing; it's to die for. Drew somehow got Mrs. Romano to come off the recipe."

"OMG, THE Sunny Italy dressing? I haven't had that since senior prom!"

"Yep, that's the one. I'm pretty sure he got her tipsy and charmed it right out of her."

"Knowing the old Drew, that sounds about right." She cranes her neck to get a closer look at him. He most definitely looks more fit and handsome than she'd expected. "But this version, this one has me perplexed. I feel a bit like I'm in a twilight zone. It's a real oxymoron; so many things are the same but also so different. The past is around every corner here. So many good memories but also the painful ones."

"I can't imagine from your view. The changes around here over the last ten years have been hard enough for locals to keep up with."

"I went to the cemetery today," Michelle says softly.

Allie reaches across the table and grabs her hand. "That must have been difficult."

"Beyond difficult, but I did it. It's just so weird Allie. How after 20 years does it seem like yesterday but also like he never existed?"

"I don't know. The longer I live, the more I think that by the time we have some bearings on life here, we'll be swept up by Jesus."

Michelle wipes a tear that has slowly emerged. "Okay, enough about me and my ghost adventures today. What's going on with you? How are the twins?"

"Good, just so busy. I'm ready for them to drive, but then every time I see a teen driver come in the ER, I'm like 'Nope, I will drive them around for life."

"And Dave?"

"What about Dave?"

"You know—your husband, your missing piece, the one your soul has longed for? Wasn't that your wedding toast?"

"Well, one day, Michelle, you'll be married for almost 20 years and have kids, and I feel it's my duty to tell you that you will be miserable."

"Ouch, that's harsh. What's going on? Is he cheating on you? First Katie, now you. I can't believe this; all men are snakes."

"No, I don't think so. I'm just so lost and fried. I mean, I love my kids, but after 15 years I feel like they're vampires and have sucked the life out of me. I used to be so ambitious and creative. I have no idea what happened to that part of me. My job is no longer a calling and passion; it is a job. The way I pay my bills. I've become everything I never wanted to be. My marriage is just a routine. I mean, in the middle of sex, I am mentally writing the grocery list."

"Yikes, I'm so sorry, Allie. I wish I could have been here to help you more. You and Dave need a vacation. Can you take some time off?"

"I've put in to take a sabbatical for four weeks in January. I haven't talked to Dave yet, but I just have to do it."

"I have a great idea! You guys should come to Germany to visit us. It will be amazing."

"I definitely will take you up on that, but I've already decided where I want to go."

"OOOHH, do tell! Tahiti? Hawaii?"

"No, Sierra Leone, and Dave isn't going."

"Oh my God, you're finally going. Have you found information on your parents?"

"Not yet, but I hope to."

"You must be feeling so many emotions."

"Yes, so many, but I just feel like it's now or never. I see so much life and death every day, and we're not getting any younger."

"You are so right. All this with Katie has really put a lot of things into perspective for me as well."

Soon their salads arrive and they're lost for the rest of the evening in happier conversations of days gone by.

Michelle exits the bathroom and runs slam into Drew.

"Let me walk you to your car."

"I'm a big girl. I think I can walk to my car alone in Chatham." Her response is snarky, as she's still upset at their earlier encounter.

"Ah, but you have no idea what has transpired since you left. A male escort can't hurt."

"Sure, if you must stamp your Southern gentleman card tonight, even though I'm pretty sure I could outshoot you any day."

He laughs. "You're probably right about that. Your daddy made sure of that before the air force ever got a hold of you." Time has changed a lot of things for both of them, but the blue in his eyes is the same as when he was a young boy.

"Michelle, I'm sorry about earlier. It's really not my place. I lost a best friend, but your relationship with Benjamin was so different, and it's not my place to judge."

"Drew Jones, what has gotten a hold of you? That's an apology spoken like someone who's been to a good therapist." She looks at him inquisitively.

He remains quiet.

"Why didn't you tell me that this was your business?"

"You never asked, and I gave your messages to the owner."

"It's wonderful to see things going well for you." She glances down. "Most of the reports I got sounded like things weren't going so well."

"Yes, there were dark days, but that's the past and I've made peace with it … well, most of it."

"Yes, I hope in my time here I too can find that peace."

They both stand in silence waiting for the other to speak.

"Well, it's been a long day. The time adjustment is hitting hard, and I still have to get settled at Nana's tonight. Goodnight."

She reaches to close her car door and he catches it with his hand. Leaning in, he says, "Hey, you like the wine so much, how about I show you the vineyards one day this week? Grapes are almost at their peak, so it's a great time to check it out."

She initially hesitates and then replies, "I would very much like to see this business of yours."

"I have a busy morning, so how about tomorrow afternoon?"

"Yes, Mom is giving me tomorrow to adjust before she begins ordering me around in the kitchen like in eighth grade."

"Remind me again how you're qualified for this job?"

"Strictly family debt, no skill."

"Meet me at the Taproom, say 4:00 tomorrow?"

"That will work."

"Sunsets over the vineyard are pretty spectacular this time of year."

Drew Jones slides into his truck seat and sits heavy with thought. Try as he might to forget Michelle Richardson, he could not. He had tried for 20 years. No matter how many women he dated, she was the bar they all had to measure up to. For years she had been the one constant and voice of reason in his insane world. She was the reason he made it to graduation, and probably the reason why he never followed through with his plans to make Curtis mysteriously disappear. But when he thought of her, it was always with a tinge of guilt. Benjamin was the absolute best friend a guy could ask for. That's why the waves of guilt were so strong. It broke every guy code in the world to long for your best friend's girl, even after his death.

# Chapter 8: Nana's House

Michelle clicks her lights to high beams and scans for deer along the winding dirt road. Another automatic response that came back courtesy of dear old Dad. She was fairly certain that the last words from her father's lips would be, "Watch for deer." The quiet hum of the road under her tires quickly changes to the crunch of gravel, a sound that as a child signaled she was nearing Nana Lucy's house. The winding driveway now seems short, but as a child it felt that it went on for miles. Very few dirt roads are left here, or really anywhere these days. This relic is a reminder of a time when more roads were dirt than paved, and seatbelts were seen as a nuisance versus a life saver. She ponders if they should have kept some of the dirt roads. Maybe the pace of life would have stayed slow. Gravel roads force a driver to take things slowly, unless they want the paint chipped off their car or to be carried off in a cloud of dust.

While things are more laid back here in the South, her time in Europe showed her that much of Western life has lost the art of relaxation and leisure. Even though by American standards life in the South is a slower pace, even leisure here isn't what it once was. Maybe that's what intrigued her so much about remaining in Germany. People just didn't seem to be in a hurry and obsessed with being busy. Just a few months here and then she and Alex could settle into a more leisurely pace.

Nana's vacant house offers Michelle the opportunity to have her own space. Even if her move is temporary, moving back after all this time is a lot to absorb. She's relieved to have her own space during so much chaos in her head. As Nana's dementia worsened, her sons insisted that she move out of her house. Of course that went over like a lead balloon. Oh no, Nana treasured her independence, and she fought for it to the last second like a revolutionary soldier charging Bunker Hill. She had called Michelle ranting and raving: "Can you believe these sons of mine? Their daddy would beat them senseless if he was still here. Claiming I need to stop driving and be babysat everywhere I go. We will see about that! I am going to take those boys to court."

Lucy Richardson was known for a lot of things, and following through on threats was one of them. Unfortunately, in a battle between tenacity and dementia, the latter will generally win. The day of her competency hearing arrived, and everyone sat eagerly looking at their watches, waiting for Lucy to present herself for her defense. Right on time, at nine on the dot, she made her dramatic entrance. Wearing her vintage Christian Dior black wool and satin suit, she sashayed right up to the perfume counter at Spainhour's department store and demanded to be directed to courtroom A. Needless to say, when Judge Haskins got the call from the store manager, no other witnesses were called. It turned out Nana had been the star witness in declaring her own incompetence.

As Michelle turns the key and enters the house, she immediately wonders if she's made a mistake. Opening the door to this house is like walking back in time. A proverbial museum of memories. Her boots create a rhythmic clicking that echo in the quietness and magnify the lack of human presence. She turns on the living room lights. This is one place literally frozen in time, just like she remembered it.

Nana did rustic cabin decor long before it was hip on HGTV. The images of deer and bears in the forest seem to belong more on a wall painting than a textile pattern. The wearing of the fabric on one cushion leaves no mistake which was the preferred seat. She leans in and takes a sniff of her grandad's worn leather recliner. After all these years it still has the faint scent of Prince Albert tobacco—a scent that she still associates with happy times. She picks up the frame that holds two photos: one of Nana and Grandad on their wedding day, and another taken of them on their 40th anniversary. While they had aged, the look they gave each other was still the same.

A towering bookcase in the corner houses a collection of framed photographs, an eclectic collage of photos that told not only the story of their family but also the fashion trends over the last 50 years. Wedding dresses that changed from knee-length baby blue to flowing white gowns with oversized headpieces and veils. Images of chubby babies, snaggletooth school pics, and even the coveted mall Glamour Shots. Her eyes go to the next picture, and her brain signals a pause. She gently lifts the photo. She holds it softly, as if the frame were as fragile as the memory. Attending senior prom with Benjamin was one of her last joyous events before his death.

She remembers feeling like a Hollywood celebrity trying on that black sequined gown. Her mom had told her it was too expensive, but she convinced her by offering to pay half with her babysitting money. She shakes her head and giggles softly. Boy, did she earn every penny of that money! Babysitting Christy Jordan's twin boys was definitely a prequel to basic training. If the energy those boys emitted could have been somehow collected, it could have powered the entire town for days. The worst of it was having to call her dad to help her get Jason's head unstuck from between the banister rails. Somehow, likely by divine intervention, they managed to avoid juvenile hall and now have families of their own.

She recognizes the dress, but not the girl. The twists and turns of life have replaced her youthful naivety with a mixture of cynicism and caution. Her mind begins a rapid fire of questions, like a magic eight ball. If Benjamin had lived, would they still be together? YES. Would she be miserable like Allie, strapped with all the adulting and loss of fun in the marriage? MAYBE. Would he have cheated on her like Katie's husband? NO. She shakes her head to clear the imaginary answers and racing thoughts as she places the picture back on the shelf. All a pointless waste of time to focus on events that will never happen, and the questions certainly can't be answered with a simple YES, NO, or MAYBE. At this stage, she's learned that life is more gray than black and white.

She kicks her boots off on her way into the kitchen. She calls out to Nana, as if she can hear her. "Nana, I'm leaving my shoes in the middle of the floor." That used to drive Nana crazy. She would always say, "Elizabeth Michelle, you are going to be the reason I trip and break my neck." She smiles and wishes she could hear that voice right now in this space. Dementia is so cruel; the body is still there, but the person you long for only shows up in flickers. Not to mention the almost demonic hatefulness that comes out that is not one fiber of the person you love.

Turning on the light, she sees a cellophane-covered basket with a hot pink ribbon. She opens the card: *Welcome home, sis! Love, Katie.* She peels back the cellophane to reveal a basket full of local wines, preserves, crackers, and snacks. With a sneaky suspicion, she opens the fridge to find it fully stocked. This is one time she loves reaping the advantages of having a Type A, super planner sister. Most of her life it just created feelings of inadequacy, but today, she extends her appreciation to this super power. Katie was the girl you wanted to dislike because she excelled at everything she did and was always so positive. The problem was, you couldn't dislike her, because the deeper you got to know her, the more you realized that this was indeed authentic. While no one should get cancer, it just seemed so unfair. Not just because she was her sister, but because every ounce of Katie permeated with optimism. Even in the midst of mothering and cancer, she was always thinking of others.

Opening the cabinets, she finds coffees, teas, and other supplies. Her eye is drawn to a clear canister on the counter filled with Bullseye caramel candies. She really had thought of everything. She opens the top and removes one; slowly she peels the wrapper, popping the sugary center out first. The creamy, sugary concoction melts on her tongue, and she quickly tosses the caramel in and savors the buttery flavor. She may have experienced some of the finest chocolates in the world, but this was a taste she hadn't had in years.

She picks up her phone and texts, "Thanks for the food and goodies. I can't believe you remembered the caramels."

"You're welcome! Who could forget? I'm pretty sure you helped pay for Dr. Harrell's mountain cabin in Asheville with all those cavities. Sleep well."

"LOL. You too."

She picks up a bottle of wine from the basket and notices it's from Rushing Streams. *Drew Jones owns a winery? What kind of twilight zone have I landed in?* She opens the bottle, pours a glass, and finds her way over to the recliner. She takes a sip and relishes the harmony between the acid, tannin, and fruit. Not only did Drew own a winery, he or someone who works for him really knows their craft.

She collapses into the chair and feels the worn leather envelope her like a warm embrace. The jet lag is setting in, and she lets out an audible exhale. *Geez, less than 12 hours home and two ghostly encounters already.* Her eyes return to the prom picture and she feels the tears begin to well up. Again, like earlier in the day, she chooses to let them flow rather than fight them. She can tell that the visit to the cemetery has stirred up deep feelings. But that was part of her mission here—to heal and move forward.

Her eyes wander to the corner of the room and she makes her way over to an old Steinway piano, which sits like a faithful hound, patiently waiting for some attention. Michelle runs her fingers over the keys of the piano. Placing her glass down, she sits on the bench. She gently presses a chord, and the sound hangs in the air as she settles onto the bench. *Could definitely use some tuning, but not as bad as it could be.* Like a muse taking over, before she even realizes, her hands begin to play. Taking piano lessons had been her mom's requirement, which she initially met with the same excitement as brushing her teeth each night at age five. She spent many hours playing scales to the tick tock of the metronome as she feverishly worked to perfect her skill. Eventually, instead of a tedious chore, playing the piano became something that she just had to do. It was the ultimate escape to lose herself.

She had spent hours playing after Benjamin's death. At times each note felt like a suture that held her heart together and kept it from completely ripping in two. Midway in Beethoven's *Moonlight Sonata*, without conscious thought, she shifts to Nana's favorite hymn and hears Nana's voice singing along: "Whatever my lot, thou hast taught me to say, It is well, it is well with my soul." Like most women her age, Nana's faith had been tried and tested with her own fair share of loss and disappointment in this life. She often sang this song as a solo in church, and when she sang these words, her conviction shined through.

Nana had always been there for Michelle, but she leaned on her the most after Ben's death. She was the only one she felt could truly understand. Everyone else could say that they knew how she felt, but that was simply not true. She became sick of hearing the platitudes: "You are so young, honey, you'll find love again." "He's in a better place." Or her all-time favorite, "He died a hero." Does it really matter how someone dies? They're gone, and that doesn't change the pain for those who love them. Nana had lost the love of her life, and she had also lost him suddenly, without warning.

The day of Grandad's death started out the same as every other weekday. He got up and went to work at Chatham's, the local textile plant where he had been working since high school. Nana got the call at school that he had suffered a heart attack. Too upset to drive, Mr. Huffman, her principal, drove her to the hospital. He was already dead when she arrived at the hospital.

The months following Grandad's death were some of the darkest Michelle had ever experienced in her family. At the tender age of eight, it was also her first exposure so close to death. She can remember seeing her once jovial grandad in the casket, and for once in her life she was frightened of him. For weeks after his death she had nightmares that he was coming to get her and taking her to heaven with him.

Then what seemed like overnight, Nana changed. After months of withdrawal and depression, she suddenly moved to Alabama to be near her sister Liz. This had the whole town whispering rumors that she must have had a breakdown to go live with her crazy sister. Daddy had always said that Aunt Liz was a few screws short of a hardware store. Michelle can remember being on the phone one night with Nana not long after she had moved and then hearing a loud *BANG*.

"Nana, what was that?"

" Oh, that was just Liz shooting at another armadillo. Liz, put that gun away before you shoot yourself."

But the biggest scandal came as Nana started dating. The talk at Cindy Hedge's parlor likely went something like this:

"Lord y'all, Lucy's lost her mind. She's traveling the world, and Harold's barely dead. We need to pray that she finds her way back to her senses."

Michelle recalls one night Nana called and her dad hung up the phone and said, "Linda, my mama has gone pure crazy. She's going on a singles' cruise at her age!"

"Oh Steve, that will be good for her. They'll play bingo …"

Michelle whispered to Katie, "Sounds like a swingers' party to me." Michelle can still hear her and Katie bursting into laughter.

"I bet Nana's got more than bingo on her mind."

"Elizabeth Michelle, hush your mouth! That's my mother you're speaking about."

She lifts her foot off the pedal and gently rolls the cover over the keys as the final chord dissipates into the air. After 48 hours of travel, she decides that a hot bath is just what she needs. No telling how long it's been since the water's been turned on and run into the house. The pipes moan and groan like an old man as the water makes its way through. Germany seems so far away, yet she feels like she needed her passport stamped again after entering Chatham. *Oh God, Alex.* She grabs her phone. *It's 3:00 a.m., and I don't want to wake him. I'll call tomorrow.*

The hot water seeps into every muscle, and she feels her tense body release into the water. Her mind pings from one thought to the next like a pinball machine. Multiple thoughts in seconds. Benjamin … Katie … Nana … Allie … Drew … so many emotions. She feels very unsettled. While her trip to the cemetery had been taxing, she had prepared herself on the flight home that it was past time to face this pain. She had locked it up in a box and run away, and now it was time to address it.

Seeing Katie, her defender and big sister, looking so fragile made her fearful. Michelle had thought the transplant would be done and she'd be fine, but seeing her in person and so frail made the fear of losing her more real. Nana? There were no words; it was just heartbreaking to see her this way. Allie and the hollow look in her eyes and the heaviness of her problems. Reviewing it all now, she feels a sense of guilt for not being there for them all. She feels like she took the easy way out, just running away and only dealing with herself.

Out of it all, what was most surprising was her encounter with Drew and how rattled she was by seeing him. Drew Jones—now that's a thick file to retrieve from the dusty corners of her brain. She's still reeling from their recent reunion. She had known that she would have to deal with him at some point, but this was not how she'd expected to find him. Many times she had envisioned running into him at a bar, but not sober, and most certainly not as the owner. She never expected to feel anything positive or negative again for him, but this new version has her curiosity peaked. This trip is beginning to shape up like an old episode of *Scooby-Doo* on Saturday morning cartoons. She sinks deeper into the water and closes her eyes. Yes, she certainly has some work to do to unravel this new mystery.

# Chapter 9: Rushing Streams

Drew is engrossed in arranging deli sliced meats, cheeses, and crackers along with a variety of olives and nuts on the wooden board when Michelle arrives.

"Wow, that's quite a spread. You really didn't need to go to all that trouble," Michelle says, swiping a pepperoni from the board and popping it into her mouth.

"No trouble at all. We serve charcuterie boards here at our tastings, so throwing one of these together has become like making a PBJ sandwich." He opens a bottle of wine and pours it in her glass. "So you're staying in your nana's house while you're here."

"Yes, I couldn't imagine living with my parents for several months. I mean, don't get me wrong, I love them, but I've been on my own for so long, and they still think of me as an 18 year old who knows nothing."

"Don't blame you there. When I left the Marines and came home, I lived with Grandma Rose for a bit, and that was hard on us both. We definitely do better with our own spaces."

He opens the patio door. Major, excited by new company, bolts straight for Michelle.

"Major, nein. Sitz." Drew speaks sternly.

"Aww, who's this sweet pup?" Michelle rubs Major's head and he quickly rolls to his back to shamelessly beg for belly rubs.

"Sweet pup … where?" Drew looks about the room and then back at Major. He raises an eyebrow and points to Major, who then flops over and runs to his owner. "Oh, you mean him. Do not be fooled by this needy mutt; he's only sweet to the ladies. Major, meet Michelle. We are"—he glances up at her—"old friends." He looks up at her to gauge if she agrees to this definition of their connection.

Michelle smiles and reaches for Major's paw. She gives it a gentle shake. "Schön, dich kennenzulernen, Major."

"I have no clue what you just said."

"It's German for 'Nice to meet you.' I heard you speak some German earlier."

He looks at her perplexed. "Afraid I am far from fluent, only a few dog commands. I paid a K9 buddy to do a little training with him when he was a pup."

"I like the take on the military name. Perfect name for a vet's dog."

"His official name is Major Pain—that's just short."

"He has the cutest face."

Major prances around, seemingly pleased at the compliment.

"The best the vet can tell is that he's a mix of pitbull and shepherd. My guess is a cocky pitbull charmed a fancy breeder's dog and they just set them out. No money in these."

"That's a shame. Someone missed out on a great pup."

"Yeah, as annoying as he can be, I'm glad to have him around. We'll come back to the food after our tour, but I can grab you a to-go box if you want to take some along."

"No, I'm good for now."

They head outside and climb into the side-by-side, and Major jumps in the back. Michelle laughs as he pokes his head in between the two of them and licks her face with his rough, wet tongue.

"Sorry, told ya he loves the ladies," Drew says, pushing Major back in his place.

As the side-by-side crests over the hill, Michelle can't believe her eyes. "Drew, this is incredible. I had no idea all this was even out here."

Stretching as far as the eye can see, the perfectly neat rows of grapevines create a patchwork quilt of green and yellow blocks. As they come closer, she can see that each carefully manicured grapevine is hanging full of ripening grapes in a variety of purples, reds, and greens. If she didn't know better, she would think she was in the Bordeaux region of southwest France or the hills of Tuscany, Italy.

Drew stops and Major jumps down and begins to bark, chasing a bird away as if he was protecting his master's kingdom.

"Ironic, huh? Here you've been traveling the world in search of the perfect wine, and it's been growing in your back yard the whole time." He bends down and pulls some grapes from the vine, tossing two in his mouth and handing her the others. "Almost there."

She cradles the grapes in her hands and takes a moment to explore the color and texture before depositing them in her mouth. "These are definitely different from the sweet grapes we got in trouble for sneaking out of Miss Mabel's back yard. Do you remember?"

"How can I forget? I still have a scar on my ankle from her dog."

"Mr. Sniffers? He was a harmless toy poodle!"

"Tell that to my ankle. The grapes we were swiping at Miss Mabel's were muscadines, sweet grapes that are native to NC. These grapes are Petit Verdot. They're smaller and more thick-skinned, and they grow very well here in Chatham. We leave most of the sweet muscadine wines to our friends down east in Duplin County. They've had a corner on that market for years. At Rushing Streams, we focus mostly on creating Cabernet, Chardonnay, Merlot, and Riesling wines. "

"It's just mind blowing to me. You know, when we were in high school, this is the last place I would have seen as a wine Mecca."

"You're telling me. It's really insane. We now have hundreds across the state, and a huge chunk of those are right here in the Yadkin Valley. It's definitely been a game changer for not only the landscape but the economy."

Michelle looks around and raises her shoulders. "So where is the grape stomping pit?"

"Still watching old reruns of *I Love Lucy* I see. Thankfully, those days are over and the stomping is done by machines today."

"Good. That may be the old traditional way, but it just always grossed me out thinking about foot fungus or bacteria in my wine."

He laughs. "I'm pretty sure the alcohol would take care of that."

The side-by-side comes to a halt and she takes his lead and follows him out. Major jumps out and stays in step with his owner.

"Watch your head coming under the separator." He reaches out and gently places his hand over her head as a reminder. "We harvest most of the grapes in September. As soon as the grapes are harvested, they must go straight to be crushed and pressed. They travel up this auger, into the separator, and then are pressed to separate the juice from the debris. In a few weeks, Billy and I will be working seven days a week, non-stop. I have a young buck named Jordan Smith from NC State doing an agricultural internship this year. Always nice to have another set of hands during harvest—well, until they think all that fancy education trumps years of hard earned wisdom."

They walk back to the warehouse, and Drew opens the door to a room with large barrels, some wood and some stainless steel. "Next we move into fermentation. This is where yeast enzymes are introduced to the grape juice. The yeast begins turning sugars into alcohol."

"So what happens to all the leftover grapes and seeds?"

"We sell them to a company that makes grape seed products and supplements."

"Smart. Using that Boy Scout 'waste nothing' principle I see. How long do you ferment it?"

"It really depends on the wine. On average, reds typically take 5 to 30 days to ferment. Whites ferment for less time than reds, depending on whether the wine is meant to be sweet or dry."

He opens another door, and she feels a slight chill despite the warm evening. He grabs her hand. "Careful, there are a few unexpected steps here. After the wine ferments, we clean it up with clarification. There are many ways to clarify wine; here we use racking. Basically, we move the wine from one barrel to another to help the leftover solids filter to the bottom."

She continues to follow him and Major as he points to various containers. She's fascinated not only by this process of winemaking but the process that has created a whole new man.

"After fermentation and filtering, some of our wines are ready to drink, but Driftwood, your choice, is our premiere wine, as it's matured in oak barrels for a year before bottling."

"Ah, so that's the oaky flavor and hence the name. Very clever."

"Oak barreling can add vanilla, clove, or smoke flavors. Plus, the porous oak also slowly allows oxygen into the wine, changing the wine from astringent to smooth. All our other wines are housed in stainless steel wine barrels." Drew opens the door to bring them back outside.

"So that's your *CliffsNotes* version of winemaking. I truly am amazed. This is quite an undertaking."

"Well, it was about time I did something with my life that was productive. Let's head back to the tasting room and I'll let you sample a few other wines."

The sun illuminates the rolling hills and vines like a nightlight. Drew was right, this sunset is spectacular. She realizes that she's feeling more and more comfortable with him. She would have thought that all the years apart would terminate a relationship, but not this one.

She looks at her phone and sees a missed call from Alex; she had totally blanked on their scheduled time. She quickly sends a text: BUSY WITH FAMILY. CALL YOU LATER.

"So how did you learn how to do all of this? I don't remember winemaking as an elective at East Chatham High."

"When I first separated from the Marines, I was trashed. Years of pushing my body to the limit in training, and then Iraq and Afghanistan, caused serious injury to my back and knees. I was on painkillers, muscle relaxers, you name it, but still in agony. I kept trying to get my disability through the military, but that can be a nightmare."

"I've seen so many friends go through it. Very frustrating," she says.

"I just didn't know what to do with myself. You know, my days were so structured as a Marine; my day was planned out from sun up to sun down. Once I got out, everything felt so overwhelming. I mean, I went straight from living in Grandma Rose's house to living on base. I'd never set a budget or paid for household fees. So I just escaped. I added booze onto the pills, and some weeks I didn't even leave my house. One thing that I didn't leave behind in the service was my hot temper. So I got stupid one night and ended up in a bar fight. But it probably saved my life because the judge ordered me to counseling. It was the same judge who sentenced Curtis, so I feel like he took pity on me and hoped this would help me not to retrace my father's steps."

"Well, at least you now admit to it. Back in the day, it was everyone else who had the problem, according to you."

"You're not wrong about that. I own that. I've been working with my therapist, Dr. Dan, for over five years. Can you believe anyone would put up with me for that long?"

"Well, he is paid," she says, teasing. "But if you've stuck with him that long, you guys must be a good match. "

"I had no idea just how great a match he was until later in our sessions. Despite his hippie peace appearance, Dr. Dan knows the reality of combat. He's a Vietnam vet who knows the smell of death and the sting of loss. He saw it first hand as a medic. He lost friends on the field and then so many to suicide after the return home."

"Unfortunate for him, but so glad that you found someone you could trust and relate to. Not everyone gets the military culture, especially combat."

"Once I understood he really got what I'd been through, he helped me get into specialists for my back and get off the pills and booze."

"So you own a winery but don't drink?"

"I do taste our wines and occasionally have a glass or two, but no more liquor. I'm not an alcoholic like my father. I was just self-medicating myself to an early death. Dr. Dan asked me one day, 'If you could do anything and know it wouldn't fail, what would you do with your life?' The answer was so easy. I would run this farm just like Papa Silas"

"So the answer wasn't 'I want to open a winery?'"

"Not initially, but tobacco isn't the crop anymore. Hell, I stopped smoking myself. So I figured I'd get in while the getting was good, and wine was where it was at. This industry has brought life and jobs back to this town. I went to Surry Community College and studied viticulture and worked hard. "

Michelle reaches in her lap to pet Major, who has decided that even at 80 pounds he still wants to be a lap dog.

"I know, it's really good to see this town come to life again. Mom and Katie are doing really well at the inn. I know all they've done to make this small business work, and I just don't think I would be brave enough."

"Everyone wants to talk about the American dream of being self-employed, but it's scary as hell. I've received a lot of support from business classes at the community college as well as the Chatham Chamber of Commerce. You really have to band together and support each other."

"I think it's great how you partner with the bakery for desserts. I mean, you could just make your own."

He chuckles. "Trust me, I'm looking to sell desserts, not kill people."

"But the food at the Taproom is so good."

"That's thanks to Scott. I lucked up when I found him. I tell him that working at the Taproom is like the Mafia. He's never allowed to get out. And Billy has been a Godsend. He's way too modest; that dude could be making bank in Napa, or really anywhere in the world. I may have learned how to grow the right grapes, but he's a master vintner. Just glad he decided he wanted to raise his kids hillbilly style." Drew flashes her a smile.

"He seems like a great guy."

Back at the Taproom, he pours a flight of wines. She looks at Drew and places her hand on his shoulder. "I am so proud of you, and I know your papa would be as well."

There were only a few people in his life that he had ever cared whether they liked him or were proud of him, and she was one. It feels good for once in his life. Things seem to be going in the right direction.

# THE CRUSHING

# Chapter 10: Katie

Katie stirs her coffee and grabs her blanket. The porch door lets out a screech as she makes her way to her rocking chair. She pulls the worn blanket around her shoulders. Most people would have thrown this torn and tattered blanket out years ago; it certainly wasn't an original design. These animal print blankets were made right here in Chatham and were a dime a dozen in the 1980s. But this blanket had been a Christmas gift from Nana Lucy, and just like Linus and his blanket, this one had been with her through thick and thin. When she was a child, her mom told her that the tiger would keep all the bad dreams away. This same blanket absorbed the tears shed after the heartbreak of breakups. It had kept her warm in her dorm room during long study nights as well as late nights of rocking her babies to sleep. Her ex-husband could take a few notes on loyalty from this blanket, that's for sure.

Until recently, she couldn't remember the last time she actually sat on her back porch. Life was just too busy, or if she did have the chance to sleep past 5:00 a.m., she sure took it. But since her diagnosis, she's had a great desire to soak in the little things. She wishes she could return time like an unwanted holiday gift. If she could, she'd return all the wasted fretting and worries over silly things and exchange them for more sunsets, sticky kid hugs, and even more romantic times with Brian. Maybe they would have remained connected and still be together.

She takes a sip of her hazelnut coffee and really lets the aroma and taste linger on her tongue. How many times had she thrown this same coffee in her travel mug and run out the door, both as a teacher and then with the bakery and inn? She reflects on how many times she had truly paid attention to a meal, or really anything, before her diagnosis. Sad, but it had taken facing her own mortality to wake up to living.

As the sun peaks its rays over the rolling hills, she begins to hear the bellowing of the cows, and she briefly closes her eyes to thank God for another day. Something else that she rarely did before getting sick, even though she'd been raised in church and took her kids every Sunday. With the hecticness of jobs, kids, marriage, and community obligations, as embarrassed as she was, God was next to last on her list. She had really come to treasure these times not only with God, but with herself. Motherhood was something she had always wanted, and she was glad she had her children, but she had really become lost and disconnected not only from God but with herself during this time. She opens her journal and begins to write.

Dear Lord,

My pain is increasing by the day, but I know I must keep pressing on. No need to bother anyone with it, and I know you're the one who renews my strength each day. The last two years have been hard, and you've helped me to keep things as normal and I can for the kids. It was exhausting before, but now it's like trying to move with weights strapped to my feet. I have found out that school fundraisers, dance classes, and ball practices don't care about cancer, and life keeps spinning with three kids. This is hard, but I give thanks for all you have brought me through. You were with me through the incredible pain of the double mastectomy and the hellacious chemo.

Dr. Chambers has assured me that once I get my stem cell transplant, things will finally be on the upswing. I want to feel hopeful, but I'm still scared. I know I'm supposed to surrender to your will, but I pray for this healing. I want to be here for my children. I know, though, that I can do hard things. If I went from running 5ks to competing in a triathlon in only a year, surely I can make it until my match is found. I wish I didn't have to be sick, but one thing that has come out of this is that Michelle is home. Thank you for bringing her home. I've missed her, and now that she's back home our family seems complete. I want her to be happy, but I wish she could find happiness here at home and settle here. Am I selfish to pray for that? The kids really love having her here, and she's such a blessing to me and Mom. Lord, please bless my children and protect them during this hard time. In Jesus' name, Amen.

Katie closes her journal and lets out a deep breath. Soon she'll need to leave this sacred space to get the kids up for school, but she basks in a few more minutes of peace before the chaos ensues. Her mind turns to Brian. As much as having cancer sucks, she never thought she'd be doing this without him. While the physical pain is bad, the hurt of his betrayal has nearly killed her. Before her cancer diagnosis, Katie's life had been pretty much a fairytale by Chatham standards. She was the valedictorian of her class and attended Appalachian State near home in Boone. She had always wanted to be a kindergarten teacher and loved her time training as an educator. Each year she walked into her classroom, and every kid was full of possibilities. She loved the idea that she was the teacher who might make a child love learning for life.

She and Brian had met at App and married shortly after graduation. The first few years of marriage were full of hope. They chose to wait on kids while they built their careers and house. They thought they had plenty of time, but they didn't count on infertility. The brutal years of hormone treatments and the financial and emotional stress had taken a toll on their marriage. With the busyness of teaching, Brian's real estate appointments, and kids, there was no time to fix it.

While Katie had known that they had become roommates, she never expected him to have an affair. It wasn't just a fling either. Thanks to social media, he had reconnected with his old high school flame, Sally Thompson. She was divorced from her husband, and soon Brian had moved in with her and her teenage kids. He tried to reconcile and come back home after Katie was diagnosed, but cancer or not, she was no one's second choice, and she sure wasn't up for a pity party return.

Now she wishes that she hadn't watched so many Disney movies as a child. If only parents had known what that Sunday night *Wonderful World of Disney* brainwashing was doing to future psyches. Cluttering brains with all that happy ending nonsense. So much so that society keeps searching for that happy ending. True, the beloved characters do experience loss and pain—Bambi and Simba lose a parent—but society is still conditioned to believe that somewhere in there lies a happy ending.

She feels a little tap on her shoulder and turns to see Joel. She still can't believe that her sweet baby has just turned four.

"Mommy, what are you doing out here?"

"Hey, honey, talking to God."

"Really, like Moses on top of the mountain?" he says with wide eyes of disbelief.

"Kind of, just at the bottom of the mountain." Katie places the blanket around his shoulders. "Come on, Superman, let's get some breakfast going."

"Superman wants pancakes, but no blueberries. They are his kryptonite!"

"Well, I can't turn down a request from Superman, and his food allergies are noted"

She opens the screen door and watches as his tiny arms soar with the blanket streaming behind. Super cape, yet another versatile use for the old Chatham blanket. Before her diagnosis, Katie would have rushed to the stove. Instead, she pauses to watch her tiny superhero as he saves his universe, one action figure at a time. Maybe old Mr. Disney had it right after all. Childhood should be full of fantasy and happy endings, because real life will catch up to you soon enough.

# Chapter 11: Baking Lessons

M ichelle follows the glow of the porch light and makes her
way into the kitchen There she finds her mom elbow-deep
in some sort of meat mixture.

"Morning, sunshine," Linda calls without lifting her gaze.

"I think the proper greeting is good evening, until the sun
actually rises. What is that disgusting meat blob?"

"Don't turn your nose up, sassy. It's meatloaf, and to refresh
your memory, you used to love it. There's a fresh pot of coffee;
hopefully that will change your tune. I'm about to put the meatloaf in the oven and then get started on blueberry muffins for the
inn guests."

Phillip makes his way down to the dining room. He seats
himself at a small table by the window. This is one reason why he
choses to stay at small inns on his travels. He craves the peace and
tranquility that these intimate spaces bring. Living in the city has
plenty of perks, like the finest restaurants, museums, and nightlife,
but the traffic and busyness takes a toll. He's always felt that he has
an old soul, and in these old spaces he really connects. Almost as if
he's lived much longer than his chronological years.

He gazes into the parlor, which features a plush velvet sofa and two wingback leather chairs. He pauses for a moment and pictures it as it would have been long ago, with a roaring fire while "Rhapsody in Blue" played on the old Victrola. He ponders all the possible conversations that likely occurred over the century in that space. Talks of looming wars. Concerns about the economy, or just a weekly ladies tea with talk of community events and irritations with husbands.

Linda clears her throat to gain his attention. "Good morning, Mr. Matthews. I do hope that you slept well."

"Oh yes, sorry, just lost in thought. Thank you, I did, and I am happy to report that my room did not spin, just as promised."

Linda smiles as she settles the basket of fresh blueberry muffins in front of him. "Glad to hear it. I have fresh muffins for you. Would you like coffee, or perhaps you prefer tea?"

"Coffee will be fine."

"Our breakfast options are there on the display. I'll be back to get your order."

"I will also have two more joining me this morning, so if I could get two more cups of coffee, that would be great."

Linda disappears into the kitchen, and Phillip reaches for his phone. He scrolls through a list of multiple unread messages and decides nothing needs his immediate attention.

The bell jingles above the door, and Phillip looks up to see his potential business partners enter. He rises and extends his hand. "Good morning. Phillip Matthews."

"Robert Smith," one of the men says, shaking hands, "and this is my brother Jeff."

"Pleasure to meet you both. Please join me and help yourselves. They brought enough to feed an army."

"Yeah, if you leave Chatham hungry or without a few extra pounds, that's your own fault. Linda Richardson is the epitome of southern hospitality."

Linda appears and fills Robert's and Jeff's cups. "Well, good morning, boys. Good to see you. How are your folks enjoying retirement?"

"Good morning, Mrs. Richardson. Apparently they're doing real good. We rarely hear from them. I have to call them to make sure they're alive." Jeff says.

"I'm sure they have plenty to keep them busy down in the Keys. Can I get you boys something to eat?"

"Oh, nothing for me." He looks at Robert.

"No, thank you. I'm good with coffee."

"Well, I'll leave you all to your meeting."

Robert moves the basket of muffins to the side and opens his laptop. "This is the architectural rendering of the plans for the resort. As you can see, it has everything a family could want to enjoy while on vacation."

Phillip studies the plans carefully.

Jeff points to the screen. "We have two beautiful pool areas: one for families with kid-friendly splash pads, and another for adults only. There's also a beautiful spa facility, which we know will be popular not only with hotel guests but locals as well."

"What about a restaurant?" Phillip asks.

"We went back and forth on that but decided not to include one. There are so many great restaurants around town and at some of the wineries, and we didn't want to impact their business. We'll offer a complimentary breakfast and a snack bar."

Robert swipes at the screen. "Now let me show you my favorite part. The interior of the rooms. Take a look at this. The rooms are designed to look like old mountain hunting lodges."

Phillip takes the tablet and admires the details that have been thought out for each room.

"You guys certainly didn't miss a thing. It definitely seems like a great investment. The land is near Carter Falls, right? I'd really like to see it."

"It's a beautiful property that includes walking trails all around Carter Falls for guests to enjoy," Jeff says.

"Oh, yes. Robert says, "Carter Falls is not only a hidden gem but has significant historical value to the town. The falls powered the water wheel for the old grist mill owned by the Carter family. Later a dam built at the top of the falls actually fueled electricity for the town for many years. The town has wanted to get this land for years, but the family was never willing to sell. This is a rare opportunity to acquire it."

Phillip puts his hand up and interrupts. "Whoa, wait just a minute. To acquire it? You don't already own this land?"

Robert glances over at Jeff. "Well, not yet, but we will soon. The current owner inherited it from his grandfather, but we know he's so far under back taxes that he'll be forced to sell soon."

"You guys mean you brought me all the way here to sell me on a hotel investment to be built on land that you don't even own?" Phillip stares intently at them.

"Mr. Matthews, I can understand you being upset. But trust us, this is all but a done deal. There's no way this isn't going to happen."

"You have no idea that this guy is going to be forced to sell. He may have other backers or family members who can help him out."

"Trust us, Drew Jones is in way over his head, and he doesn't have anyone to bail him out."

Phillip stands up. "I have another meeting at the Old Beau Golf Resort. Let me know when you boys actually acquire the land, and then we'll talk further. Until then, don't waste my time."

The bell on the front door jingles and Katie enters.

"Hi, honey, how was your transfusion?" Linda asks as she removes the piping hot meatloaf from the oven and sets it on the cooling rack.

"Just another day as a human pin cushion. Hopefully I'll feel the energy impacts soon. I saw Robert and Jeff Smith out there meeting with someone," Katie says, wrapping the apron around her withering waist. "Wonder what scheme they're up to this time?" Katie opens the fridge and grabs a carton of eggs.

"What do you mean?" Michelle asks.

"Well, a few years ago, they basically stole Mable Reeves' house right out from under her. After her husband died, she was left financially strapped, so they told her they would buy her house and let her rent it back from them. A few months later, they terminated her lease and then turned around and sold the land to a gas station chain and made a huge profit." Katie taps the eggs one by one on the side of the bowl.

"Well, those apples didn't fall far from the tree," Linda chimes in. "Their father started that real estate company, and he's been doing underhanded deals for years. How do you think they could afford to retire so early in the Keys? Such a shame too; their Mama is so nice. I don't know how she can be married to such a devious man."

"Okay, sis, let's get you baking. We're going to start with the red velvet cake this morning. I've helped you out by measuring out all the ingredients for your first lesson."

Michelle reaches for the eggs and begins to dump them into the large mixing bowl. Katie grabs her arm. "Wait! What are you doing?"

"Baking a cake?"

"Not like that, you're not. You have to start with your wet ingredients and then add in your dry ingredients slowly."

"What's the big deal? It's getting all mixed up anyway." Michelle shrugs her shoulders and looks at her sister.

"Michelle, I hate to admit it, but your daddy is right. He always says you have all the book sense but no common sense," Linda says with exasperation.

"Really? Let's see how many of you can survive in the jungle on just rain water and bugs."

The bell rings outside on the counter.

"Oh Lord, let me go see what Prissy Weeks wants this time. I'm sure she's got her knickers in a wad about something. I swear, you would think her daughter was the only girl who's ever gotten married!"

Nana, who had been lost in her word search book, slowly moves over to Michelle.

"Bless your heart, Michelle, you always were a fish out of water in the kitchen. Scoot over and make room."

Nana scoops the measuring cup into the flour container and reaches for a knife. She skillfully levels each scoop before sifting the flour with baking soda, baking powder, cocoa, and a dash of salt. She moves over to the commercial grade mixer and plops a softened stick of butter into the bowl. She briefly searches for the power switch. "Humph, where is that thingamabobber? We didn't have these high-tech gadgets back in my day. Can you girls imagine, we used to actually have to stand and mix this by hand."

Her hands subtly shake as she slowly pours in the sugar, making a creamy concoction. The mixer continues to hum as she gently folds in the eggs one by one, followed by vanilla extract and red food coloring. Then with the precision of a well-oiled machine, she begins to alternate between the flour and buttermilk vinegar mixture. Michelle and Katie watch with amazement. She doesn't miss one step.

Nana shuts off the mixer and lifts the paddle to reveal a vibrant red batter that already smells decadent. Michelle resists the urge to stick her finger in and sample the cake batter. Nana used to have one beater for each girl to lick when no one cared about the possibility of salmonella poisoning from raw eggs.

With a look of accomplishment, Nana steps back and says, "Now that's how you mix up a cake fittin' for the preacher!"

"Here, Nana, let me help you pour the batter." Katie pours the rich batter into neatly greased and floured pans. Nana gently makes her way back to the table and resumes her word search.

"What was that?" Michelle looks in disbelief

"What was what?" Linda says, walking through the doorway.

"Behold the power of dementia," Katie says. "Nana was with it enough just now to mix an entire red velvet cake from memory."

Nana calls from the corner, "You know I can hear you talking. I am sitting right here."

"You sure are, Lucy. We see you," Linda calls to her with an elevated voice.

Linda carefully runs the knife along the side of the baking dish, freeing the meatloaf from the edges. "Like we said, some days are good and some bad. We take it as it comes and enjoy the moments of blessings."

"Sis, how are you getting settled back here in little ole Chatham? Missing the big city life yet?"

"I have to say I've been pretty impressed with all the changes here. There are so many beautiful venues, more food choices than just BBQ or buffets, but the wine is definitely the most impressive. I never expected to drink wine as good as I do in Europe while I was here."

"Well"—Linda turns her head to the side—"it sounds like the prodigal daughter isn't just tolerating her hometown but enjoying it."

Michelle plops a large three-ring binder down on the counter. "Well, I hope you're ready for a full day. Baking might not be in your blood like weather forecasting, but we're about to give you a crash course."

Michelle settles in between her mother and sister and prepares to learn. There would be no other choice when face to face with two former educators but to pay attention and learn. She had never had the slightest desire to bake anything other than a frozen pie. Yet as her time with Drew had proven, time moves on, and life changes in ways you can never predict.

# Chapter 12: Dr. Dan

It was late September, and with the trees just beginning to tease the color show to come, it made for a nice drive. Many people look forward to fall, and the economy here sure reaps the tourism rewards, but fall for Drew is a cautionary signal that winter is next. He feels a shiver run through him just thinking about it. Summer is it for him. Give him an 80-degree day, his rod, and some biting fish, and he's content.

Drew starts the ignition and begins his hour drive to Boone. It's time to check in with Dr. Dan. Since the stabilization of his PTSD over the years, his appointments have become less frequent. Dr. Dan and Drew are thinking of extending the gap between them even more, but Michelle's return has set off a firestorm of emotions to be handled. Now he may consider stepping up the sessions.

It's a commitment to drive the hour to Boone one way, but he really doesn't mind the drive. There are only a handful of therapists in Chatham, and he knows every single one of them. Plus, they're all female. He doesn't consider himself a misogynist, but he needs to work through these issues man to man.

Initially, Drew was pretty sure that Dr. Dan was a participant at Woodstock. His gray, long ponytail, and his office with eclectic decor and crystals, screamed old hippie. In his late sixties, Dr. Dan still sported Birkenstocks with his jeans and blazer. Definitely a stark contrast to Drew's well-worn Carhartt Jacket and cowboy boots. Drew learned quickly to never judge a book or person by their cover. Despite his hippie appearance, as Drew had shared with Michelle, Dr. Dan knew about combat from more than a textbook. Being a Vietnam vet, he knew the smell of burning flesh and the sting of loss of his friends. Additionally, he knew the confusion and loneliness of returning home to be spit on and hated, all because you did the job you were recruited and trained to do.

"How's it been going, Drew? So good to see you." Dr. Dan stands up as they shake hands. "Catch me up since our last visit."

"Well, my anger has been pretty controlled. Just a lot going on. I have a lot of financial stress on me." Drew settles into the couch and crosses his ankle atop his thigh.

"Tell me what's going on there." Dr. Dan places his coffee mug to the side table.

"Well, you know I've already told you that the land the vineyard is on I inherited from my grandfather."

"Yes, I believe you told me he was a very successful tobacco farmer."

"Yes, he was. So he left the land to me and my brother, but my brother left Chatham years ago and didn't care about the land, so he signed it all over to me."

"What about your grandmother?"

"She has lifetime rights to the house, and believe me, my grandfather was a wizard with investments. He looked out for her, but to see her shop at the grocery stores, you'd think she was going broke tomorrow. I try to get her to splurge on herself, but it's pointless."

"I get it. They came up during the Great Depression, and you don't forget that kind of poverty."

"So the land is mine free and clear, which is a blessing, but the property taxes must still be paid each year, and with the land values here soaring what seems like daily, the increase each year is unbelievable."

"Do you have anyone you can ask for a bridge loan?"

"No. I'm currently maxed out with the renovations at the tap room and the work on the old mill building."

"What about your grandmother?"

"No, I'm going to do this on my own. If I can just make it through the holiday season, I'll have more than I need to get the cash flow going."

"So for now, this is a wait and see game. Let's focus on getting through each day and keeping the stress down until a resolution can be found. Remember, we don't have a crystal ball, so we can't predict the future. How about flashbacks?"

"Only one episode of flashbacks."

"Were you able to use the calm, safe space to help ground you?"

"Doc, as much as I hate to admit it, yeah, I did."

"And?"

"Yes, it worked."

Dr. Dan chuckles. "Why do you hate to admit that something like that works?"

"I don't know, it just seems like some new age magic mess or something."

"The human body is magical, and we're just using what we know to stop that process. Maybe it would be helpful for us to process that flashback. Was it related to your father?"

Drew wrings his hands and stares down at the floor. "No."

"Your mother?"

Drew feels his stomach sink at the mention of his mother. "No."

"Oh, so Iraq?"

"No, it's something we've never discussed, and I'm not sure that I'm ready to even now. Doc, there are some doors that should probably remain closed."

"Well, of course it's your choice whether you share that or not, but I'll play the therapist card and argue that keeping doors closed is not the best path to healing. Don't you think opening the other doors have helped you tremendously? You're certainly not the same man who walked in my door a few years ago."

Dr. Dan was right, but Drew didn't walk in here willingly. His inability to manage his addictions and anger had landed him in a bar fight, and a judge ordered him to counseling.

"I thought I was in such a better place. I've worked through so much and found my passion in the winery and rebuilding the old mill."

"You're still in a better place to use your words. You're not going backwards; there's just a new kink in the road that has to be worked out. What has you so rattled?"

"A girl, Doc, a girl. Isn't that always the story?"

"Okay, now we're getting somewhere. So tell me about this girl."

"Michelle Richardson. We've known each other forever."

"Interesting. For someone so significant, you've never mentioned her before."

"There was never a reason to. She moved away right after graduation, so she hasn't been a part of my life for a long time," he says looking out the window and watching a cardinal settle onto the bird feeder.

"So if this girl who lived near you and hasn't been a part of your life in over 20 years has you rattled, I don't think you need to be a therapist to know there must be a story here."

Drew shifts his gaze to meet Dr. Dan and nods his head. "Yep, a story that impacted and changed many people's lives. A story I wish I could rewrite."

"Drew, it appears that whatever you don't want to share is causing you a lot of distress. Remember, as you've experienced already, those can trigger huge episodes of depression and the potential for relapse as well."

"Maybe next time, Doc, but for today, our time's up. I promise I will step up the meetings."

Drew walked out knowing that as much as he dreaded it, he must finish what he had started in therapy. He couldn't just deal with his war wounds and ghosts. He had to slay these demons from his childhood. His sobriety was counting on it, and he valued that way too much.

# Chapter 13: The Offer

Phillip makes his way down Highway 21 and thinks how his grandfather's descriptions of these foothills were so accurate. It was truly astonishing how vividly his mind had burnt these images, considering he'd been a young man when he left. The sun sinks further below the horizon, splitting the blue sky like pie into equal slices of red and orange. As a child, his grandfather had told him stories about how he grew up in the shadows of these Blue Ridge Mountains, where his brothers and cousins would pass the day away playing cowboys with tobacco sticks for horses and corn cobs for pistols.

Phillip's dad, and subsequently his children, had grown up with very comfortable finances, largely supported by his grandfather's success as a physician. So this type of existence sounded like abject poverty to this yuppie, yet his grandfather lit up full of joy as he relayed these stories. He used to say, "What we lacked in wealth, we made up for with the richness of community. No one would ever go without as long as we had community. If you had extra, you shared it, whether it was tomatoes, clothes, or money. We weren't consumed with having more than our neighbor, like we are today. We were working to survive together."

As his grandfather's workhorse body started to break down as a result of Lou Gehrig's disease, he talked nonstop about Chatham, and especially Rose Holcomb Johnson. Rose and his grandfather were raised on the same street, attended the same church, and ultimately that connection led them to be high school sweethearts. While Phillip knew that his grandfather, John, had loved and been devoted to his grandmother, who they had lost to breast cancer many years ago, Rose had always held a special place in his heart. He openly admitted that Silas Johnson had been the better match for her. John knew he was too ambitious and selfish to ever love Rose the way she needed. He felt that she deserved someone who could appreciate her kindness and love and make her feel valued, and he knew no matter how much he adored someone, medicine was his first love. Before he lost his ability to speak, he shared with Phillip his regrets for not retiring in Chatham and enjoying the last years of his life there. He begged Phillip not to make his life all about work, and that if he found someone he couldn't live without, to make her the priority. These words echoed in his head frequently as he struggled in this crazy world to find the right partner.

His GPS alerts him that he has arrived at his destination: the Taproom Bar and Grill.

"Get home to your family, Billy. I've got this." Drew motions to the door as he wipes down the bar.

"If you're okay, man, I know my wife would appreciate a second pair of hands to wrestle the kids through bath and bedtime."

"Tell Lorie she's welcome. Thankfully, Major has a bladder the size of the Goodyear blimp. See you tomorrow."

Phillip takes a seat at the bar.

"Howdy, welcome to the Taproom." Drew grabs a menu and places it down along with a glass of water. "On the front you'll find food, and the back lists our beer and wine selections."

Drew disappears into the back briefly and then returns, asking, "What can I get for you?"

"After a long afternoon of golf, I think a beer would really hit the spot. Whatever lager you have on draft will do."

Drew returns with his drink. "How was golfing today?"

"Great, if you count the weather. My golf game needs a bit of practice."

"I hear you, man. That's why I fish. You can always have poor outcomes or poor weather, or the fish just weren't biting. Visiting from out of town?"

"Yes, and the town has definitely lived up to the charm I was told about. I've had a lot of business stuff today, but I'm hoping to explore more of the area over the next few days."

"Well, there's no shortage of things to do, especially if you enjoy the outdoors. Hiking, kayaking, and some great streams for catching trout."

"I was hoping to meet the owner of this place," Philip says, settling his beer on the coaster.

"Well, you're in luck today." Drew slings the bar towel over his shoulder and leans in. "You are speaking to him."

"Lucky me. Philip Matthews." He extends his hand, and Drew accepts.

"Drew Jones. Nice to meet you."

"I've heard a lot about your vineyards and, of course, the Taproom. Where are your vineyards located?"

"About 10 miles down the road. What makes you so interested?"

"I'm looking to invest in some of the businesses or properties in the area. Any interest in a business partner?"

"Who sent you here?" Drew says with suspicion.

"No one. I'm here on my own accord. My Grandfather John knew your Grandma Rose, and he spoke so highly of this place that I don't know. I just feel led to invest in property here."

"Oh, Dr. Matthews. I heard that he and my grandmother were quite the item back in the day."

"Yes, high school sweethearts is what he said. He spoke fondly of your grandmother, and more frequently before his death."

"Sorry to hear of your loss. My grandfather was influential in my life. Both of my grandparents were saints. They raised me and my brother after my asshole father murdered our mom."

"Oh, I am so sorry. I had no idea what a horrible tragedy for you all. I certainly didn't come here to cause trouble."

"No ill feelings, man. You had no idea, and that was a long time ago." Drew grabs a handful of glasses. "Hey, that drink is on the house. Let me know if we can get you anything else. Sally here will take care of you."

"Well, here's my card. If you ever change your mind, give me a call."

Drew places the card in his shirt pocket and walks into the storeroom, away from the eyes of Phillip Matthews.

He had sensed a shift in his body earlier but tried to ignore it. He feels the beads of sweat form and knows the sensation of smothering will come next. He hears Dr. Dan in his head, *Sit down and ride it out.* He sits on top of a crate in the far corner, and before he knows it, the room fades and in an instant he's sitting in the back of a police car in 1983.

The strobe of blue lights continuously flash as he looks at his brother, Chris', tear-stained face.

"It's okay, Chris, I got you; it's going to be okay," Drew says with the voice of a 12 year old that sounded more like an adult.

Chris, who is seven, lifts his water-filled eyes and looks at his big brother with the hope that he can provide the safety and protection needed.

Drew hands Chris the brown and white teddy bear that had been provided to them by the officer. "Here, take Mr. Bear and lie down." Chris lays across Drew's lap.

Drew looks out the window of the car; the blue lights illuminate his father, Curtis, being pinned to the ground as an officer places handcuffs on him. He hears the dispatcher on the police radio say, "Copy Unit 4, EMS has confirmed one gunshot fatality on scene, scene is now secure, medical examiner is in route, ETA 20 minutes. Social services will meet you at the hospital for the children. No ETA on that." Drew is old enough to know that all that chatter means one thing: his mom is dead. He takes his hands and wipes away the remnants of Chris' tears, who's now fast asleep in his lap. He quietly whispers, "It's okay, it's okay." Looking back out, he sees Curtis Johnson being shoved into the back of another patrol car. Drew makes a vow to God that either he will take Curtis out or he will take matters into his own hands.

Drew stands up and begins to move. So much for the past being left in the past.

# Chapter 14: Shadows

The tea kettle whistles and she pulls on her pajamas, which still carry the faint scent of Sophie, her cat. Sophie had attempted to pack herself in her suitcase, and once removed had proceeded to pout under the bed in protest of her leaving. She had talked with Alex after work today, and it had made her homesick for him and Sophie. She missed their long walks through town after work and dinners together. Most nights he cooked while she savored a glass of Reisling and they talked through their days. Other nights they enjoyed the vast selection of culturally diverse restaurants that surrounded them. She had been so busy getting settled here that this was the first time her heart had registered how much she missed Alex.

But no matter where she lived, a cup of hot tea always soothed her. Stirring her milk and sugar in, she thinks about the hours she and Nana talked over tea. Every afternoon she had hot tea and some type of sweet treat waiting after school. Revolutionist descendant or not, there was still a hint of British in that southern belle.

The summer following Benjamin's death, Michelle and Nana spent hours conversing while drinking tea and assembling puzzles. Hot tea in the morning while watching Regis and Kathie Lee, and iced tea on the porch in the afternoon. She recalls one very impressionable conversation, one that penetrated her heart and began to inspire her change.

It was a hot July day, and Benjamin had been dead for almost a month.

"Come on," Nana said, "let's get outside and get some vitamin D. You need to see something besides that TV and these four walls. We'll walk down the path to the garden and see if we have any ripe watermelons."

Michelle reluctantly slipped on her flip flops. Thankfully the path was shaded by a canopy of pine trees to protect them from the sun.

"Michelle, I loved your granddaddy dearly, and his death is still the deepest pain I have ever experienced in my life. Once I came to grips with the fact that he was truly gone, I knew I couldn't bring him back. One day I woke up and said, 'Lucy, you have spent your whole life taking care of others. It's time for you to live and do what you want.' After your grandfather's death, I realized I was the next contestant on 'Get into Heaven.' My friends were dying right and left. Hell, I was at the funeral home more than the staff. I endured a lot of critical eyes, even from my own kids, I'm sure you remember." Lucy looked at Michelle with raised eyebrows.

Boy oh boy, did Michelle remember. Her spunk and spirit always made Michelle believe that she could do anything. When people ask her where she gets her sass from, there's no doubt it was Nana Lucy. So her words that day carried extra weight.

"What I'm trying to say is that I know the pain of losing deep love, and I know it's so hard, but you have two choices. You can sit in misery forever, or you can start to take small steps to start anew.

I questioned myself every step of the way, but in the end, I had to do what was best for me, and I am glad I did all the things I did."

She clearly remembers standing in the watermelon patch that day, and despite Nana Lucys's words, she felt more lost than ever.

"But how, Nana? How did you do it?"

"Start by communicating with your friends. Go to lunch. Allie, that poor girl, is worried sick and calls you every day."

"It feels wrong, like Benjamin meant nothing if I just move on. How can I enjoy living when he's dead? It's not fair."

"You're right, it's not fair and it never will be. If you wait for it to all make sense, you'll run out of time. You do it minute by minute ... hour by hour ... day by day. My darling, grief is painful and very complicated, but in time, I promise, you will begin anew. No one will ever replace Benjamin; he was irreplaceable, and a beautiful chapter of your life. It's time to write new chapters."

Nana's love and support had extended past the sacred days spent here. Nana had written to her every week in basic training. While basic training was intense, the physical and mental demands needed to succeed felt easier than grief and served as an outlet from the crushing pain. Nana's letters and calls had pulled her through.

Michelle senses the warmth as tears wash down her face. She wishes that she had a magic way of rescuing Nana from the horrors of dementia, just like she had rescued her.

She sips her tea and settles into her chair. Her body is tired after a long day at the bakery, and her mind is racing with so many thoughts, many of which include Drew. She recalls the thin strip of woods that separated her back yard from Drew's house. In their elementary school years, he had been more like an annoying little brother. Drew and his younger brother, Chris, spent afternoons playing in the Richardson back yard. They tortured Michelle and Katie, kidnapping and hiding their Barbies all over the back yard.

Thankfully, they had not yet progressed to hardened criminals, and a bribe of cookies or popsicles magically produced the lost dolls.

Michelle was a good student and rule-follower, while Drew had a frequent flier pass to the principal's office that was issued starting in kindergarten. One day, Michelle caught him and Bobby Parks as they attempted to send Bubbles, the class fish, back to the ocean by way of the toilet bowl. Michelle's alarming high-pitched scream had alerted Mrs. Simmons to the scene of the crime, and the boys' evil plot was quickly aborted.

Her thoughts turn back to Drew, and one memory stands out. It was the summer before eighth grade. Michelle had set out on her bicycle on the path through the woods to the old mill. This had been their daily hangout to cool off in the water on hot summer days. As she started through the woods, she heard shouting. She looked over and saw two figures actively engaged in a physical struggle. She quickly climbed off her bike and stood behind a tall pine tree. She placed her hands on the sappy trunk and peered in to get a closer look. Her heart pounding, she realized the two figures were Drew and his father, Curtis. They rolled around on the ground and punches were thrown. Her heart raced, and she thought should she get help, but her feet wouldn't move. She was frozen. Words were yelled, but she couldn't make them out. Michelle gasped as Drew's dad pinned him to the ground with a boot kick to the face. He stumbled away, and Drew slowly rolled to his side. As he did, he caught Michelle's intense stare. Michelle ducked behind the tree, but it was too late; her cover has been blown.

Drew wiped the blood from his mouth and walked towards her.

"Drew, are you okay?."

"I'm fine. What are you doing spying on me?"

"I wasn't spying. I was just heading to the mill and heard the noise."

"Well, go on and mind your business."

"We need to get you some help. I'm going to call my dad."

As she turned to go, he grabbed her wrist with a force she had never felt. "No," he said with a stern face. She had never been as afraid of anyone the way she was in that moment. "Drew, you're hurt, and your dad shouldn't treat you this way."

Realizing his force and sensing her fear, he gently released her arm. "Michelle, I'm sorry for hurting you, but I'm telling you, mind your business. You're out of your league, and I've got this handled."

Her gut still told her to get help, but for some reason she felt she needed to honor his wishes. "Okay, well at least let me help you clean up." He sat outside on the steps while she tended to his wounds with a washcloth and peroxide.

An odd sound captures her attention—a rhythmic tapping pattern, almost like Morse code. *Tap tap tap. Tap tap tap. Tap tap tap.* Following the sound, she discovers the screen door unlatched and giving way to the movement of the wind. She slowly swings the door fully open and gradually steps out onto the back porch. The wind settles and she feels the change as the blazing heat of the day fades into a pleasant summer night. She's captivated to see the first of the lightning bugs fill the air. Soon the back yard is twinkling with them, their lights blinking on and off like a hundred tiny planes in the sky. Her eyes track their flight up to the stars in the sky. No matter where she had lived, she was sure the stars would never shine as brightly as they do here.

A rustling in the woods quickly shifts her attention. Her military training kicks in, and she checks to see that she's close to the door in case she needs to make a quick exit. The sound moves closer, and Michelle slowly reaches for the door handle. The wind picks back up and the air becomes heavy with the scent of gardenias. The scent immediately registers because gardenias had been her favorite flower for as long as she could remember, yet it's odd, since they bloom much earlier in the summer. Her eyes do a quick scan along the tree line, looking for any sign of gardenia bushes, then she sees it. A shadowy figure now approaches the porch. She can't make out distinct features, but the silhouette is male. She freezes, her mind telling her to move, but her body won't obey the commands. Finally, her body catches up to her mind, and she quickly runs in and turns the lock.

*Stay calm, there's nothing out there. It's sleep deprivation causing me to hallucinate.* Sleep—she just needs sleep. She distracts herself by opening her computer and sending an email to Alex. He will soon be up to go to work: "Good night. Sorry I didn't get a chance to call today; it was hectic with getting settled and seeing everyone. I really miss you! Talk tomorrow. Love, Me."

The satin sheets feel cool against her hot skin as she slips into bed. She pulls up the quilt around her, and for the first time since she was a young girl, she sleeps with the light on.

# Chapter 15: Mothers and Daughters

Between baking for the day, getting breakfast for inn guests, and tending to regulars, the morning has gone by quickly. Linda opens the oven and slides two German chocolate pies in. She then plops down in her chair and tears open a pack of Nabs.

"You girls want a Nab? I'm starving." She extends the pack of crackers.

"Me too!" Katie grabs a peanut-butter-filled cracker and takes a bite.

Michelle reaches in and grabs one for herself. The taste of a salty cheese cracker with peanut butter takes her through several memories all at once. A southern staple, Nabs—or four corner crackers, as some call them—had sustained generations of factory workers and field hands. Her first skills in survival training came long before the military. It was common knowledge that every vehicle should have an emergency pack of Nabs in the dash.

"Katie, do you remember when Leroy Dotson came in and wanted to know if we could make a cake made of nabs for his wife

Louise's birthday? Lord, bless his heart. He said that was all she ate, so he figured it would be the perfect cake."

"Yes, thank goodness we swayed him to a different choice," Linda says.

"What did he get instead?" Michelle asks

"We sold him on the chocolate layered cake with peanut butter frosting."

The room grew quiet as they ate their crackers. Linda took a sip of her Coke before asking, "Michelle, what do you cook for Alex? After seeing your skills, I feel sorry for that poor man."

"First of all, Mom, this is not the 1950s. Alex and I both work. Did you ever think he might be an excellent cook?"

Katie looks to her mom, awaiting her response, while finishing her cracker.

"Well, that's true. Plus, I forget my daughter lives in a fancy European town with fine dining all around. Must be like living in a storybook."

"Sometimes it can feel like it. There's just something so soothing about walking streets that have been around for not just hundreds but thousands of years. I just feel very connected to ancient history when I'm there."

"Well, Mom and I are going to take a business trip"—Katie makes air quotes with her fingers—"to see you once I get well. I would love any excuse to sample European chocolates and perfect my Black Forest cake recipe."

"Oh please, I do want you guys to come and visit. It will be a great time. We can spend some time in Heidelberg. It's full of cobblestone stress, castles, and wonderful vineyards. Then we could visit Frankfurt; they have a wonderful art museum there that you would love, Mom. And of course, we can visit as many German bakeries as you like. Trust me, Germans love their cake and coffee in the afternoon."

"Ah, but do they know the fine art of snacking on a Nab? Pairs well with Coca Cola." Katie tosses the last of her cracker in her mouth and makes a gesture like "tada." She places two blocks of cream cheese in the mixing bowl. "Germany sounds wonderful, but tell us more about Alex. I'm looking forward to meeting him at Thanksgiving. I still can't believe that my sister has dated someone for all these years and I've never seen him except for on a screen." She switches on the mixer and begins to blend the ingredients.

"You and Allie, I swear I feel like I'm under interrogation with you two sometimes."

"Well, there is a lot that you keep under wraps."

"Do you have the kids this weekend?"

"No, Brian does. Why?"

"I may not know how to bake a good cake yet, but I do make a mean pitcher of sangrias. Allie's coming over to the house Friday. Come join us."

"You know, that sounds great. I can't drink right now, but I can enjoy juicy gossip just as well with a glass of sparkling grape juice."

"Mom, you should join us. It would do you good to get out."

Linda wipes her hands on her apron. "It's sweet of you to offer, but I'll leave girls' night to you young girls. This old hen will be out like a light after a half a glass of wine and listening to your father watching the same reruns of *MASH* he's seen a hundred times. Here comes Drew. I'll get his desserts for him, and then I'll see you girls later this afternoon, I have an errand to run."

"What is Drew doing here?" Michelle asks Katie.

"He's here to pick up the Taproom desserts." Katie raises her eyebrow. "Speaking of juicy gossip, did you tell Mom about your little adventure to the winery with Drew?"

Linda puts down her pan and turns to Michelle. "No, she did not. Some things never change; she is still telling me nothing. What did you think?"

"It was mind blowing. He just had so much knowledge, and to think of all that he's managing with the Taproom and the winery."

"He's really turned his life around, and I believe it has added years to Rose's life. Lord knows she has worried herself sick over that boy," Linda says

"Seems that he's made a 180. I hope it lasts, but I fear the track record is just not there," Michelle says with a hint of concern.

"No," Katie says, "this is not temporary. He's heavily invested with us in the small business association and chamber of commerce. I think he finally found his passion in the winery."

Michelle watches through the diamond glass cutout as her mom hands Drew several boxes. She hopes her sister is right, but she knows that addiction is a daily battle. Only time will tell if this time he's for real. For his sake, she hopes so.

# Chapter 16: Secrets

Linda gently taps on the door by the sign that reads, "Chaplain Available, Please Knock."

Allie yells, "Come in." Looking up from her desk, she's surprised to see Linda approaching her.

"Hi, Linda, is everything okay? Oh no, has Katie been admitted to the hospital again?"

"No, dear, everything is fine. Sorry to alarm you, but I'm here to see you."

"Well, that's a nice surprise," says Allie. "Please sit down."

Linda sits down and places her purse on the table by a stack of brochures on organ donation. She takes a deep breath and prepares herself to tell a story that she hasn't shared in over forty years.

"First, Allie, I'm not here as your friend's mother. I have to be assured that for now, this conversation is clergy protected. I do not wish for my family to know this until I'm ready."

"Absolutely, Linda, you know I'm a professional. What's going on? You're really making me very concerned here. Are you ill?"

"No, this is something that happened a long time ago." She looks around the room and for a moment considers leaving. She knew this would be hard, but it's proving a harder story to tell than she'd imagined.

"When I was a senior in high school, I had a child and gave him up for adoption." Linda lets out a long exhale. There, now it's out there, and she can't take it back.

They both just sit listening to the small clock on the table tick.

Allie grabs Linda's hand. "Oh Linda, that's an incredible burden to carry around all these years on your own."

Now tears are gently flowing down her face in a steady interval. Allie gets up and grabs a box of tissues and hands them to Linda.

"I've wanted so many times over the years to tell my family and try to find him, but I just could never muster up the courage. Now that there's a chance he could be a match for Katie, I will never be able to live with myself if I don't do everything to try to find him." She brings a tissue to her face and dots each eye.

"I have lived 40 years with the pain of losing a child, and I will sacrifice what it takes to never feel that again."

"I am so sorry. I think about my kids, and I can't imagine not knowing what happened to them or if they're okay." Allie glances down at the floor as tears fill her eyes. "And I can't help but think of my own mother. I have so many questions about her and the circumstance that led to her giving me up."

"That's exactly why I'm here. I knew you'd understand and could help me search for him. I can't speak for your mother, but in 1965, things were not like they are today. Pregnancy out of wedlock was like a death sentence. We were told no one would marry us and that our children would be outcasts as bastard children. We were sent away to special homes with other teenage mothers and assured that once we had the babies and gave them up, we could just move on as if it never happened. Never in my life have I ever been told such a vulgar lie."

"Of course you can't just act like it never happened. You carried this tiny human for nine months. How anyone could think that would be easy is beyond me," Allie says.

"The people I turned to for help made me feel like a trashy person, like all I did was run around and have sex with boys. I got pregnant the first time I had sex, and I was not alone. Many of the girls I befriended in the maternity home had similar stories. It was also as if we became pregnant on our own. No blame was placed on the males it took to create these children."

"When you say 'the people you turned to,' who are you referring to?"

"Almost everyone. The first place I was taken was to Pastor Smith, who made me pray to Jesus in front of my parents and his wife for forgiveness for the terrible sin I had committed. I already felt that I had brought shame on myself, my family, and my friends. I felt so alone and like the worst person ever. My father was absolutely mortified, mostly that his little girl had even had sex, but also about what others would think. My mom did have great sympathy for me, and she told me shortly before she died that it broke her heart for me and she wondered every day about her grandson. That was the first and last time we ever spoke about it."

"Did you even get to see him?"

"Oh yes, I was able to spend four days with him after delivery. I think I can remember every little detail of those four days because that's all I have of him. As I approached the birth, like most first-time mothers, I had no idea what to expect. Lord knows I'd been given no education or support about the birthing process from anyone. All I had to go on were the many scenarios of how this would feel, but none of them fit the actual moment. All anyone had told me was that I would be glad it was over."

"But it didn't go that way. Right?" Allie says.

"This tiny human, while inside me, had seemed a temporary inconvenience. In my mind, I was just a giant incubator and had felt no real connection to the life growing inside me. I couldn't wait to get it out and move on with my life. Then there I was looking at this fragile infant. This was not a problem to be solved—this was my baby."

Allie crosses her hands to her heart. "Oh Linda, that must have been such a horrible feeling."

"Yes, and in my panic, I looked across the room at my mother, who I thought surely after seeing her grandchild would stop this."

"But she didn't? What did she do?"

"My mother had definitely been prepared for this moment. She sprung up from her chair and walked to the bedside. I couldn't even speak. Unable to speak. All I could do was look at her as the tears just fell like a flood. I was hoping she could read my mind."

"I'm going to assume she didn't," Allie says with emphasis.

"The words flowed out in a robotic tone, as if this had been rehearsed for months. 'It's for the best, for you and the baby. You can still go to college, and the baby will have a life you can't offer right now. One day you'll be married and have more children when you're ready to be a mom.'" Linda pauses to collect her breath between her tears. "Those words echoed over and over in my head. *When you're ready to be a mom.* I thought, *Does she not realize that I am now a mother and always will be?*"

Allie rises and hands Linda a bottle of water. "Do you need to take a break?"

Linda takes a sip of water and places the bottle on the table by her. "No, I'm okay. This feels good and has needed to come out for a while."

"How could your mom just let that happen to you and her grandchild?" Allie asks with a confused look on her face.

"My mom was a hostage of society. There was absolutely no choice but for me to give the baby away. As painful as it was for us all, my parents truly thought they were helping me make the best choice for me and my son."

"Yes, very true. Different times, different standards," Allie agrees.

"Every part of me wanted to fight, kick, and scream, but no matter how unfair and wrong this all was, I knew I was outnumbered. I had already endured months of shame, guilt, and emotional torture to know that no one would come to my rescue. Anyone who would be my ally was not aware. My parents wouldn't even allow me to tell the child's father.

"When they took him for the last time ..." Linda places her hands on her face and begins to sob uncontrollably. Allie moves over and puts her arm around her until Linda's breath regulates and tears slow.

As Allie holds Linda, she knows two things. She will do whatever possible to find Linda's child, and she has to do whatever it takes to find her mom. She can't risk waiting one more day.

"Linda, thank you for trusting me with your story. It's okay, let it all go. This has just been too much to carry by yourself all these years."

Linda opens her purse and removes her compact. "Oh, I look a mess." She attempts to dry her eyes and remove traces of mascara from her cheeks. She closes the compact and looks at Allie. "So where do we start?"

"Well, I'm more versed in international adoptions, but I have a friend from grad school who works here in NC at The Mountain Home for Children, and I have a great connection in medical records here. I'll give them both a call. Did you have the baby in North Carolina?"

"Yes, it was a maternity home in western NC, called St. Joseph's. Thank you, Allie. I hope we find him before time runs out."

Allie hugs Linda. "I'm going to give it all I have, and we're going to back that with a lot of prayer."

Allie sits and stares at her computer. Her mind is trying to take in all she has heard. This was certainly not her first time hearing such shocking information, but even though she knows she has to, it will be hard to keep it from her best friend. Seeing Linda's pain makes her wonder if her own mother is still alive and feels the longing of Linda to know her. She begins to type:

Subject: Visit

Hello Beatrice,

I was so excited to hear back from you. I'm taking a four-week sabbatical in January and would very much like to take you up on your offer to stay with you in Freetown. I look forward to meeting you and all the children upon my arrival. I will be in touch soon with my travel itinerary.

In peace, Allie

Allie's mind is still trying to adjust to all she just heard. She thinks about where to start. She closes her laptop and picks up her phone and dials the extensions for medical records. In her head she hears an imaginary clock ticking, and her heartbeat seems just as fast and loud. Katie's life could literally depend on her finding this missing person, and she isn't about to waste one second.

Allie picks up her phone and texts Michelle: *Running a little late. I will meet you at the salon.*

"Medical records, Nellie speaking. How may I assist you?"

"Hey, Nellie, it's Allie. I need your help. We have few facts to work with, and we have to work fast and discreetly. Are you in?"

# FERMENTATION

# Chapter 17: Girls' Night

Michelle reaches to open the bright yellow door to the Cuticles and Curls Salon. Her nose is immediately met with an interesting concoction of hairspray and nail lacquer infused with modern day lemongrass oil.

"Hey, ladies! Come on in." Elizabeth Terry waves them in with her neon orange nails as she finishes checking out a customer at the counter.

Allie rushes in the door. "Sorry I'm late, last minute emergency."

"Oh, you're not late; we just got here ourselves." Michelle walks over and gives her a hug.

"Michelle, O.M.G. It's been so long! I haven't seen you in a month of Sundays. Give me a hug!" The years may have impacted her physical appearance, but time had made no dents in her personality. Two things remained true: Elizabeth Terry had never met a stranger, and she was going to hug everyone she saw. It was clear that these traits were not only alive and well, but from the looks of things, helping her run a successful business.

Michelle reluctantly allows her into her personal space as she feels like she's being squeezed by an anaconda.

"Miranda, take these ladies back and get them soaking. I'll be right with you all."

Michelle watches as Elizabeth's bronzed-spray-tan frame slips outside and lights up a cigarette.

"Great idea to start our girls' night out with pedicures. Since returning, I'm all out of my routine and way past due for one," Michelle says.

"Due one?" Katie looks at Allie and they laugh. "Spoken like a woman of luxury with no kids. When was the time you had a pedicure, Allie?"

Allie stares down at her feet as if they would respond. "Not counting the one Shannon gave me with glitter fairy polish when she was five, I'd have to say before my wedding."

"Dang, you guys really make me think twice about having children," Michelle says as she sorts through the hundreds of choices of nail polishes.

"Oh? It sounds like you and Alex are already talking about kids. So, he's okay with more kids, even though he has one in college," Allie says with a subtle smile.

"I know it seems crazy for him to start all over, but he really loves being a parent. He wanted more children, but his ex-wife didn't."

"It changes your priorities, that's for sure." Katie wiggles down and relaxes into the large massaging chair, enjoying the gentle vibrations against her tired body. "It's going to be a tough change for you and Alex. There's no more sleeping in or taking off on spontaneous weekend getaways."

"Ummm huh, and forget sex." Allie gives Katie a confirmative nod of the head. "Plus it's gonna be hard for you guys with no family to babysit. My mom has made me nutty as a fruitcake over the twins, but I can't imagine how we would have made it through without her and my dad." She perks up and looks at Michelle. "But wait, let's get you down the aisle first. What's the holdup?"

"Allie, you're asking her the same question I keep asking," Katie says with her eyes closed, relishing in the warm sensations as they radiate through her achy feet. Normally her neuropathy, one of her long-lasting side effects from chemo, wouldn't allow her to enjoy a pedicure, but today's a good day.

"No major holdup that I know of. When we first met, he said that after his divorce, he wouldn't marry again, but he's definitely changed his mind on that over the last few years," Michelle says.

"I know that feeling. That's how I feel now about marriage," says Katie. "It's hard to truly believe that it will be forever after you've been through the pain of divorce."

"Well, when he gets here for Thanksgiving, we're just going to have to tell him to get things going," Allie says with a nod.

A few splashes make their way to the floor as Allie swirls her feet in the warm water. "So Katie, I know probably a question you're tired of answering, but really, how are you doing?"

"I never know how to answer that question. Do people want to know how I feel physically or mentally, or do they just feel obligated to ask?"

"Just give it to me straight with no filter."

"The week has been a good week. I'm feeling a little better since I had a transfusion earlier this week. It helps for a while and then the fatigue just takes over. I thought no fatigue could beat that first trimester of pregnancy kind of tired, but boy, was I wrong. But motherhood doesn't stop for anything, so I just keep doing what the kids need and try not to think about it. So thankful to have Michelle here. She's been such a help with the kids and bakery, and surprisingly hasn't burned the place down yet."

"Hey! So much abuse I've been dealing with since my arrival," Michelle interjects.

Allie smiles. She reaches over and squeezes Kaite's hand. "You know the air is full of prayers, and this will happen. In the mean-time, our physical therapist, Carlos, is a cancer survivor, and he runs a support group. You should pop in one day. I'll text you his info. There's nothing like people around you who can relate to what you're walking through."

Allie glances down at her feet and just wishes she truly believed that. Her faith recently feels like a pack of meat stuck way in the back of the freezer. You know it's still there, but you're just not sure if it's still good to use. Her brain tries to reconcile the conversations earlier with Linda, and touching Katie's frail hand, she senses the weight of her mother's plea.

"Thanks, I will certainly think about that," Katie replies with a smile.

"Okay, ladies"—Elizabeth turns the corner and flashes her big Miss America smile—"how are we doing? Feeling relaxed?"

They all look at each other. "I would say we are feeling fantastic," Michelle says.

"Wonderful, that's what we like to hear. Now can I get you ladies some wine? I have a local prosecco that is to die for."

"None for me, thanks," Katie says.

Allie looks at Michelle, and they simultaneously nod their heads. "We'll take some," Michelle says.

Elizabeth hands them each a glass of sparkling wine and assigns Miranda to work on Allie and appoints another manicurist for Katie.

"You ladies better get the sandblasters out for these two. They probably have talons for nails by now," Michelle laughs

"Don't you worry, gals, we got you covered. We see it all here. Don't we, Miranda?"

Miranda keeps her focus on Allie's feet and nods her head in agreement.

"Just last week, Jane Ellis tried to make an appointment for me to do her poodle, Gigi's, nails. I mean, she's a good customer and all, but I just had to draw the line there. Can you imagine? What does this look like? A Pet Palace?"

Elizabeth sits down and begins to remove the polish from Michelle's feet. "Now Michelle, tell me all about this sexy European man who has swept you off your feet."

"Well, I'm not sure it's that exciting. Dating him is like dating any other man. You know, we have our ups and downs."

Elizabeth looks up with disappointed eyes. "Honey, lie to me, and make it good. I'm a married woman with kids. I need some fantasy in my life. Soooo, tell me, how did you guys meet?"

"We met when I was working on the military base in Germany. He's an IT contractor, and let's just say that I had a lot of computer issues that required his assistance," Michelle says with a wink.

Elizabeth looks up from her filing. "Mmmhmm, go on."

"Well, at first it was kind of cute how shy he was, but finally I had to ask him out."

"Okay, one of those, huh? Playing hard to get?"

"No, I don't think so. He really is very shy. That's probably why he's been single so long. He just needed someone who was willing to make the first move."

"Is he hot?"

"Well, I don't know about hot, but I think he's cute. He's very kind and really cares about me."

"That's important. Looks fade, but the heart remains. Lord knows me and my Mark sure don't look like we did in high school, but he still brings me flowers and makes time to take me out on the town occasionally. Just last weekend we dropped the kids off to Mama and rode up to West Jefferson. We had lunch at Louise's Sweet T Cafe and went to St. Mary's church to see the frescoes. It was so nice."

"Oh, those frescoes are so beautiful. I haven't been in years," Katie says.

"Yes, just standing inside there, I feel so close to God. Gives me chills right now just thinking about it," Elizabeth says.

"That's great that you and Mark are still finding time together. That's what killed it for me and Brian," Katie says. "We stopped pursuing each other, and eventually I guess we fell out of love."

"I wouldn't say that me and Dave fell out of love. I just think that after the twins came along, we just got out of synch. Everything became so serious and task-oriented. I don't remember the last thing we did for fun," Allie says as she places her glass down.

"Well, honey, your twins are old enough to fend for themselves. I can't wait for the day my kids are. You need to tell them to put a pizza in the oven and you and Dave need to hit the town one night."

"Elizabeth, whatever happened to Candace Jackson? You guys were thick as thieves back in school," Michelle inquires.

"Girl, now that is a story." She looks around to check who is within ear shot and leans in closer. "So you all know she was smart as a whip in school."

"Oh yes, last I heard she had graduated from UNC and then attended NYU law school." Michelle takes a sip of her wine.

"Yep, that's right. Once she graduated law school, she stayed in New York and got married. She met her husband, Blake, in law school, and they were both working hard to make partner. Well, I don't know if she fell and hit her head or just went plum crazy, but the next thing I know, she had up and quit her job, packed up her whole family, and moved back to Chatham."

"Doesn't she own the Zen on Main yoga studio?" Katie asks.

"She sure does, and you know what else? She went and changed her name to Vira." She looks up and makes a face.

"Vira? Why?" Michelle raises an eyebrow.

"Lord only knows. She says it means warrior in some yoga language that I don't understand."

Allie eagerly jumps in. "Oh yeah, in Sanskrit it does mean warrior and symbolizes the inner ability to overcome ego and ignorance."

"Thank you, Allie, the world's first original Google," Katie says, laughing.

"What can I say, I enjoy learning." Allie raises her glass in the air.

"Is she practicing law here?" Michelle asks.

"No, she homeschools her four kids and runs the yoga studio, but her husband has a small practice down the street. She says she just got tired of the stress, and she never saw her kids. Besides being a little nutty, she seems happy, and her parents are thrilled to have the grandkids nearby."

"And how about your other sidekick, Barbie Jo?" Michelle takes a sip of her wine.

"Poor Barbie Jo has been through it. You know she has always had the knack for picking the worst men in the history of men."

"Didn't she date Jeff Smith in high school?" Michelle asks

"Date him? Honey, she married him. Boy, he's a piece of work, but that's for another time. That was husband number one. She's currently on marriage number three, and last I heard, that one was on its last breath. Then a few years back, her daddy stole her identity and nearly bankrupted her. I promise, you can't make this stuff up. If anybody wrote a book about this town, no one would believe it."

"I had forgotten how much info I could get at the local beauty parlor," Michelle says with a satisfied look.

"Oh no, no, the term 'beauty parlor' is so passe. This is a full-service spa," she says in a scolding tone, looking up at Michelle. "Can I set you girls up with a manicure while you're here?"

"Thanks, but not today, Elizabeth. We have some takeout that's calling our name, and from the sounds of it, I have way more town gossip to catch up on," Michelle says with excitement.

"Well, next time for sure. Thanks for coming in, and Michelle, I sure hope to see more of you while you're in town. You girls don't get into too much trouble tonight, and I better see you at church Sunday," Elizabeth says, waving her pointer finger at them.

The streetlights have just begun to glow as they head to their cars.

Michelle hands Katie the key. "Why don't you guys head to Nana's house. I'll pick up our dinner on the way. Everyone still good with pizza from Tap House?"

"Yes, sounds good to me," Katie says while wishing she could remember the taste of a good slice of pizza. Another lingering side effect of her chemo treatments.

"Allie?"

"Yes, sounds great, and ask Drew or Billy for a bottle of Summer Crush; it's one of my favorites."

"All right, see you guys soon."

The Taproom is most certainly a popular spot in Chatham on Friday nights. Michelle is glad they ordered ahead, as every table is full while people wait for tables to free up. They are so busy that she sees Drew across the way taking orders.

"Hey, Billy"—Michelle walks up to the bar—"I called ahead with an order. Is it ready yet?"

"Let me check. It should be, but we're pretty slammed."

"Certainly looks like it. I mean, you've got the boss man waiting tables." She opens her arms and shrugs her shoulders.

"Don't let that serious face fool you. He loves being in on the action," Billy yells back as he heads to the kitchen.

Michelle watches Drew interact with his patrons, and it's true. She can tell that he is genuinely in his element. He catches her eye, she gives a subtle wave, and he makes his way over.

"Looking for a table?" Drew asks.

"No, thankfully I called ahead. Girls' night at my house with Allie and Katie."

"Too bad, we have live music starting in an hour. You guys should move the party here."

"Maybe next time." She hates the sudden wave of anxiety that comes over her each time she sees him. "Oh, Allie wants me to get a bottle of Summer Crush. Do you have any left?"

"Do I have any left?" He walks over to the display, grabs a bottle, and pretends to blow the dust off. "Enough to keep her in it for life if she likes. Here, tell Allie this one is on the house."

"Are you sure?" Michelle shifts her footing and relaxes a bit more into her stance.

"Yes. I'm just happy to know that someone appreciates the efforts. Tell her to enjoy it and that it's a rare batch, as I won't be making that one again."

"Why is that?"

"In winemaking, like most businesses, the only way you find out is by experimenting. Sometimes those experiments are a bust, and other times a huge success. Here, take this one and try for yourself. It's similar to the Driftwood that you love but has the Petit Verdot grapes I showed you at the vineyard. I think you'll like it. Let me know what you think."

She takes the bottle and reads the label out loud: "Santiago? Sounds Spanish. I thought the Petit Verdot grapes were the ones from the Bordeaux region of France."

"Very good. I must be a better teacher than I thought. You are correct. Santiago is indeed Spanish. This wine is named after a character from my favorite book."

Billy returned with a large pizza box and a bag, unknowingly interrupting the conversation. "Do you need plates and silverware?"

"Yes, that would be great, and extra Sunny Italy dressing please." She tilts her head and raises her eyebrows. "How did you ever get Mrs. Romano to give you this recipe? She always said people would have to pry it from her dead hands."

"A sharp businessman never reveals his secret tricks."

"Well, I better get going."

"Enjoy, and let me know how you like the wine."

"I will, and thanks again for the tour. I really learned a lot and had a good time."

"It was my pleasure. See you around."

She carries the boxes to the door, and he opens it to let her out.

He had been perfectly content with his life until she had rolled back into town. Now she's awakening in him a part he thought was long gone, and it feels good, almost too good. Like Santiago, he might just have to take his boat out into deeper waters than he ever imagined if he wants to get the catch of his life.

# Chapter 18: Reminiscing

"Wow, let the 1980s soundtrack play. This house is full of so many memories," Allie says.

"Allie, put your leg warmers on and give us your best Solid Gold dancer routine," Michelle calls out from the kitchen.

"I'll need a few more of these first." Allie raises her glass and looks at the faces of her dear friends, who are more like sisters. She wants so desperately to tell them that they have a brother out there, and that he could be a great source of hope, but she knows that she can't.

"After the few nights I have been here, I'm not so sure that we don't need to get out the old Ouija board and perform an exorcism here," Michelle says, settling into her seat.

"Oh Chelle, you always were a scaredy cat. What are you afraid of? Is Old Tom Dooley's ghost after you again?"

"Hey, I'm sorry. History or no history, that is a horrible story to make elementary children learn and sing about."

"What are you two talking about?"

"Come on, Allie, you remember the legend of Tom Dooly. Oh wait, that might have been the year your parents switched you to private school."

"Probably. I am so glad they finally came to their senses. Don't get me wrong, it was a great school, but I missed you guys so much, and those uniforms were hideous," Allie says with a disgusted look on her face. "I think I vaguely remember the song, but I never really knew the story."

Katie crosses her legs and sits back in her chair. She begins to speak as if orating in a large theater: "This is a story full of scandal, betrayal, and get ready—STDS! Trust me, Netflix has nothing on this one. So old Tom Dooley was a Civil War vet accused of murdering his lover. Oh, what was her name?" she says, snapping her fingers. "Something Foster."

"Laura Foster," says Michelle, taking a slice of pizza. "Don't ask me why I know that. Carry on."

"Yes, that's it. Turns out ole Tom was quite the ladies' man. It was rumored that he was sleeping not just with Laura Foster but also both of her cousins, Ann Foster Melton and Pauline Foster."

"Eeeewww," screech both Allie and Michelle.

"So unbeknownst to the cousins or Dooley, Pauline had actually moved home to get treatment for syphilis, and she infected them all. When Dooley discovered he had syphilis, he vowed to kill the woman who gave it to him, and he thought that was Laura."

"See, just like I said, such a crazy story to have elementary children sing about, but at least they left the syphilis part out of the song."

"Oh wait, that's not the kicker," Katie says. "In the end, just as the song says, Dooley was hanged for Laura's murder. "Buuuttt"— she draws out her word for emphasis—"it's actually believed that Ann, her cousin, murdered Laura and that Dooley, out of love, died to save her life." Katie sits back, taking pleasure in her memory of her story.

"Well, good luck finding a man to take the fall for you these days," Allie says.

"Michelle slept with the light on for weeks after that field trip to the Wilkes County Courthouse," Katie says.

"Well, I've been sleeping with the light on again here."

"Seriously, what are you afraid of in Nana's house? This was your second home. Not to worry, any ghosts here are harmless family ghosts. Several of Grandaddy's relatives died in this house," Katie remarks

"Ooohhh, creepy. I wonder if there are really ghosts here," Allie says. "Which ones died?"

"Let's see, both of his parents died here, and they also had two children who died—one as an infant, and one died of smallpox, I think around age five."

"That's sad to lose so many children," Michelle says.

"Happened all the time in the days before all the medical discoveries."

"Like Daddy said, you'll hear some creaks and groans in this old house." Katie reaches for another slice of pizza, delighted that her taste buds seem to be more receptive tonight.

"It's more than creaks and groans. I don't know how to describe it; there's just something unsettling, and I could have sworn I saw someone standing out there the other night. With Curtis Jones now out of prison and roaming about, it just makes me feel creeped out."

"What would Curtis Jones want with you?" Allie asks with a curious tone.

Suddenly Michelle realizes she has overshared and acted quickly. "Okay, I have to change the subject or I'll have to go sleep somewhere else. Allie, how is your Summer Crush?"

"So good. I can't believe Drew is upset about how this turned out. To me it has the perfect balance of sweetness."

"Here, try some of this. I know you don't usually like the dry ones, but Drew gave it for us to try. I think it has a very nice body." She takes a clean glass and pours some in.

Allie picks up the glass and swirls the rich red wine and takes a sniff. "It has a great aroma." She takes a sip. "Very nice, if you're a Cabernet Sauvignon fan. Katie, just a sip?"

"No, thanks." She wrinkles her nose. "I have a complete aversion to wine now after chemo."

"Yes, I've heard so many patients talk about how chemo changed their taste buds, and all kinds of crazy things. It's such a beast," Allie says with an empathetic tone.

"You're telling me." Katie reaches for a bottle near her and picks it up. "But I do love the names Drew chooses. Night Fishing, Perfect Catch, Hooked up—so clever."

Michelle says, "Sounds like a one-night stand to me. Figures that they were named by Drew."

"For your information, smarty, those are fishing terms. From what I'm hearing, the only one-night stands Drew Jones has now are with fish. To my knowledge, he hasn't dated anyone since he and Suzanne broke it off years ago."

Michelle wants more details about what happened there but decides to leave it for now.

"Well, this Santiago name sure doesn't go with his theme. He said it was named after a character in his favorite book."

"Oh, it most certainly does go. Think eleventh grade American Lit class," Allie says.

Michelle shrugs her shoulders and looks to her sister. "I'm clueless. Katie was always the one with her nose in a book."

"I'm at a loss here as well," Katie says.

"Santiago is the main character in *Old Man and the Sea* by Ernest Hemingway."

"Again, ladies and gentlemen, we present to you Allie Luffman, *the* original google." Katie laughs and then looks at her sister. "Tell us what your plans are now that you've retired."

"I may have retired from the military, but it's really no different. After I return, I'll be doing pretty much my same job, working full-time as a weather tech, but just as a civilian with no uniform and no deployments."

"And you and Alex?"

"Not much more to tell than what I told you earlier. We plan to travel now that Leo is out of the house."

"Okay, we've heard this. I agree with Elizabeth's observation earlier—something juicy. Honestly, Michelle, the way you describe the man, he sounds like your golden retriever rather than your lover," Allie says with a snicker.

"What's wrong with a loyal, intellectual, stable man who has mad cooking skills?"

"Nothing, I guess I just don't hear—"

"The passion," Allie interrupts Katie.

"You know I'm a private person. I'm not going to give you all the gory details. Plus, you guys have no idea what it's like dating after a certain age. The apps, the online mess, the crummy bar pickup lines, and then you think you find Mr. Right, only to learn that he's already married."

"Wait, what?" Katie says, nearly spitting out her soda.

"Oh yeah, I hear all the dating drama I want at the hospital," Allie says. "I'll just keep Dave."

"Let's talk about something fun … like your wedding," Katie says with excitement.

"Ah, a German wedding. Anyone else hearing the overture to *The Sound of Music*?" Allie lets out a deep sigh of delight.

"No way, no big wedding for us. I think we'll just do a destination wedding somewhere, just the two of us."

"You can't do that. Mom and Dad will just die," Katie protests.

"Why? Daddy will be thrilled to save all that money, and I think Mama is still on anxiety meds that she started due to planning your wedding."

"Not true." Katie gives her a disapproving look.

"Good grief," Michelle argues, "at times it felt like you were Princess Diana. You were a bridezilla before there ever was such a term."

Katie looks off with a dreamy look. "That might be fair. It was a beautiful wedding, and if I may say so, I did look like a princess. Too bad he turned out to be a frog and no prince."

"I can think of a few more choice names than a frog," Michelle says.

"Well, cancer has made sure I stay single. Definitely not the partner I was looking for at this stage of life," Katie says, trying to suppress a yawn.

"That's about to change," Michelle says as she retrieves a plate of leftover bakery treats and places them on the coffee table. "Once we find this donor, the men will all be lining up for this catch."

"It appears they'll have to get in line behind a certain Chatham firefighter whose car has been seen in your driveway on several occasions," says Allie with a hint of mystery.

"Oh really?" Michelle puts her cookie aside and looks at her sister, motioning for more details.

"Oh please, so he's dropped off some meals and picked up the kids a few times. He's a former Eagle Scout turned firefighter. That's what these people do." A hint of crimson spreads across her face.

Allie and Michelle both look at her, waiting for more, but Katie isn't offering.

"My, my, look at the time. I'll leave you two to speculate about my non-existent love life. The reality of putting three kids to bed now calls. Allie, so good to see you outside of the hospital, and Michelle, I'll see you tomorrow—that is, unless the ghosts get you."

"Very funny; see you tomorrow."

Allie closes the lid to the leftover pizza and slides it into the refrigerator.

"It's hard seeing her so sick, Allie." Michelle refills her glass and settles into her grandad's chair.

"I know, it really is. I don't know how she keeps on going, but it's not just an act for you. Every time I see her, she is so positive, but I know from the time I spend with cancer patients that deep down she has to be scared."

Michelle leans into her friend. "Allie, I know that you're bound by confidentiality, but is there anything about her case that you can tell me. I've been getting just the bare details."

Allie feels the words rise to the back of her throat: *You have a brother out there who could save her life. We just have to find him.* But she quickly pushes them down with the last sip of her wine.

"I'm sorry. I know what you know." She uses her shrewd communication skills to redirect the conversation. "So what are your plans for the rest of the weekend?"

"Tomorrow I have bakery duty until 4:00, then I'm heading downtown with Drew to check out the spot for the bakery truck for the Pumpkin Festival."

Allie gives her a suspicious look. "Oh really?" Allie says.

"Oh really what?" Michelle says, tossing the last bite of her cookie into her mouth.

"What's the deal with you two?"

"What deal? It's business. He's the head of the festival committee or something like that, and we needed to make sure we had access to electricity for the food truck."

"It's just that you've always been so cryptic about Drew. I still don't really know what went down with you two the summer after eighth grade."

"It's hard to tell you the answer to something that I don't know. After his mom died, we spent a lot of time together. My heart was so hurt for him, and I just wanted to help any way that I could. What he had been through, to lose his mom so young, and in such a tragic way, was horrific. No kid should have to witness their mother being killed, especially by their own father."

"You're right, no kid should. Those are the cases that I just can't shake from work. Kids hurt or having to see things they will carry for the rest of their lives."

"Like I told you, I went to the cemetery when I first got to town. It's the first time that I've been to Benjamin's grave since his funeral. It was hard, but I had to do it." She looks at her ring.

"Seems like that day happened in a whole different life. So much has happened since then to us all. It truly does seem impossible that we're all twenty years older. Sometimes I think about how different life would have been had Benjamin and I married and I'd stayed here, but that was not the plan God had in mind, I guess."

"I guess not," Allie adds with a tone of sadness.

"While I was there, I went to Sheila's grave, and I realized that she was only a few years younger than we are right now when she died."

"Yes, and my kids are barely older than Drew was at the time."

"You're right, though there are a few things I never told you about. After his mother's death that summer, there were so many nights I snuck out to meet him."

"How did you ever get that by your eagle-eye dad?"

"I'm still not sure, but we would meet in the church cemetery. Honestly, it was the saddest thing I had ever seen in my life. He would just sit in the dark for hours at her grave."

"You guys just literally sat in the cemetery in the dark of night? Doing what?"

"At first, I sat and listened to him rage about all the ways he was going to kill Curtis, while he chain smoked and drank Jack Daniels."

"Is that why you mentioned Curtis earlier?"

"Yes, kind of makes me worried now that Curtis is out that Drew might do something."

"I don't think so. I mean, you never know, but he has so much going for him now."

"I hope so. Eventually the rage calmed, and we would just sit in silence. He told me that he was going to come there every night until his mom showed him a sign that she was okay."

"That poor kid, and you as well. That's a lot to carry around for another person. You guys were both kids."

"I know that now, but at the time it seemed that we were so much older than we were. Allie, what happened in that silence was so powerful. I don't know how to explain it. "

"I do. Your presence, choosing to literally sit with him in his deepest pain, you showed up for him. Sometimes actions are way more powerful than any words."

"As far as what happened between us, I guess you would say that it was …" Michelle pauses to find the words. "Well, like the name of that wine, a summer crush." She pauses and wonders if Drew thought about that as he named the wine. "The relationship grew, and about the time we realized it had grown into something, he just turned on me. He stopped talking to me, and he just changed. Then along came Benjamin, and you know the rest of the story."

"Yeah, it's remarkable that Drew made it out of high school at all. The odds were not in his favor."

"No, they weren't. I expected to run into him, but I never expected to see him doing so well."

"Are you sure that's all that is unexpected?" Allie questions.

"Of course! That was a lifetime ago, and we both have very different lives now." She rises and walks to the door. "We could both do this all night, but I'll be hating myself when that alarm goes off for work tomorrow."

"Just like old times, kicking me out." Allie laughs and gives her a hug.

Michelle closes the door and checks the locks several times. Yes, it feels just like old times, and she's loving every moment of it. More than she ever expected.

# Chapter 19: The Accident

"I was glad to see you on my schedule today. It's been a while." Dr. Dan softly closes the door to his office.

"Harvest time, Doc. I've been working long days and nights." Drew settles into the left corner of the couch. The same place he always sits.

"Ahhhh. Yes, I should have thought about that; it's that time of year." Dr. Dan stirs his coffee, takes a sip, and continues. "So what are your early thoughts on your yield this year?"

"Very close to last year, and that was one of our best harvests since I've been in the business. As always, though, the grapes look great, but the final product will tell the true tale."

A familiar scent of strong, black Folgers coffee now permeates the room. "Any solutions to your financial situation?"

"I'm still feeling the pressure. I had a strange visit from an investor who wanted to go into business with me, but I just feel like he's in with Jeff and Robert Smith, the scheming brothers I told you about."

"Is this investor local to the Chatham area?"

"No, he's from Boston but has ties to Chatham through his grandfather. He said he saw the growth down here and wanted to get in while he could. I shut him down pretty quickly. I'm not interested in sharing this land with anyone outside my family."

"I know how strongly you feel about that, but you might have to consider other options."

"I'll cross that bridge when I get there."

"And your lady friend who arrived back in town … I'm sorry, her name escapes me."

"Michelle. I took her on a tour of the winery, but our time together has been limited. I've been busy with harvest, and she's been helping her family out. That's what brought her here; her sister is having some health issues, so she's helping run the family business."

"Looks like your families have the entrepreneurial spirit in common. How has it felt to spend time with her?"

"Initially it felt a little odd, but we quickly picked up where we left off."

"Do you still have feelings for her?"

"Still? They never left."

"Do you get an indication that she feels the same way?"

"I don't know, but it doesn't matter. She has a boyfriend and a life outside of Chatham."

"Well … she's not married, and I've never known you to back down from a challenge this easy. What gives?"

"She deserves better than me, and once she had that kind of guy."

Drew reaches across the way and hands Dr. Dan a yellowed newspaper clipping. Dr. Dan removes his glasses from his pocket and begins to read.

## Local Teen Drowns while Saving Child

Frank and Julie Rodriguez held back tears as they thanked their son's classmates and all the EMS workers for their valiant efforts as they tried to save their son last week. Benjamin Rodriguez, 18, of Chatham died June 6 after a sudden flash flood sent him and three-year-old Milicent Anderson into the rushing waters of the Yadkin River. The swollen stream carried them away until they were pulled out downstream by local EMS. Benjamin, along with classmates Drew Jones and Allie Luffman, both 18, were helping others cross when Benjamin and Millicent were swept into the waters.

East Chatham's high school principal, Richard Mooring, made an emotional statement: "We are saddened to learn of the death of our recent graduate, Benjamin Rodriguez. Our thoughts and prayers go out to his family and friends. I am proud of the courage exhibited by all involved to preserve life under such extreme circumstances."

Steve Richardson of Chatham Fire and Rescue, who assisted in the rescue efforts, urges people to check weather reports and be prepared while enjoying nature: "We just have to have respect for mother nature and know that within seconds, a situation around water can change. Go out and have fun, just be prepared."

Dr. Dan gently places the article on the table by him and turns his attention to Drew. "This is what you were referring to last time. Why have you never shared this with me before?"

"Didn't seem important. He's gone. Can't change that."

"What was your relationship with Benjamin, the young man who died?"

Drew slides to the end of the couch and glances down at the floor. "He was my best friend."

"That's a tough loss. How did you guys become such good friends?"

"Of course you know my brother, Chris, and I went to live with my grandparents after my mom's death. That was the summer before I started high school. So many things were up in the air. Benjamin and his family had just moved to Chatham, and he was getting adjusted to a new school. I was so angry at Curtis, and I wanted to do everything in my power not to be anything like him. He was just a first-class guy. He just gave off the spirit of the kind of person I would like to be."

"How does Michelle factor into this story?"

"Benjamin was Michelle's fiancé. Not too long after he moved to town, they began dating. It was hard to see her with someone else, but I knew I could never give her the life that Benjamin would have—at least I didn't think I could ever be good enough. I knew she would be well taken care of."

"That's a very unselfish kind of love to display at such a young age."

"As hard as I tried, I still lacked the discipline to get my shit together, even for her. I was still drinking, smoking weed, and driving like a bat out of hell, and just in general living out a death wish. I never wanted that to be her life."

"You know that was more than a lack of discipline. That was your trauma taking over your brain and making it difficult for you to make clear decisions. All of those things were not your fault; you were severely abused, and those were just reactions, not who you are at the core. Look where you are now. Do your current actions match those of your past?"

"Well, trauma, demons, whatever you want to label it, Doc, I knew it wasn't going to end well. I never thought I'd see my 21st birthday, and maybe a part of me didn't want to. I mean, I really saw no bright, shiny future. My classmates were all making plans to go to college or get jobs and start families. I had screwed around and barely passed and had zero direction."

"You didn't see your decision to join the Marines as a positive direction?"

"Not originally; it just really was a way to get the hell out of Chatham and away from the past, or so I thought."

"Yes, we can change our zip code, but it has been my experience that our past seems to always find our forwarding address."

Drew rises from the couch and begins to pace, as he has done in the past when sharing difficult memories with Dr. Dan.

"We were all preparing to go our separate ways after graduation. Michelle and Ben were staying local and attending the community college. Allie was headed to App State, and I was headed to boot camp down in Parris Island the following week. I guess you could say it was a farewell party to our teen years before we had to start being adults."

Drew pauses and draws in a deep breath.

"There is a lesser-known waterfall near the county line along the Yadkin River. We liked to hang out there because we generally had the area all to ourselves, but that day when we arrived, a couple of families were there. It's a nice size waterfall that was perfect for sliding, so can't blame the kids for wanting to hang around."

Dr. Dan chuckles. "I think I still have a few battle scars from my sliding days as a kid, but well worth it."

Drew smiles at him and continues to pace around. "Yeah, those kids were wearing out a new path to the top, sliding over and over again. We set up our stuff and settled in. It was nothing for us to be out there until well after dark. We had hoped that as dinner time approached, the families would clear out and we'd have the place to ourselves again. Kind of hard to crank up the Motley Crue full blast with little ones around."

Dr. Dan nods his head in agreement.

"There really wasn't a lot of warning, but then again, we really weren't paying attention. We had music on and were tossing around a football. We did hear a crackle of thunder now and again, but it was summer, and that didn't always mean we'd see a storm. So many parts of this are still a blur, but the one thing that is clear is the rain came like nothing I have ever seen before. It went from not a drop to someone turning the shower on wide open. Within seconds, we could barely see each other."

"So at this time it was the two families and you, Michelle, Benjamin, and Allie?"

Drew shakes his head. "No, it was Benjamin, Allie, another friend Kyle, and my girlfriend at the time, Heather."

"So Michelle wasn't with you on this day?"

"Not at that time. She and some other friends were coming after they finished working, but they didn't arrive before the storm."

Dr. Dan crosses his leg and nods with an understanding to proceed. Drew returns to sit on the couch.

"We all huddled together on the small bank we were on. The trail to the car was short, but the problem was we had to cross the creek to get to the path. Normally this is no problem, as it's just a small bank creek, and we stepped across a few rocks to get across. By now, the rain was quickly running off the banks, escalating the water from a trickle to a rushing force, which made it tricky and dangerous to cross."

Drew picks up his water bottle and pauses to take a drink.

"Take your time, Drew," Dr. Dan says. "This is a lot to unpack after so many years."

"The rain finally let up, so I crossed to one side, and Benjamin and I began shepherding people across. First the adults and then the kids. The last child was a terrified toddler who was clinging to Benjamin for life and screaming for her mother."

Drew clasps his hands tightly and begins to rock slightly on the couch, highlighting the intensity of the memory.

"Benjamin was handing her to me when his footing lost grip and he slipped on the rocks. They both fell in and were quickly swept downstream with the rush of water."

Dr. Dan sits in the heaviness of the moment, and after a pause says, "Do you need to stop, or are you okay to proceed?"

"No, I want to go on." Drew draws in a deep breath before proceeding. "Allie and I ran down the bank, and we saw Benjamin holding on to a large tree branch that extended over the bank along the river. We scoured the area, looking for anything we could use to pull them to shore. Nothing was sturdy enough. Allie managed to toss two ring floats that the kids were using, and Benjamin was able to reach one. Then the branch snapped, and they were afloat again. I ran along the bank until I lost sight of them." Drew buries his head in his hands and begins to rub his hands through his hair. "That's the last time I saw him alive."

Despite his efforts to suppress them, a steady stream of tears begin to flow, each tear seeming to carry the weight of his memories. "I could have done more; I should have done more."

Dr. Dan sits quietly for a few moments before speaking. "It sounds like you did the best you knew how under incredible circumstances. What exactly do you think you could have done differently that day?"

"It should have been me. It should have been me, Doc." Drew rises and begins to pace with more vigor. "I was living recklessly and did nothing but waste my days. Benjamin was a great guy. He did all the right things and didn't deserve to die before he ever got to live."

"The level of goodness of a person doesn't protect people from bad things. We've been here before. Your mom, your Marines that you lost, and now your best friend. Sometimes life just absolutely sucks and makes no sense. War, weather, death, and ... well, basically most things are out of our control."

Drew walks to the window and gazes outside. He watches an elderly lady pull into her parking space at the rate of a snail while other cars zip up and down the busy street.

Dr. Dan rises from his chair and joins Drew at the window. "See something interesting out there?"

"Just thinking of the irony of people going about their daily tasks while on the other side of the glass I'm bearing my soul."

"You've experienced more loss than most people your age, and it changes a person. Brings to mind a favorite quote: 'To live is to suffer, to survive is to find some meaning in the suffering.'"

"Going all Dali Lama on me now?"

"Actually that's Friedrich Nietzsche, but most major religions have some connection to suffering and what it means."

"I don't know what I believe anymore."

"And I think that's your next step in healing. We are mind, body, and spirit. You've worked on your mind with me and cleared your body of substances; now I think it's time for you to work on your spirit."

"So what do you suggest I do? Go meditate on a rock, go to an ashram in India, a trip to the Holy Land?"

"I can't tell you where you'll find spiritual healing; that's a path only for you to discover, but I do think it's a crucial step for you making peace with the past and finding meaning in your present life."

Drew sits in his office at the Taproom. He tries to focus on the orders he needs to place, but his mind keeps circling back to his session with Dr. Dan. Two things consume his thoughts: *Michelle is not married yet, and his spiritual unrest.* He opens his wallet and pulls out a worn business card that reads "Captain Sam

McDonald." He might not know what he needs spiritually, but if it exists, he knows where to find it.

He's just about to hang up the phone when a familiar voice answers: "Captain Sam here."

"Sam, it's Drew."

"Well I'll be a monkey's uncle, good to hear from you. Wait, are you in trouble?"

"No, not in the sense of needing you to bail me out of jail, but I could use some time on your boat."

"Well what are you waiting on? Get your ass on down here."

"I'll be in touch. I have a few things to take care of here before I head your way."

Hearing Sam's voice confirms that this is a step in the right direction. Now it's time to handle one more thing. He opens the envelope stamped FINAL NOTICE and then pulls out the business card Phillip Matthews had given him. It's the last thing he wants to do, but he has no other choice. It's his only option to keep the business and land his family has passed on for generations. He's inches from having everything he's ever wanted, including Michelle, and he has to make this work.

# Chapter 20: Pumpkin Festival

"Hey, Captain," Josh calls out from the back of the truck. "How much of this equipment do you want with us at the festival tomorrow?"

"Just leave it all out; I'll sort through it. What are you still doing here anyway? Your shift ended hours ago."

"I could say the same to you," Josh says.

"Well, my story is different. I'm an old man who has already sown his wild oats. It's a Friday night; you're a young buck, so go have some fun. Now get out of here. I don't want to see you again until tomorrow morning."

"Yes, sir. Have a good night."

Tomorrow will not be an ordinary day; they'll be stretched thin assisting Chatham PD with safety at the festival. Everything from responding to minor fender benders to heart attacks. Something about a festival just makes everyone's cardiac events amp up. However, working in a small-town fire department, Steve Richardson had learned that there's no such thing as an ordinary day. The worst thing to do is to wish a first responder a calm day. You can bet all hell will break loose.

Much to his mother's horror, he'd started his career as a junior fireman while still in high school. She accused him of trying to send her to an early grave with worry. He guesses they're even now, as she has given him more than a few scares over the last few years with her dementia. Once she took off in the middle of the night and was in Atlantic City, New Jersey before the authorities located her. Despite his mom's anxious worry and pushback, he knew from the first call he responded to that it was in his blood to be a first responder for life. From responding to structure fires, medical emergencies, or even helping Betty Jane Forsyth find where she parked her blasted car for the hundredth time, he still can't imagine doing anything else.

A lot has changed over the course of his career. Thanks to improved building codes and smoke detectors, structure fires are no longer the majority of the calls. For the most part, days in Chatham are pretty calm, and he and his colleagues look more like grown-up Boy Scouts going on calls to assist the elderly who had fallen, or giving talks at the local elementary school on fire safety. But small towns aren't immune to major crises, and when they do arise, his team often has to improvise. They just don't have the resources or manpower of the larger cities.

He picks up an envelope from his desk and slowly tears it open. The letter arrived a few days ago, but he just hasn't worked up the courage.

Dear Chatham Fire and Rescue Family,

I hope this letter finds you and your families all doing well. I am happy to share with you that I was just accepted into medical school at East Carolina University, where I plan to specialize in emergency medicine. I hope to get up to Chatham next summer for a visit before I start school.

With love and gratitude,

Millicent Anderson

He removes an old, worn manila envelope from his desk drawer. He deposits the letter in the envelope, which is already bulging with a thick stack of cards. Benjamin was lost, but Millicent was a success story from that tragic day. Today Millicent is 23 years old. Each year on her birthday, the family sends a donation and card to the Chatham Fire and Rescue, expressing their gratitude. It's always bittersweet to get her updates. He's happy to see her doing so well, but it also reminds him of what they lost that day. While he feels pride in the ability of him and his team to help so many, no matter how many you save, it's the ones that you can't that linger. It leaves him with a nagging feeling and asking himself, "Could we have done more?"

He places the envelope back in the drawer, which lets out a loud squeal as it closes. He sorts through the gear laid out in the bay and loads the truck with the necessary items. He throws the extra items into the back of the all-terrain rescue vehicle and heads out behind the station.

He pauses before unlocking the door to the outside storage building. A plaque by the door reads: *In Memory of Benjamin Rodriguez.*

The initial call that day didn't come from the command center. It had come from Michelle. She just had a bad feeling after the storm started that something wasn't right. He had just hung up the phone with her when the official call came in from the ranger station.

Steve and his team were the first EMS team to arrive. Rangers had managed somehow to pull a child and Benjamin on to the bank. Steve can still recall every moment of that day with clarity. "Pendergrass and Cox get to the child; Gary and I have Benjamin," he remembers shouting as they arrived on scene.

Together, like a choreographed dance Steve and Gary had done hundreds of times, they performed a rapid exam on Benjamin. Steve gently stabilized Benjamin's head while Gary rolled him to his side, clearing water from his airway and checking for any injuries on his back. Steve checked for a pulse and began compressions.

"Cox, what do you guys have there?" Steve yelled out.

"Loss of consciousness, no visible fractures or open wounds. We have a pulse, but it's weak and thready."

Backup units from neighboring counties were arriving on scene. They assisted with blankets and rotating rounds of CPR for Benjamin.

"Let's load and go, people; time is ticking."

A rotation of medics had performed CPR all the way to the hospital, but Benjamin never regained consciousness. In Steve's career, he had delivered bad news more times than he would like, but there was no amount of training that would prepare you to tell your daughter that her fiancé was dead and her life forever altered.

He recalls walking out and seeing her sitting in the hospital waiting room, wrapped in a blanket.

"Dad, how is he? Is he conscious? Can I see him?" She jumped up from the cold plastic chair.

"Michelle, honey, sit back down." He picked up the blanket that had fallen off and gently wrapped it around her. "I am so sorry."

Even today, when he recalls this memory, he can still feel the lump in his throat and the wave of nausea.

Looking at her face, he knew once the words came out, her life would never be the same. He wiped a tear and lifted his gaze to meet her eyes. "Michelle, Benjamin didn't survive. He's gone, baby." The room faded away as she collapsed into his arms. Benjamin was already becoming like a son to him. No loss is easy, but this one cut deep.

The door lets out a creak and the scent of a musty basement hits his nose. So many donations had poured in after Benjamin's death that it allowed them to purchase this extra space and more specialized equipment. After decades of North Carolina dealing with multiple catastrophic hurricanes and flash flooding, they were finally given training and equipment to train in swift water rescue. Since then, he and his team had participated all over the state in multiple rescue operations in both western and eastern North Carolina. He places the gear in the storage box and does a quick inventory of supplies in each storage unit. Satisfied that it's up to par and everything is in place, he locks the door and wishes it were that easy to lock away the memories. He walks away and prays that he's long retired before that swift water equipment has to be used again.

Michelle has a full morning of deliveries to make. As she makes her way about town, she notices that the traffic has picked up significantly. Yes, it's most definitely October in western North Carolina. Visitors from all over are driving in to catch a glimpse as the leaves hit their peak colors. Subtly, the soft hues of red, orange, and yellow will crescendo into a peak grand finale with a brief pause of color explosion before the leaves surrender to the ground. It truly is incredible to think that one subtle leaf here and there can lead to such a grand finale of the brightest colors imaginable.

Not only has the traffic increased, but the pace at the bakery has picked up considerably. They are especially busy preparing for the upcoming Pumpkin Festival. In just a few days, the streets will be lined with people marveling at craft vendors and sampling every food concoction you can dream up. A ribbon of scents will swirl through the air as the smell of fresh wood handicrafts mingle with the hot fried dough of funnel cakes. Whiffs of ripe lemons being squeezed to make refreshing glasses of lemonade. Popcorn in various varieties, from sweet kettle corn to special seasonings like dill pickle and cheddar cheese. And of course, anything that isn't nailed down is fair game to be fried: pickles, okra, Oreos, crickets, and even rattlesnake. The gentle fall breeze will carry the smell of the award-winning BBQ from the Happy Hog.

One thing that is certain about North Carolinians—they are serious about their sports and BBQ. Few questions will incite a family riot bigger than the following: Are you a Duke or Carolina Fan? Eastern NC or Western NC BBQ? The debates can heat up quickly and be contentious regarding whether Eastern NC, with its vinegar-based sauce, or Western NC, with its tomato base, is best. The Happy Hog decided that it was not only safer but more profitable not to pick sides but rather to serve up both sides of the state.

As the festival edges closer, she feels the mood of the town grow lighter in anticipation. Even with all the extra work, she's feeling a bit more cheerful. She guesses inside of everyone there truly is the heart of a kid who adores a good festival. The spirit is so contagious that it seems to have even temporarily infected Joe Simpson, the old town curmudgeon. Just this week she thought she saw the corner of his mouth curl up in an attempt to smile as he left the bakery with his morning coffee and doughnut. Always the same order. One plain doughnut and one black coffee followed by the inevitable statement: "Back in the day, I could get a dozen doughnuts for what one costs today."

While she attended many festivals in her childhood, this will be her first time experiencing the Pumpkin Festival. The event started after she'd left for basic training. The festival kicks off with the annual Great Pumpkin Weigh Off. Growers all over the East Coast line up to hit the scales to see who will take home the bragging rights and cash for the largest gourd this year. According to her dad, some years the winner weighed in at more than 1,500 pounds. Though Steve Richardson has been known to tell a few tall tales related to the size of fish he caught on the river, these weights were confirmed to her by others.

The town prepares year-round for this festival. Once this year is done, plans will begin anew for next year. Businesses and crafters know they'd better register early if they hope to secure their spot for the next year. In addition to food and crafts, the festival gives businesses and nonprofits a chance to showcase what they have to offer the town.

Thanks to Allie, along with free blood pressure checks, the hospital agreed to use their mobile medical unit to test potential donors for Katie. Michelle is keeping a positive face on the outside, but inside, she's growing more concerned daily that a match won't be found in time. Since Michelle arrived here, Katie has already suffered two severe colds that put her in bed for weeks. At the bakery, she's stopping to catch her breath more often, and she has more bruises than a linebacker for East Chatham High. Michelle tried to persuade her last week to stay home, but she insisted that she needed the distraction to keep her mind from getting the best of her. Linda and Michelle have at least been successful in convincing her to take the day off to enjoy the festival with her kids.

"Hey, Dad, can you give me a hand?" Michelle calls out the window of the Street Sweets rolling kitchen, another of Katie's genius business moves. The food truck is set up at most local events and is also contacted to do corporate and private parties. The state-of-the-art food truck is stocked with the pre-baked favorites from the bakery but is most often booked to fry up hot doughnuts, which guests then top with their favorite toppings. Their sweet or salty cravings can be satisfied with a selection of classic glazes and toppings, or more adventurous ones like bacon and jalapenos. But today, they'll have a steady line of folks waiting for a handheld fried apple pie drizzled with Dogwood Bakery's signature caramel sauce. Folks have to get these while they last because they're only offered once a year during the festival.

"Toss me the extension cord so I can get it plugged in over here."

Steve untangles the long, orange cord and manages to successfully find what seems to be the last available outlet on the crowded street.

The sounds of banjos, fiddles, and dulcimers begin to fill the air. Soon the leader begins to sing.

"Oh good grief." Michelle looks out at her dad with exasperation. "Seriously, from Baghdad to banjos, my journey home is now complete."

"I see your dislike for bluegrass music hasn't changed. I had hoped one day you would grow an appreciation for your heritage." He begins to claps his hands together and tap his foot to the medley as he sings along with the band:

*Froggy went a courtin' and he did ride, uh-huh*
*Froggy went a courtin' and he did ride, uh-huh*
*Froggy went a courtin' and he did ride*
*With a sword and a pistol by his side, uh-huh, uh-huh, uh-huh."*

"I have always wondered what is this song even about," Michelle says, checking the connections to the truck.

"It's clear as day. Mr. Frog is asking Miss Mouse to marry him. Listen." Steve proceeds to clap and sing.

*"He said, 'Miss Mouse, will you marry me?' uh-huh*
*He said, 'Miss Mouse, will you marry me?' uh-huh*
*He said, 'Miss Mouse, will you marry me?'*
*And oh so happy we will be, uh-huh, uh-huh, uh-huh."*

Michelle's dad was right—she had hated the sound of bluegrass music growing up. The songs to her seemed to just reinforce the hillbilly stereotypes that they were all poor, uneducated, and apparently often had trouble with the law. Songs that lamented about lost loves, barely scraping by, and prison woes, as Billy Bob confesses why he had to murder Joe Schmoe. Yet she adores jazz and blues music. So if she really thinks about it, there are a lot of similarities.

Steve continues to hum along with the song as he runs the gray duct tape down the electrical cord to the sidewalk.

"Don't need any broken hip calls today." He steps back to survey his work with satisfaction just as Linda walks by. He links his arm into the crook of hers and begins swinging her around.

"Steve Richardson, I don't have time for your nonsense today."

"Yes, Daddy, you two can do-si-do all you want later. Mom and I have a line of customers waiting."

Michelle carefully removes the hot pies from the grease, trying to avoid the rapid pops of grease, and lays them on a plate lined with paper towels. As the months have progressed in the bakery, she's not only become more proficient with her baking skills but has discovered that she actually enjoys it. There's something very satisfying about merging all the ingredients into a final product that brings others a tiny bit of happiness.

She's quite surprised at how quickly she's settled comfortably into her life here in Chatham with her family. When preparing to retire from the USAF, people wanted to know if she'd return to her hometown to live. She never saw herself as being able to return home. She felt like she was so different from when she'd left that it would be like a polar bear trying to live in South Florida.

Initially, as she'd anticipated, she did feel a bit like an outsider in her own hometown, but it didn't take long to feel back at home. Living here now feels like slipping on her favorite stretchy pants after a big meal. One thing that she has truly treasured is the time and conversations with her sisters and mom. It's so true that it's hard to miss something you never knew was there to miss.

Since she left so young, she hadn't experienced these types of intimate interactions as an adult with her mom and sister. The ability to have what seems like small interactions with family members is likely taken for granted by most who have them. This is why so many military families build strong bonds. In the absence of family, they're forced to find surrogate families to lean on. Something is happening that she never saw coming. She's falling in love with her hometown again, and each day is making it harder to think about leaving.

She slides the plate down to Linda, who drizzles the decadent buttery caramel sauce on top.

"Here you go, Jean. How's your mama doing?" Linda reaches out to hand her two fritters.

"Oh, she's in bed today." She shakes her head, taking a bite of her fritter. "Down with her bursitis again. How's Lucy doing?"

"Oh dear, I hate to hear that. Lucy is the same; memory comes and goes, but mostly goes these days."

"Such a sad state, isn't it? I mean, about getting old. My mama and Lucy were some of the most active women in this town. Served on every church and community committee around."

"They sure were, and some of the best-dressed around as well."

Jean shakes her head and giggles. "Oh, you're right about that. They never missed a sale at Spainhour's department store." She licks the final drizzle of caramel from her spoon. "Linda, I don't know how you do it year after year, but these pies never disappoint. Looks like both your daughters have a knack for the business."

Linda looks over at Michelle. "Yes, it's been such a blessing to have her home during this time. I was a little hesitant, but her skills have shaped up nicely."

"Do you mind boxing this fritter up for me? I'll take it to Mama later. And add a lock and key if you have one, or it might not make it to her."

"Don't have a lock and key, but I'll tape it up to make it a little less tempting."

"Thanks, and it goes without me saying that we're all praying for Katie. God's got this; just keep the faith."

"We appreciate it. Give your mom my best. Hope she feels better soon. Enjoy the festival; we sure lucked out on the weather today. Absolutely gorgeous day for the festival."

Jean waves and collects her box.

Drew arranges the bottles of wine on his table and looks across at the Street Sweets truck. It's more than a coincidence that the Rushing Streams wine booth is across from the Dogwood Bakery truck. Being on the Pumpkin Festival planning committee at times had its perks. No one argued when he volunteered to help set up the map of vendors this year. His current view is worth all the hours, even the battles with Evelynn Darnell, the mayor's opinionated wife.

"Hey, Billy, hold down the fort. I'll be right back." Drew weaves his way through a thick crowd of people. Most people he passes seem in good spirits to be at the festival, except for one distraught little girl crying over her lost balloon.

"Hey, Drew!" Allie waves from across the way.

"Hey there. Where are the twins?"

"They're too old to be seen with their mama. You know teenagers—they'll pop up when they run out of money."

He laughs. "You look dressed for business and not fun."

"I'm headed over to the hospital table to help support screenings today. We're encouraging as many people as possible to get swabbed for possible matches for Katie."

"I did mine a while back and will definitely encourage everyone to do the same. It was fast and easy. I was especially glad to find out that no needles were involved," Drew says.

"Seriously, the big bad Marine with a hundred tattoos is afraid of a tiny needle?"

He looks around. "Don't let my secret out; you'll ruin my badass reputation."

She laughs. "It really is simple, and even if people aren't a match for Katie, once in the registry, they could save someone else's life. Where are you headed to?"

Drew fidgets and adjusts his baseball cap. "Oh, just heading over to get my fried apple pie fix."

Allie looks at him suspiciously. "Hmmmm, and to see a certain someone who just so happens to be preparing these apple pies?"

She notes a hint of red come in his cheeks as he tips his hat to her and says, "See you around, Allie. I'll send folks your way,"

Drew continues to cross the street. It's been over a month since their day at the winery. He had every intention of showing her his next dream at the Old Mill. True, they were both busy, but he had to work up the courage for this. Showing her the winery was one thing, but this is different. They have so many memories attached to this place, and he wonders if she'll appreciate this new version he's put so much sweat into. He hears Dr. Dan in his head: *Only way you'll know is to ask.* Why then does he feel like he'd rather take on enemy fire right now than make this ask.

He waves at Trevor Settle, who's being swindled out of a few bucks by his daughters for a ride on the apple cart. The girls win and slide on the seats with triumphant smiles. The Chatham Shrine Club are the masterminds behind this fleet of golf carts masquerading as giant red apples. For a donation of a few bucks, they'll take you from one end of the festival to the other, take you on a spin through the corn maze, or more than likely help you find your car lost in the sea of cars parked throughout the town.

Drew walks up to the back door of the Street Sweets truck and taps lightly.

Michelle flings open the door. Her face is red from the heat of the fryer, and her apron is dotted with powdered sugar. "Only knock if you're here to work."

"Looks like business is good."

"That it is. How many do you want?' Michelle turns to reach for a box.

"None right now. I was wondering what you're doing tomorrow."

"Well, at this rate, sleeping all day. Why?"

"Tomorrow looks like a great day for some hiking, and I was wondering if you'd like to join me." He shoves his hands in his pockets and thinks, *Okay, that was lame.*

She brushes off her apron and straightens her hat. "Sure, just not too early."

He glances up, surprised at her quick but affirmative answer. "Of course not, I have to show up at church. Even at age 38, Grandma Rose will tan my hide. How about 1:00?"

"Sure, I think I can be among the living by then."

"Great, I'll pick you up. Dress for the outdoors."

"Okay, see you then." Michelle closes the door and looks at her mom, who she can tell is fighting the urge to say something. "What?"

Linda has always had a soft spot for Drew Jones. Many in town thought he would turn out to be a bad egg just like his father. But he had not only been a neighborhood kid but one of her third-grade students. That year in her classroom, he seemed to be a carefree kid. In that brief year she saw glimmers in him that many never had the opportunity to see. She knew that given a better home life, he and his brother could have had a better chance in life. It truly kept her up some nights to know how dire the home life was. Each night she prayed over them and so many of her other students who lived in difficult homes. It had been so wonderful to watch him over these last few years find his own path. And although she hadn't met Alex yet, and it probably wasn't fair to him, she wouldn't put a stop to Drew pursuing her daughter.

"Nothing. I have absolutely nothing to say."

"All right then, let's get back to work."

Michelle drops the pie into the fryer and glances at her mom to see that she's no longer looking. She lets out the breath she's been holding in and feels her face relax into a smile.

At the hospital booth, Allie types the information for each participant into the registry and carefully checks that the number on the vial matches their name in the system before handing it to Christy Johnson, the lab tech. Christy is the daughter of her high school classmate Felicia, who runs a very successful floral shop in Chatham. So crazy that these kids are old enough to be out of school and making their own lives. Seems like just yesterday she and Felicia were waiting tables at the China Inn restaurant, trying to earn money for summer camps. Mrs. Chou was always all smiles to the customers, but behind the kitchen doors, she and Felicia didn't need to know Chinese to know when she was less than pleased with their serving skills.

The line remains steady most of the morning as one by one people are swabbed. Allie looks up to find Joshua Taylor standing in front of her. Allie isn't the only one who knew; it's no secret around town that ever since Katie's divorce, Josh has had his eye on her.

"Well, well, if it isn't one of Chatham's finest," Allie teases.

Joshua had worked his way up in the Chatham Fire Department and would be chief as soon as Steve Richardson retired—which means dies, because everyone knows he will never stop working.

"Allie." He tips his hat to her.

"Are you here to get tested?"

"Yes, I am. I wanted to come earlier, but I had to wait for a lull. Glad people are enjoying the day, but this day is a nightmare for us in law enforcement. People can get really feisty about these parking spaces."

"I don't doubt it. Here you go. If you'll just read this consent and sign, Christy will explain the procedure and get your sample."

"With all these people today, don't you think someone will be a match?"

"We sure hope to beat the odds by finding that needle in a haystack, and we appreciate you participating."

"How is Katie doing?"

"Why don't you ask her yourself?"

He turns to find Katie standing behind him.

"Hi, Josh. Talking about me again?" Katie gives him a friendly wave.

"Katie, good to see you. So how are you?"

"Well, today is a good day. I guess I'm just energized by the festival and possibly a lot of grease and sugar. I do, however, feel a bit overwhelmed to be the poster child of Chatham. It's definitely humbling to see all the support."

"People here truly care about you and your family. They want to help any way they can. Plus, the need for high quality sweets in this town is really inspiring the sugar junkies to help out their favorite supplier," Josh says, feeling more at ease.

Katie reaches over and places her hand on his shoulder. "Very funny. Well, thank you. I appreciate you getting screened."

"Speaking of family"—Josh looks around—"where are your kids?"

"Off with their dad, probably eating things that they'll regret later after a few rides on the Ferris wheel."

They stand in awkward silence, then Josh says, "Well, I better get this done and back to car duty before the chief comes looking for me."

Allie hands him the pamphlet on what will happen if he's a match. Katie and Josh continue to chat as they walk over to the testing area.

Allie watches as Katie walks away. She knows she was lying. She might fool people with her smile, but her frail body tells a different story. She looks down at her phone. She's heard nothing from her contact regarding Linda's request. Although she knows they will contact her if they have info, she steps away from the tent and makes a call.

"Hey, any updates? Is there anything else we can do to increase our chances of finding them? Sorry to be pressing you. I know this is complex, but we're running out of time."

Michelle sinks deeper into the hot water. She had no idea that cooking could be so brutal on the body. She feels throbs pulsing in her feet, and her lower back and hips are so stiff that she's sure only injections of motor oil could loosen them up at this point. Tired as she is, it's a good tired. Even though she spent most of her day inside the food truck, she loved being in the thick of the festival today. Once the crowds thinned, her mom had encouraged her to take a break and walk around. She couldn't remember the last time she'd felt such a sense of peace. The smells, the views, the people. She knows that she was experiencing nostalgia, a honeymoon period of sorts, and that living here would likely dull the feelings over time. Yet most people whom she knew here seemed very content and happy with their lives.

Drew asking her to meet up was most certainly a part of the day that she had not foreseen. She had talked with Alex after the festival, and originally had planned to tell him about her plans with Drew the next day. She had told him about the tour at the winery but that seemed like a reasonable thing to explain. She just doesn't know how to explain how Drew fits into her past. "It's complicated" doesn't even begin to cover it. She's feeling a bit of guilt in saying yes, and had typed Drew her cancellation message but then erased it a few times, reminding herself that part of her reason for returning was to heal old wounds, and this one still lingers.

She puts on her PJs and rummages through the various bottles of wines she has accumulated since arriving. She settles on the left-over bottle of Summer Crush that Allie liked so much. Even though she doesn't typically care for sweet wines, it sounds good today. She pours herself a glass and then slips under the covers. She reaches for the remote and begins mindlessly flipping through channels. It doesn't take long for her eyes to become heavy as the exhaustion of the day and wine begin to take over.

She turns off the TV and quickly becomes aware of the silence in the pitch-dark room. She'd heard odd noises or smelled the gardenias on a few nights, but she hadn't experienced any more sightings of the mysterious shadow man since her first night. Katie is probably right: per usual, she's letting her imagination get the best of her. As she drifts off, her mind relishes a memory from long ago that she rarely recalls. She feels a rush of warmth wash over her body as she recalls these memories. A sweet summer when she was just a fourteen-year-old girl falling in love for the first time. After her long day, the night air had been mild, so she'd raised the window to allow the cool breeze to circulate.

Now deeply asleep, Michelle is oblivious to not only the sheer white curtain flapping erratically but also to the man standing at the end of her bed. No, she hadn't imagined him that night, and he didn't go away. Tonight, he is very much there, as he has been each night since she arrived, watching her sleep.

# Chapter 21: The Old Mill

Michelle looks like an out-of-work lumberjack as she walks out with her faded jeans and plaid jacket. The jeans are hers, but the jacket she found digging through Papa's closet. People made a lot of judgments about how Nana had moved on so fast after his death, but his closet remained the same as the day he died. Apparently, Nana could never face that final chore. Michelle figures if she's going to get something dirty, it might as well be this dog bed of a jacket. Plus, it was incredibly warm, and depending on how long they stayed out once the sun set, it would cool off quickly in these hills.

A few minutes past one, Drew pulls up in the driveway. Michelle grabs her keys and closes the door behind her. When she turns around, she can't believe her eyes. Drew is standing beside his 1989 white Jeep Wrangler.

"Seriously, you still have this same Jeep?" Michelle taps on the hood with her fist.

He opens the door for her to climb in. "Why get rid of a good thing?"

"Honestly, you men will keep cars and T-shirts forever."

"It's called loyalty. A quality that I thought most women had high on their list. Plus, I had to bag a lot of groceries at the Cash and Carry to pay for this baby."

"Now that part you are so right about." She settles into the seat. "Man, it just all seems so long ago, doesn't it?"

"Like a whole other life ago." He glances over at her before returning his eyes to the road. "I only take her out on special occasions. I love her, but she's not reliable."

She turns her attention to Major, who appears to be sleeping in the back seat. "Hey, Major, how are you today?"

"He's a little mad at the moment; you have his seat. He usually rides shotgun, but he's a gentleman and acquiesced to the lady."

She reaches back and scratches his head. Major lifts his head long enough to acknowledge her and then goes right back to sleep.

"So where are we heading to hike?"

"Just hold your horses. You always were so high strung."

"Hey, maybe true, but living in Europe has helped me learn to live life at a different pace. Well, that and yoga."

"The old work-to-live-not-live-to-work philosophy. Probably not going to work for this farm boy, but you sound really happy there."

She stares out the window and admires the colors of the leaves. They are really starting to change. She hesitates a moment before responding. "I am."

"Good, I'm glad."

"You seem really happy here. Are you?"

"I've never really been a fan of the term happy, but I would definitely say that I'm content."

"Any special lady friend?"

"No, I guess you could say that I'm married to my work."

"Well, that's no fun."

"Funny, that's what my ex, Suzanne said about me."

"That you were no fun?" she asks with a touch of sarcasm.

"Pretty much. We were living together, and I was at the vineyard all day and then got home late at night from the tap room. She said if she had wanted to live alone, she would have rented her own place."

"How long did you guys date?"

"Off and on for about three years."

"Any chance you guys will work it out?"

"Oh no, that ship has sailed; she's married and has kids now." He turns the Jeep into a small gravel parking lot. "Hate to interrupt your game of twenty questions, but we're here." He parks the Jeep and she steps out to be surrounded by a canopy of colors.

"Know where we are?"

She looks around and senses a familiar feeling, but she still isn't sure. "Not yet. I'm still getting my bearings after being away for so long."

"Come on, you will soon." He grabs a backpack from the back of the Jeep. Major takes off like a shot; it's obvious that he's familiar with this place.

She follows them down a winding path through the woods. With no one in sight, each step they make through the fallen leaves seems to echo through the woods. The air is heavy with the aroma of pine sap as the sun's afternoon rays radiate through the open spaces between the trees. The path begins to curve and leads them by an old dilapidated shed that's slowly eroding into the earth. The closer they edge, the louder the sound of rushing water becomes. Abruptly she stops and stands still to listen. In the stillness she can hear the rushing water and the distinctive bird call and response of bobwhites.

He smiles. "You know where we're going now, don't you?"

"Absolutely!" She can't mask the excitement. She hasn't been here in so long. Each step they take closer, the sound of the water becomes louder. Eventually they come to the clearing and there it is: Carter Falls. Though she's sure that some trees have fallen and the brush grown in new ways, to her it's the same.

"Wow, it's been so, so long!" Her eyes light up like a child on Christmas morning.

"I thought you might like to visit the old stomping grounds." He reaches his hand out and she takes it. He steadies her while she makes her way to a large rock that overlooked the falls. They sit in the stillness, each engaged in their own silent series of memories of this spot.

"Do you come here a lot?" She turns to ask.

"Only every day."

"Every day? No wonder Major knows the way around here."

"Yep, it's become our second home. Come on, let's go see the old mill."

"Ummmm, I would be surprised to still see it standing."

She follows Drew down the hill, and Major races ahead, barking and chasing every squirrel that crosses his path.

"Here, we're going to take a shortcut through this bamboo. Careful, there are a few briars around."

He leads the way, creating a path for her as he breaks the bamboo down with his feet. As they work their way through the last section of bamboo, that's when she sees it. Not only is the old mill still there, but it's completely restored.

The first thing that draws her eye is the working water wheel. The water travels down the flume and falls with a force against the paddles that kept the wheel turning at a constant rate. As a kid, she had tried to imagine what it looked like when working, and now she could see. The decayed siding had been skillfully replaced with various shades of weathered browns to give the illusion of her former appearance.

"What do you think?" Drew looks at her with an obvious sense of pride.

188

"Drew, I am speechless. You did this? This had to be such a labor of love. I can't imagine the time and money you've spent to get this to this level."

"And you haven't even been inside."

"How in the world did you ever get the old water wheel to work?"

"The old one was beyond repair, so we had a new one built. No easy task considering these are specialized wood workers who do this. Then we had to bring in a crane to take the old one out and put the new one in."

"That's a lot of work for a water wheel."

"Well, what's a grist mill without a working water wheel?"

"People built things better back in the olden days. The rock foundation was solid on her. Even with natural erosion over time, this foundation is going nowhere. Things like the siding and other repairs I was able to do on my own. Took longer but saved me a bit of money."

"Papa Silas definitely gave you great handyman skills."

"That he did."

She follows him up the steps, which have been meticulously restored with accuracy as well. He opens up the door, and the scent of fresh-cut lumber fills her nose.

"Watch your step, I've still got things scattered all around on the floor."

Drew opens the door to reveal an open space with elegant hardwood floors and a beautiful long bar in the far corner. They walk over to the bar.

"Wow, this is a very unique look. What is this made out of?"

"It's actually from some copper I found in the mill as I was working. I had it melted down and really liked the look. When I could, I tried to incorporate things that were here to keep the history."

They walk over, and in between two windows is a beautiful table.

"This was made from wood from the original water wheel."
The spokes of the wheel had created a stunning rustic table with a
beautiful glass overlay. "I figure this will make the perfect location
for a cake cutting at weddings."

"So is that what you see this as mostly, a wedding venue?"

"That's the initial thought, but also family reunions, corporate
parties, and such."

They walk outside.

"Looks so different from back in our day. Who would have
ever thought that it could have such life breathed into it."

"Definitely just me; so many people thought I was crazy."

"I wouldn't say you're crazy. I think this took a lot of vision
and bravery."

They make their way outside just as the sun begins to fall
behind the trees and the first lighting bugs begin to illuminate
the fast-approaching night. Years ago that would have signaled
that it was time to head home, but today, sitting in this sanctuary
of memories, neither one is in any hurry to leave. It seems as if
their childhood wish has been granted; they are adults and can
linger in this place, where all problems are suspended, for as long
as they want.

# Chapter 22: Clues

Allie removes the plastic lid from her coffee cup and deposits two packs of sugar along with a splash of cream. She quickly mixes the ingredients and raises the coffee to her lips and then sets it back down. As much as she needs the caffeine rush, she doesn't want to risk burning herself. Many of her co-workers avoid the hospital cafeteria, but she has always found it to be a comforting contrast to the sterile hospital environment. It's also one of the only places where she can sit inside and experience the sun. Her office, the ER, and the chapel, where she spends most of her hours, are all virtual caves, which doesn't help with her feelings of depression. Here, she can sit and gaze out the window and feel a bit connected to the outside world.

She takes a deep breath, holds it for a second, and lets out an audible sigh. Gazing out the window, she notices for the first time this fall how beautiful the leaves are, and she observes a squirrel retrieve a nut and scamper up the tree. Most days are such a whirlwind that it's nice to sit and be. She's now able to take a sip of her coffee, which reminds her of drinking coffee at her grandparents' house. Nothing fancy, no flavors, just coffee, cream, and sugar.

She'd been paged at 4:00 a.m. to assist with a family who was considering organ donation after a car accident left their 20-year-old daughter brain dead. She sits lost in her thoughts, always hoping that she handled the situation the right way. Over the years, she's grown more confident in her abilities to tell families their loved ones died or soon would, but now she just hopes that it didn't come across too easy, unintentionally cold and callous. Among the clattering of trays and silverware, she hears her phone vibrate.

"Chaplain Allie speaking." She places her hand over her other ear to block out all the background noise. "I'm in the cafeteria. Send her down. Thanks, Liz." In the frenzy of the early morning, she hadn't thought about her meeting with Linda. Thank God for Liz. She's been her assistant now for over five years, and she's the only reason she can keep it half together these days.

A few minutes later, Allie watches as Linda navigates through the rows of rectangular tables, stopping occasionally to acknowledge friends and neighbors. She doesn't need to be privy to the conversations to know what's being said. In the south, it's proper etiquette to know about who is in and out of the hospital and what for, and you should always inquire about these events. So she watches as Linda weaves in and out of tables, hugging different ones and likely offering the standard responses of "Well, bless your hearts" and "We'll get them added to the church prayer list." For most, it's genuine compassion and kindness, but also deep in the heart of each southerner, they're all just a bit nosy. Eventually she makes her way over to the table, and Allie rises to give her a hug.

"Good morning! Would you prefer that we go to my office? Rough morning, so I was in need of a change of scenery."

"Oh no, dear, this will be fine. You said you have some information. I've just been on pins and needles since your call. Have you located him?"

Allie hates to put a damper on Linda's excitement. "Not yet. Like I said, I don't want to squash your hope, but I want you to be grounded in the reality that this is a long shot."

Linda smiles, but Allie can sense the disappointment.

"But I have learned something that may help us."

Linda patiently looks on as Allie shares with her what her contact told her related to adoptions that occurred in NC around the time her son was born.

"The bad news is that those records are pretty much sealed, but the good news is that thanks to social media and DNA registries, many people are having success being reunited."

"What's my next step?"

"Linda, before you take this any further, have you thought anymore about telling Steve? I just feel like you need that support."

"No, I just can't deal with all that right now, and like I said, I just don't want to get anyone's hopes up. We don't need any more let downs around here."

She opens her bag and grabs a sticky note. "Here's the website. You'll need to go make a profile."

"Oh Allie, I hate to impose, but could you please help me. I get so flustered with these dang computers. Katie has just changed us over at the inn, and I just don't think this old dog can learn but one new trick at a time."

Allie really doesn't have the time to tutor her, but this is her best friend's mom, and she can't say no. "Come on, let's head to my office."

The hallways are bustling with healthcare professionals in a rainbow of scrubs, each color denoting their specialty. They navigate patients walking with IV poles, some being wheeled down the hall in stretchers, and even a mom in labor managing a difficult contraction.

Once settled in her office, Allie opens her computer and they begin. Together they fill in as much detailed information as Linda can recall. They get to the end and hit submit.

"Now Linda, if your information matches someone else's, you'll be alerted."

"So we just wait?" Linda says with a sense of desperation.

"Yes, at this point, all we can do is wait." Allie reaches across the table and grasps Linda's hand. "And pray that your son is also looking for you."

# Chapter 23: Halloween

The sun is still up when Michelle arrives at Katie's house. It will soon slip softly behind the mountain tops and be replaced with the gentle glow of moonlight. Michelle has checked the forecast, and it's going to be perfect weather for their Halloween night. No rain and clear skies, which should yield lots of stars along with a half moon. She'd been disappointed to learn in her meteorology training that despite all the movies and images of the full moon on Halloween, those are quite rare.

Michelle opens the car door, and one by one three little balls of energy slide into their seats.

"Okay," Michelle says, "I have one Superman, one pirate, and one Tinker Bell. Who's ready for some serious candy grabbing?"

"Meeeeeeee," three high-pitched voices echo in unison while bouncing up and down in their seats.

"Okay, guys, I know you're excited, but don't give Aunt Michelle too much trouble," Katie says, handing each one their candy buckets.

"Don't worry, there will be no trouble tonight." Michelle places her witch hat on her head and points her finger in their direction.

"Too much trouble here and I'll just cast a spell and turn them all into toads."

"Toes? Who wants to be a toe?" Joel asks with a perplexed look.

"She said *toad*, not *toes*, matey. It's like a frog with warts," Brett says in his best pirate voice.

"Eeewwww! Well, I don't want to be a toad either," Joel says.

"Aaaaaarrgghhh, matey, that's the point. If it were up to me, I'd have you walk the plank." Brett raises his sword in his brother's direction.

"Okay, okay, there will be no turning to toads or plank-walking tonight, because everyone will be on their best behavior." Michelle places her witch's hat inside the car.

"First, trick or treat rule number one: seat belts buckled. I want to hear three clicks."

"Aunt Michelle, I need help," Karry says as she struggles to get her seat belt around her green, fluffy dress.

"Of course, princess." Michelle stretches across Joel to reach the buckle.

"I'm clicked in," says Brett.

"Joel, how about you?" He signals a thumbs up "I should never doubt that Superman has it all handled."

"Have a great time, guys, and I'll see you in a bit." Katie wraps her sweater around herself tighter.

"Mommy, can you please, pleeeeaaseee go with us?" Karry says with her best pleading voice.

"No, sweetie. Mommy isn't feeling well, but we'll snuggle and watch a movie when you get home." She closes the car door and hugs Michelle. "Thank you for this." As Michelle pulls back, she notices the tears quickly forming in her sister's eyes.

"That's why I'm here, plus I have many Halloween nights to make up for. Now, go. Get inside and rest."

Katie waves from the porch until the car is no longer in sight. She manages to make it to the couch and lies down before she fully releases the tears she's been holding back. Taking her kids trick or treating was one of her favorite things to do. Even after her diagnosis, she would have never believed that she would ever be too tired to share this night. But tonight, she has little time to lament all that cancer had stolen from her and her kids; she's asleep before enough tears fell to even wet her pillow.

"Okay, guys, we're going to make a quick stop here at the Taproom for some pizza and then head downtown to the Trick or Treat on Main event. I need something on your stomach before this sugar dump happens." Michelle puts the car in park and then reaches for her phone.

"Everyone lean in. I want to get a selfie with the cutest nephews and niece around."

Michelle holds up her phone and snaps a pic. She quickly sends the picture and a text to Alex: "Don't worry, I am safe from vampires and werewolves with these fierce protectors. Love and miss you!"

The four of them settle around a small table in the corner, and a waitress dressed up in a 1950s-style poodle skirt bee bops over to their table.

"Oh my goodness, don't you guys look adorable. What can I get for you?"

"Just a large cheese pizza and four waters please. " Michelle hands her the menus.

After a few minutes of playing I Spy, their pizza arrives, and only then does Michelle realize how hungry she is. With her long day at the bakery and then rushing to get the kids, she missed lunch. She wonders if she would ever have what it takes to be a mom, as this must be their lives every day. Never time to think about their needs, always focusing on others. Allie and Katie are right—her life would change drastically. But looking at them, she feels a tingle in her heart and knows that she still wants it.

She scoops out a slice for each of them, pulling the long strings of extra cheese from each plate. The table grows quiet as they savor the crispy crust, sweet sauce, and perfect combination of cheeses. Drew really knows what he's doing with this place, from the wines to the food. She spots him coming from the stockroom and acknowledges him with a wave. Their time together here has been healing for her, and after all these years, she's happy that he's found such passion in life. Maybe she can return to Germany after making peace with all she had left undone here.

Drew checks on the few other patrons that had made it that night and then makes his way over to their table. "Looks like everyone enjoyed their dinner."

"It was yummy!" Karry says as Michelle wipes the remnants of sauce off her face, careful not to mess up her rosy cheeks and lipstick.

"Yes, I agree with Karry, yummy indeed. Katie is feeling pretty rough, so I offered to take these candy bandits trick or treating."

"Candy bandits, you say. Well, I have just the thing for them." He gives each of them a handful of candy, and they eagerly begin to tear in.

"Only one piece for now." They each give her a disappointed look.

Drew pulls up a chair. "Hey, kids, let me tell you how much your Aunt Michelle loves Halloween, and especially haunted houses."

"Oh no, not this story again. Don't you have some work to do?" She looks at him a bit annoyed.

Drew leans in, eyeing each kid and ignoring her question. "When we were in high school, a bunch of us on Halloween night went through a local haunted house."

"A *real* one?" Karry's eyes widen.

"No, honey, it was only a bunch of firemen all dressed up in costumes. The Chatham fire department did it every year to raise money." Karry relaxes back into her chair, seemingly relieved by his answer. "It was so dark in there that you could barely see each other. So we were making our way through the house, and your Aunt Michelle was holding on for dear life to almost everyone in the group. Then suddenly, one of the zombies started following her and calling her name" "Michelle ... Micheeeellllll e ... Mihceeeeeeellee."

Drew stands from his chair and begins to walk about like a zombie. The kids stare with wide eyes, while Michelle gives a subtle eye roll.

"Then more and more of them started to follow her." He sits back down, straddling his chair.

"Then what happened?" Joel asks as he finishes his last bite of candy.

Drew glances over at Michelle. "She ran out of that house so fast, people thought her pants were on fire. I think she actually left a trail of smoke," he says with a serious face. The kids begin to snicker.

Michelle cracks a smile. "Well, it was scary!"

"But wait, how did they know your name, Aunt Michelle?" Brett asks in his serious, non-pirate voice

"Go ahead, tell them. I hate to ruin your fun." Michelle looks at Drew and motions with her hand for him to continue.

"Well, the genius here had her high school letter jacket on with her name in HUGE letters on the back."

Brett takes his hand and plants his face into the palm. "Wow, Aunt Chelle, that's pretty bad."

"Enough about the past, but speaking of spooky houses, I've had a few hair-raising moments at Nana's house."

"Really, like what?" Drews raises his eyebrows.

"A few times I've heard some strange noises outside, and then there will suddenly be this strong scent of gardenias. It's very bizarre; you know, it's too late in the year for gardenias."

"Ah, I'm sure those woods are full of deer right now just waiting for my rifle. And you know your nana—she's probably got some fancy bottle of perfume leaking somewhere." Drew leans back in his chair and crosses his arms.

"Maybe, but something just feels off," she says as she stacks the plates on the pizza pan and hands it to the waitress.

"Yeah, Grandma Rose is at home with the house locked up like Fort Knox. You know, she still believes this is the devil's holiday. I don't argue with her, but I'd hate to tell her that I'm pretty sure old Satan can weasel through the best set of locks in Chatham on any night of the year. So what's the update on Katie?"

Michelle glances over at the kids.

Drew, heeding her warning, says, "Hey, guys, if you head out back you'll find some corn hole tossing going on."

"Go ahead, toss a few times and then we'll head downtown."

The kids head out and Michelle continues. "It's not good, Drew. I was certain we'd find a donor by now. She's really weak and can barely take care of the kids. I swear I don't know how she even does it when she's well. She's in the bakery at 5:00 a.m. then running the kids around all day in between."

"Yeah, and that ex-husband is no help. He's too busy chasing every skirt in town when he should be helping. Thank God for Linda and Steve."

"Don't get me started on Brad," Michelle says.

The door slings open and the kids whiz by them. Brett chases Karry and Joel with his pirate sword.

"Looks like your cue to load up your train for the next stop. You all have fun. Hey, why don't you stop by here for a glass of wine after you take the kids home? I'm pretty sure you're going to need it," he says with a wink.

"Thanks, I just might take you up on that." As she walks away, she feels a little wave of guilt but quickly dismisses it. *I am doing nothing wrong; just old friends catching up.*

Drew clears a recently vacated table and watches through the window as Michelle attempts to load the kids into the car. He shakes his head and smiles. Yep, resembles trying to herd cats. She catches his glance through the window and waves, and he feels a little butterfly in his stomach. He knows what he has to do. If she comes back tonight, he has to tell her how he feels. Her time here is ticking down, and he has to act fast if he doesn't want to see her drive out of his life forever again.

Allie removes her chaplain badge from around her neck and hangs it over her rearview mirror. For the first time in a long time, she actually studies her ID photo. She compares the face she sees in the photo to the image reflecting back at her in the rearview mirror. Though her physical features haven't changed much over the years, she wonders if others see the changes in her that she feels so poignantly. She believes that she always looks tired and that her eyes have lost the sparkle they once had. She calls Dave to let him know that she's stopping by Linda's on the way home. She tells him that he's on his own passing out any Halloween treats, but she doesn't even know why they buy candy anymore. The odds of trick or treaters at their doorway tonight would be as likely as them winning the lottery. They had built their house off the road, and unless they were friends or family, no one even knew there was a house back there. Dave will just kick back in his recliner and eat half the candy while he watches reruns of the same shows he's seen a million times. The twins are at a friend's house at a Halloween party. Thankfully, due to cell phone tracking, she feels confident that they are where they said they'd be. Well, at least that's where their phones are hanging out, and since they are a second appendage, she knows they are there.

As her car eases out of her parking space, her mind replays her day—something that's happening more and more often these days. She used to be able to pray with patients and leave the work to God, just like she'd learned in her training. While she has seen some things that can only be explained as answers to prayers, more often it seems that God has other plans than what families prayed for.

Images of her patients and families roll nonstop in her brain. Even in sleep she can't escape them, and they often show up in her dreams. The face of a 33-year-old mother with breast cancer, much like Katie. The worry on the faces of parents with a toddler having unexplainable seizures. Today brought extra heaviness to the ER staff, who worked for over an hour to save a 19-year-old involved in a motorcycle crash. Sadly, he didn't make it, which meant she was front and center by the chief of surgery to tell the parents. Now that the twins are about to start driving, these really hit hard. She never really thought of all the pain and suffering she would encounter as a chaplain; she'd only focused on bringing hope and encouragement. This was definitely much easier to do when you feel hopeful yourself.

Her moods had shifted so much in the past few months that she had stopped doing daily check-ins on the behavioral health unit and only went when a consultation request was put in. She feels really bad about doing it, but the line was blurring between those patients' struggles and her own mental wellbeing. Empathy is one thing, but over-identifying with their symptoms is not only ethically a problem but also extremely frightening.

This was when she reached out to her supervisor and requested the time off for sabbatical leave after the holidays. She's grateful that her supervisor values her work there and granted her the leave. She's also relieved that Dave is supportive of her time away as well. They had attended a few couples' sessions over the last few months, and the counselor had really enlightened him on compassion fatigue and the long-term consequences to not only her mental and physical health but also their marriage.

With all the day had brought, there had been one bright glimmer of hope. A call from Josie in the lab had given her some news that was both encouraging yet bewildering at the same time. She knows that she doesn't want to have this conversation with Linda over the phone. This situation calls for an in-person conversation.

As Michelle and the kids arrive, the town is all aglow with luminaries lining the street on both sides. Kids dart in and out of the local businesses, stopping only briefly to check out their latest addition to their candy collection before heading into the next store. Like most kids their ages, Michelle and Katie grew up trick or treating door to door, but in recent years, the Chatham Chamber of Commerce has started a new tradition. Trick or Treat down Main is a win for the kids and the town, as it makes it safer for trick or treating and also helps to promote the local businesses. The streets are secured by Chatham police, and recently installed speakers pipe out all the top Halloween tunes.

There is so much to participate in: costume contests for kids and adults, pumpkin carving contests, and at precisely 9:00 p.m., Miss Trudy's School of Dance will line the streets in their ghoulish costumes to recreate Michael Jackson's infamous "Thriller" video. Every business door is decorated with clever themes. Elizabeth is dressed as Glenda the Good Witch and has transformed the Cuticles and Curls salon into the Land of Oz. The Revolutionary Tea room has taken the obvious choice with an Alice in Wonderland theme, complete with Dibbles, the owner's cat, parading about in the window as the Cheshire Cat. Candace Jackson, now known as Vira, and her staff at the Zen Yoga Den have decorated a 1970s VW van to look like the famous Mystery machine from *Scooby-Doo*. Her husband is Fred, she's Daphne, and their kids are Scooby, Shaggy, and Velma. Michelle is shocked when the kids can't name any of the characters from *Scooby-Doo*. Shame on Katie for not exposing her kids to one of their childhood favorite shows. She makes a mental note of making sure this is rectified.

The sun set long ago, and just as the weather forecast promised, the clear sky sparkles with stars and half the moon. Sometimes the weather turns out just as forecasted. Michelle looks up at the sky and down at the energy and excitement on the streets. Her heart is full. Many years ago, these downtown buildings, which hold so many dear childhood memories, were abandoned, as the trend was strip malls. Those places may offer more choices, but nothing in her eyes will ever rival downtown. Saturday mornings shopping in the Roses department store, which permeated with the smell of fresh popcorn. Hours spent admiring jewelry at the Jewel Box, and wrapping up at the Royal Drug Store for hot dogs and a cherry smash. It did her heart good to see this place alive again, building spaces for these experiences for the children. In this technology-driven world, these spaces offer places to both recharge in solitude and connect.

"Hope you guys had fun! I sure did. We have one more stop at the inn to see Mimi and Pop Pop."

As Michelle pulls into the driveway, she recognizes Allie's car there. Her heart immediately starts to race. *Oh no, Katie.* She reassures herself that she would have been called by now if something was wrong.

"Trick or treat, Mimi!" the kids chant.

"Oh, just look at you guys." Linda opens the door wide to reveal tables full of various treats. "No tricks on me, because I have plenty of treats. Come on into the dessert boofet."

Kids who stopped by the inn knew that they would get a lot more than candy on Halloween. From the time she'd opened The Dogwood Inn and Bakery, every Halloween Linda had worked diligently baking mini cookies and cupcakes to create a dessert spread fit for royalty.

While the kids ravage the remaining items on the buffet, Michelle makes her way into the living room, where she finds Allie curled up in a chair with a cup of coffee.

"What are you doing here? I got nervous, thinking something had happened to Katie, when I saw your car."

"Oh no, I'm sorry; she's fine as far as I know."

Michelle feels her body relax. Here lately she's been finding herself more and more on edge as her mind keeps going to the worst-case scenario. Reality is sinking in that without a match, Katie will die.

"I just haven't seen my second mom in a while, and when you have teenagers, Halloween is just another day." It's killing Allie to conceal all she knows, but she has not only an ethical oath to keep but a deep respect for Linda's wishes. "How is surrogate motherhood going for you?"

Michelle pours herself a cup of coffee and then seats herself across from Allie. "It's fun but exhausting! How did you do this?"

She feels for her friend, who has bags under her eyes and looks like the weight of the world is on her shoulders.

Allie laughs and holds up her coffee cup. "A lot of coffee and a lot of prayer!"

"Did you talk to Dave about going to Sierra Leone?"

"Yes, and thanks to our marriage counselor, I think he's starting to understand the difference in a little tired and burnout. I'll be leaving right after New Year's and staying the whole month of January."

"Wow, that is a long time."

"Not really, it's a pretty typical amount for a sabbatical."

"What will you be doing, besides looking for your parents?" Michelle takes a sip of her coffee.

"I'll actually be assisting Beatrice at the orphanage and learning more about my home country and the struggles there."

"Your home country—that is so exciting. I'm very happy for you. I truly hope you find your parents, or at least get some answers."

"Me too." Allie takes another sip of her coffee.

Their conversation is interrupted as Steve enters the room carrying Joel. "All right, I know you two ladies could yack your jaws all night, but this superhero needs to get home."

"Yes, I need to get going as well," says Allie.

"Mom, can we help you clean up?"

"On no, get these goblins home to Katie. Your dad and I will get this."

Steve helps Linda pack up the leftovers. "It was nice of Allie to come by and visit. Any special reason she stopped in?"

"No, I think she just needed a little extra TLC. You remember parenting in those teenage years—it was hard. Go on upstairs. I'll finish this up. You know I can't find a thing once you put it away."

She pushes open the door to the kitchen with her hip and settles the boxed-up treats on the counter. Per usual, Steve is right. Allie had stopped by for more than motherly support. Linda has never been good at hiding things from him. He managed to weasel every surprise she ever tried to keep from him. Though he had acted surprised, his fresh haircut and new shirt let her know that his 50th birthday party was not the big surprise she had hoped. Nonetheless, a good marriage is built on trust, and they have always been honest with each other. She's sure he would be crushed that she had kept this secret their entire marriage, but she just isn't ready to disclose this yet. Plus, she doesn't want to get his hopes up in case this is not a match.

She busies herself cleaning the kitchen and preparing for the tasks for the next day. She knows she won't sleep tonight, so she might as well stay busy with work. Her mind replays the conversation with Allie again:

"Linda, I have incredible news. We've located your son."

Linda sat down. These were words she had longed to hear, but suddenly they struck fear in her. Her mind raced with a mixture of thoughts that reignited the shame and guilt she'd felt all those years ago.

"I don't know what to say, I can't believe it."

"I know, me too. I couldn't believe it myself, but it's true. Everyone I talked to said that it would be next to impossible with so little information."

Her son. She had found him. Even though she had hoped to find him one day, deep down she felt the odds would be too great. It truly was a miracle. Now could she hope for just one more miracle—that he would be a match?

Katie is still asleep when Michelle drops off the kids. Michelle uses her key and gets the kids bathed and in bed before softly waking her.

"Katie, we're home. Go get in your bed. The kids are all settled."

Katie sits up. "Oh wow, I was out. I promised Karry snuggles and a movie."

"Don't worry, you can do that tomorrow. She's out like a light."

"Thanks again," Katie says with a yawn.

"No need. We missed you, but we had a great time."

"Do you need some monster spray to take to Nana's to keep the ghosts away?" Katie manages a smile.

"No, I'll be fine. I'm stopping by the Taproom for a night cap, and thanks to your three munchkins, after that I'll sleep like a champ."

Katie raises her eyebrow. "Don't you think you're flirting with danger there, sis."

"Don't be ridiculous. I'm so tired of this. Drew and I are just friends, never more."

"Keep telling yourself that, but I've seen a change in both of you since you arrived back in town. Plus, I am 100 percent sure that if he thought he had a chance with you, he'd take it."

"Whatever. Get some sleep. Goodnight."

Michelle closes her car door and reaches for her phone. It's 3:00 a.m. in Germany, but she sends Alex a text anyway. "I miss you." With a heart emoji.

Does she really miss him? Sure, when she talks with him, especially on video chat, she truly misses and longs to be with him. But she has truly settled into a rhythm of life that, dare she admit it, she likes. Is Katie right? Is she flirting with danger? Something in her has been unsettled since returning and spending time with Drew. Is it just the nostalgia and the connection they shared with Benjamin? Or who knows, maybe it's just the trance of fall in western NC. She would never admit to her older sister that she might be right, but it still isn't enough to make her car bypass the Taproom Bar and Grill.

Linda turns off the kitchen light, grabs her sweater, and goes out to the porch. The street is quiet, and very few cars will likely go by for the rest of the night. She settles into the swing in the crook of her porch. Her mind floats back to that tiny hospital room over forty years ago. A wave of tingles hits her body as she remembers the feel of her tiny babe in her arms. While she has prayed and thought about this moment, now her joy has turned to fear. She feels very nervous and a little sick to her stomach. While she longs to meet him, she has to know if he's a match for Katie.

Her mind turns back to her conversation with Allie:

"Does he know the situation of Katie's health? Will he agree to be tested?"

"He actually has already been tested at the Pumpkin Festival. We should know something very soon."

"The Pumpkin Festival? "Linda looked bewildered

"Linda, there's something else you should know about your son." She paused and grabbed Linda's hands. "He has been living right here in Chatham."

As his name flowed out of Allie's mouth, Linda froze in disbelief, knowing how many times she had interacted with him. How could a mother not know her own child?

The chains squeak now in a steady rhythm, and the gentle sway of the swing has calmed her racing heart. She closes her eyes, takes in a deep breath, and speaks a prayer out loud: "Lord, thank you for this miracle of finding my son. I don't want to seem ungrateful or greedy, but please give us one more miracle. Let him be a match for Katie."

As Michelle arrives, Drew is busy wiping down counters and closing things down for the night. She sits at the bar and he pours her a glass of wine.

"Busy night?"

"Not too bad. I gave Billy the night off so he could enjoy Halloween with his kids."

"Well, from someone who just carried three candy monsters around, I'm sure he's pooped. I think you have the right idea; just have pets."

He smiles. "You got that right. Major is all I have time for with running everything."

"Drew, I am really so proud of you and all that you've created here. You should feel so good about all of this."

"Thank you. It's been a hard road, but worth it. Let's sit outside. It's a beautiful night. Unless you are afraid of ghosts?"

"Very funny." Michelle takes her glass and follows Drew out onto the patio. "Speaking of ghosts and people you don't like to discuss, have you seen your father since he got out?"

"No. Like I told you, that lucky SOB was released last year. He barely served 20 years for murdering my mom. You should see him. He's all reformed. Working at the domestic violence shelter as a peer counselor for the men, and at church every time the door is open."

"You know, sometimes people do change, Drew."

"I know people can change, but I will just never believe that man has a soul." He reaches over and fills her glass as he works up the courage to continue. "I had a very intense session with Dr. Dan recently."

"Oh, about what?"

"The accident." He looks at her intently.

Michelle feels her body tensing up. "Please, I don't want to talk about that tonight."

He brings his chair closer to her. "I understand, really I do, but I just have some things that I need to say. If it becomes too much, I promise I'll stop." Drew clears his throat and leans forward toward her. "Michelle, when you first came back, seeing you wear Benjamin's ring, that wasn't about you. It was a reminder to me that I failed both of you that day. All I ever wanted was for you to be happy, and Benjamin did that for you. I was as screwed up as they come, and he was a great guy. I feel like I'm responsible for some of your pain." He looks down. "In the end, I couldn't save my mom or my best friend."

She reaches out and touches his hand. "Drew, I had no idea that you carried the weight of all this. No one is responsible for Benjamin's death. It was a tragic accident, and the only person responsible for your mother's death is Curtis. You were a child and had to grow up way too fast." She discreetly removes her hand and thinks of her sister's warning.

"Just this week was the first time I had ever told Dr. Dan about Benjamin. He knows that my father killed my mother, he knows about the Marines I lost, but I haven't been ready to open that door yet. I just haven't been ready."

"I can understand that."

As the time inches closer to midnight, this space around them seems to be filled with shadows of memories that only they can feel. There are so many more things that he wants to say to her. The words are there but the nerve is not. He wants to tell her that she is the kindest person he's ever known, and the first person he ever truly trusted. But more than anything, he wants her to know that if he could have one wish in the world, it would be to have the chance again to make her happy. He takes a breath and reaches for her hand, but in that moment, her phone begins to vibrate.

She looks at him. "It's my mom. At this hour, this can't be good. Let me answer."

He doesn't need to hear the other side of the conversation to know that a match has been found for Katie.

Michelle ends her phone call and exclaims, "A donor has been found for Kaitie. Isn't that incredible?"

Drew and Michelle embrace, and she pulls back. "I have to go."

"That is wonderful news. Wow! Any idea who it is?"

"Someone who was tested at the Pumpkin Festival is all we know."

"Go, go, you need to be with your family." He stands up.

"Wait, what did you want to tell me?"

"Nothing that can't wait. Go be with your family and keep me updated. I'll get Grandma Rose on the prayer group first thing in the morning"

"Thank you, Drew. I haven't felt this much joy and hope in years."

She doesn't need to elaborate, because he knows exactly what she means.

He holds her coat and she slips her arms in. She turns to say goodnight, and that's when she notices. Her brain registers the body of a grown man standing in front of her, but her soul feels a connection with a boy from long ago. Drew moves closer. She knows she should leave, but she doesn't. He reaches down and zips her coat; his eyes met hers, and then without saying a word, he tells her everything he has wanted to say his whole life with one kiss.

# CLARIFICATION

# Chapter 24: By the Sea

Discreetly tucked in along the North Carolina seashore between the Intracoastal Waterway and the White Oak River lies the sleepy seaside town of Swansboro. Aptly dubbed "the friendly city by the sea," Drew can see why Sam has chosen to settle down here. Once a bustling shipbuilding hub but now focused more on fishing and tourism, it serves as a refuge to many from the frantic pace of modern life. The streets are lined with historic homes, some still featuring a widow's walk, where wives waited anxiously to greet their husbands as they returned from sea. Weathered shingles and exteriors emit a timeless charm while also serving as a testament to the many storms withstood.

After a busy harvest season and all the events of the fall, Drew is in need of a place where the pace of life mirrors the slow lull of the water. He maneuvers his truck down the narrow street towards the heart of the town, skillfully avoiding a gaggle of geese. The streets are lined with eclectic shops that he assumes offer tourists souvenirs related to the sea, but this time of year, there are few customers to be found. The rush of summer tourists is long gone, leaving the locals to relish in their waterside sanctuary until the next beach season.

Drew's GPS signals that he has arrived at his final destination, so he pulls into a parking space behind a hand-painted sign that read in all caps: PARK HERE AND SEE WHAT HAPPENS. Drew shakes his head and smiles. That is classic Sam. He's for sure at the right place.

It's early afternoon, and the sun is glimmering off the water as it slowly makes its arc across the crystal blue sky. Seagulls are crying overhead, and he watches as one skillfully dives and retrieved a small fish. He hopes he and Sam will be as lucky as that bird with their catches while here on the water. He hasn't had much time to fish since spring, and he's itching to have a rod and reel back in his hands. His senses are overtaken by the scent of brackish water and marine life wafting through the air. He pauses to take in the tranquility before making his way down the dock.

His mind zig zags through a wave of memories of his time stationed just a few miles down the road in Jacksonville at Camp Lejeune. Well, at least the sober ones that he can recall. Like many of his fellow Marines, his first experience of seeing a beach happened after joining the Marines. He and his buddies spent most of their weekends at Atlantic Beach, drinking cheap beer and trying to impress as many bikini-laden girls as they could with their hard-earned physiques.

He carefully scans the array of fishing boats tethered to the docks, all gently bobbing in harmony, until he spots Sam. Instantly Drew is confronted with the stark reality of just how much time has passed as he observes the changes in both his mentor and the boat. Years of sun-kissed days and countless seasons battling the elements have left their mark on both Sam and the *Carol Ann* in various ways. Sam's face has succumbed to deep-set lines, while the boat, once painted in vibrant hues, has faded to reflect softer pastels.

"Permission to board," Drew calls out from the dock.

"Drew Jones, you old devil dog, get over here and let me take a look at you." Drew stands tall at attention and Sam gives him a deep looking over from head to toe. "You look a helluva lot better than the last time I saw you."

"I sure hope so. Best I can remember, I was hungover as hell, and you were lecturing me about getting my life together."

Sam looks out over the water and back at Drew. "Yep, that's about how I recall it as well. Come on aboard."

Sam reaches down and grabs Drew's hand to help him over the edge and then takes off towards the bow of the boat. Drew follows along, stepping over worn-out fishing nets and gear, making his way to two mismatched chairs that serve as a front porch.

Sam stands at the bow of the boat and takes in a deep breath of salty air and lets out a loud, audible exhale. "Welcome to heaven on earth."

"I can definitely see why you love it here."

"Absolutely nowhere else I'd rather be." Sam opens the cooler and pulls out a can. "Can I buy you a soda? Afraid I only have diet ones; trying to keep that young whipper snapper of a doctor off my back. He's always fussing at me about my weight and my heart. He got me to give up my cigarettes, but I told him I ain't giving up my fried foods. I have my limits, and at my age, I need some sense of pleasure."

Drew takes the cold can, shakes the excess water off, and cracks it open.

"So what brings you all the way here to see this washed-up Army medic?"

Drew takes a sip of his soda and places it on top of the cooler, which sits between them as a makeshift table.

"My head doctor sent me."

"Oh boy, Dan Reynolds sent you here. How is that old cat? Good thing the Army paid for him to go to school for psychology, because he was the worst medic I've ever seen."

Drew laughs. "And he sends you his best, as always."

"I hope he's enjoying his hippie life up there in the mountains. Too damn cold for me there. So what wild goose chase has he got you on now?"

"He says that he has taken me as far as he can in the mental world. Apparently, he seems to think that I have some unfinished business with God."

Sam lets out a large belly laugh. "Well, son, there are a lot of things I have claimed to be, but God has never been one of them. You need a preacher or chaplain, but certainly not me. You know I do most of my worship here on the water."

"And that's exactly why I'm here. My time spent with you tying flies and out on the water, those were the last times that I felt close to God. I go to church every Sunday with my grandma, but that's just to make her happy. I haven't felt God in that building since before I left for boot camp. Guess I thought coming here would be my best option if I want to figure this out."

"What exactly do you need to figure out?"

Drew stands up and surveys the old houseboat with its sun-bleached curtains, each step he makes letting out a low creaking from the boards. In her heyday, the *Carol Ann* had been the queen of this dock.

Drew begins sharing the events that have occurred since the last time they talked. Sam sits quietly, taking in every word, occasionally nodding to signal an understanding and permission to continue. Drew finally finishes what he has to say and sits down with caution so that the wobbly chair doesn't collapse underneath him.

Sam rises from the chair and moves to the edge of the boat, propping a foot on the bow. "This is my favorite time of the day.

Some folks love sunrises, but this gentle fade from the bright light of the sun to a canvas of stars always soothes my soul."

They've been so engaged in conversation that the afternoon has evaporated away, and now the sun is bidding the day farewell. Drew walks to the edge of the bow, and they both stand in silence, watching until the sun finally slips away below the horizon.

"As I'm sure you've noticed, the old *Carol Ann*"—Sam gently taps the side of the boat—"she ain't what she used to be. Of course, neither am I. People stroll up and down this dock every day and look at her like she's an eyesore out here, and I reckon amongst all these fancy boats and yachts, she is. But while they see a dilapidated and run-down boat, I see beautiful memories. We've enjoyed hundreds of beautiful rides out by Shackleford Banks, and more sunsets at Cape Lookout than I'd ever be able to recall. We've had days when we've caught so many king mackerel, I thought we'd sink the boat, and we've ridden out storms that should have taken us both out. As I stand here, I can hear the echoes of fireworks from every Fourth of July display we've witnessed on this inlet. Sure, she's left me stranded a few times, and there are some amenities that would be nice for her to have, but I've had some of the best times of my life on this boat."

The lights from the dock illuminate Sam's face as the tears make their way down.

"And this boat, she held me while the water lulled me to sleep on the nights that all I could see in my head were the dead I had to leave behind."

The shift change between the sun and stars is now complete, and on this night, there's an almost full moon shining on the water.

"Drew, it's never about the boat or the people; it's the history that binds you, and that history is always going to have a mixture of ups and downs, triumphs and defeats. That ability to ride out the storms together, that perseverance and history, are what create strong ties that last a lifetime and beyond. There are no guarantees in life, only opportunities, and each of those opportunities comes with an equal chance of success or failure. You must be able to accept both if you choose to take the risk."

Drew steps in closer. "So, you think I should go after Michelle?"

"No, no, that's not for me to decide. Remember, you came here to talk to God, not me, and I can do my best to facilitate that conversation for you. Where are you staying?"

"A studio over on Front Street."

"Ummm ummm, sir, that used to be a dump until my friend Ed got a hold of it. He's got so many properties around here and is making a killing on these ... what do you call it ... oh yeah ... Airbnb sites. If I'd known this sleepy town was gonna get so popular, I'd have bought up half the town years ago myself."

"You're telling me! I feel the same about Chatham. We were all so bored and just looking to get out of there back in high school, and now people are flocking there by the busloads to visit and live."

"Now go get some sleep and be back here with your gear at 0500." Sam says.

Drew reaches his hand out and grasps Sam's hand, and Sam clasps his other hand on top. "Good to see you, old friend"

The moon is high in the sky as Drew wiggles his key into the slot. He drops his duffle bag on the sofa and crashes down in the large, oversized chair. His body should be exhausted after the five-hour drive earlier in the day, but his visit with Sam has left him wide awake. He sits in the dark, reflecting on the conversations and wondering if he's crazy for coming here.

He had been perfectly content with the direction of his life before Michelle returned. Should he even be contemplating a future with her? He wonders if maybe Sam has the right idea remaining solo in life. Maybe he shouldn't tempt fate and just let the old mill be his *Carol Ann*. They could grow old together with no one to argue about the position of the toilet seat or whose night it is to do the dishes. Yet Drew knows that he's getting a chance that Sam never had, and if the tables were turned and Sam's love had survived Vietnam, the memories recalled on that boat would have been a whole different story. The memories might be the same, but there would have been another person to share those experiences with. Unlike Sam, the love of Drew's life is very much still alive. Unless God sends a sign like Jonah and the whale, until he has exhausted every chance, he's going to go after her.

# Chapter 25: November

The morning fog is thick and makes for a slow drive into the bakery. It's mid-November, and the leaves have long peaked, leaving only the bare branches exposed. The ground is covered with various stages of brown leaves slowly drying and decomposing—except in Clara and Ray Tyndall's yard. The Tyndalls own another Victorian home across from the bakery. Even though their yard is covered in oak and maple trees, you rarely see a leaf in their yard. Ray proudly circles his yard with his heavy-duty leaf bagging lawnmower at least once a day, sometimes twice in peak season. If leaves in the yard were national security threats, they would be the head of Homeland Defense. Michelle's parents and the Tyndalls were always pleasant to each other, but their persnickety ways had made for some heated town council meetings. Her mother swears that at night Ray sneaks over with a ruler to measure their grass to ensure they're in code.

Michelle pulls her jacket tighter; this morning the air has an extra edge, as if forewarning of the colder days to come. For as long as she can remember, she's adored fall, feeling more energetic and alive as the arrival of the crisp autumn days set in. Sadly, it just never seems to last long enough. The anticipation of the meta-morphosis of the leaves is all too quickly replaced with a twinge of sorrow that once more autumn has come and gone. This year that passage of time is even more tender, as it means her time here in Chatham is growing shorter by the day.

She no longer dreads these early mornings, and she's already feeling a slight wave of sadness at the thought of leaving not only her family but the bakery. She still enjoys her work in weather forecasting, but it's been energizing to learn a whole other busi-ness. She's come to crave the predictability of the baking schedules and looks forward to interaction with the regulars. Well, most of them. She's getting a bit annoyed with Ruth Vestal claiming that they're skimping on the amount of raspberry filling in the dough-nuts. Like if they were going to cut costs, that would be the place.

She walks over and presses start on the coffee maker. Her mom has spoiled her, and Michelle has walked in each morning with the java already brewed, but she's where she needs to be, helping Katie recover. Michelle doesn't envy her, as she has her work cut out for her. Not with the cooking, cleaning, and carting the kids to all their activities. No, she could do that in her sleep. Her mom's biggest struggle is getting Katie to rest. So far, Katie's body seems to be accepting the infusion of the donor cells, and by the number of times Katie calls Michelle a day, you'd think she's ready to run a marathon. A bombardment of instructions tumble out in rapid-fire succession. Each time she starts with "Did you remember to?" and ends with "and don't forget to." Michelle takes each instruc-tion with happiness, as these are all good signs that her sister is recovering her lost energy and zest.

She opens her laptop to review the orders for the week. With her mom and Katie out of the game for a bit, they have relin-quished the bakery responsibilities to her. They hired Beth, a trusted family friend, to look after the inn, and Devin, a local college student, to help Michelle juggle the upcoming influx of

Thanksgiving orders. Devin will be in later this morning, but for now it's just Michelle alone with her thoughts, which may not be the best idea right now.

The weeks since Halloween has been a complete blur, with one day bleeding into the next. She barely has time to talk with anyone if it doesn't have to do with business, even Drew. There has been complete silence between them, and when she stopped in the other day to make deliveries to the Taphouse, Billy told her that Drew had gone out of town for a few weeks. She wondered where he was and if he's okay, but she didn't ask any more questions.

She takes a sip of her coffee and then begins to carefully roll the dough out on the floured surface. Over the next few weeks, it will be mind-blowing the number of pies that will be baked and sold: pumpkin, apple, sweet potato, and her least favorite, rhubarb. Apparently, she's in the minority, because according to her mom, it's a hot seller. Much to her dismay, just like fruitcake, there's a secret society of folks out there who actually eat this stuff.

The scent of cinnamon and nutmeg are already filling the air, along with the smell of tart apple filling simmering on the stove. She gently places the rolled crust into her pan and lays the pie weights in before placing them in the oven. She then turns her attention to creating the velvety filling. She combines the pumpkin purée with evaporated milk, sugar, and autumn spices until they're smooth. She just finishes stirring the apple mixture on the stove when she hears a loud commotion in the hallway. She opens the door from the kitchen and walks out to find the entryway rug all out of sorts. Otis, Nana's cat, is fast at play with a small plastic lid, probably from the milk container. She observes as his nimble paws worked fiercely, moving the small, blue, plastic top like a hockey puck across the ice. In his excitement to catch the puck, Otis builds up too much speed and is unable to stop. His momentum sends him crashing like a bowling ball into the coat rack, which nearly clips him as it lands on the floor.

"Otis, bad kitty. You're the wildest cat I've ever met." This isn't entirely true, as her own kitty, Sophie, is quite a rascal as well. "What do you have to say for yourself?" Otis peers out from underneath the couch, where he has scampered to safety. "I do hate to take your fun toy, but we don't need Nana falling over these rugs."

She reaches down and lifts the coat rack and straightens the rug and then deposits the blue lid into the trash. Otis stares her down with a look that seems to say, *You may have won this match with your human ways, but I'll be back.* He rushes past Nana's feet and up the stairs as she enters the room.

"What in tarnation is wrong with that cat now?" Nana says, making her way down the stairs.

"Oh, he's just mad because I took his milk top and interrupted his hockey match. I was just about to make a second cup of coffee. Are you hungry? How about some oatmeal?"

"Oatmeal, yuck." She makes a sour face. "What I want is one of those cinnamon rolls, with extra icing." She points to the tray of fresh rolls that Michelle is cooling on the counter.

"Now Nana, you know that won't be good for your diabetes."

"Oh pooh, now you sound like your mother. At 80 years old, something is going to kill me, so it might as well be one of those cinnamon rolls." She lowers herself slowly onto the chair. "Every morning she makes me the same old boring oatmeal. I only have a few taste buds left, and I'd like to enjoy them before they go."

"Well, she did leave me in charge, so we'll do it your way for today." Michelle winks at her and thinks how the tables have turned. As a teenager, when Michelle was frustrated at her parents, she went to Nana's house to complain about them. This morning, she's glad to return the favor. She will have her dad check the blood sugar later and adjust her insulin dose, but for now, she'll indulge her.

Nana sits quietly drinking her coffee and savoring her cinnamon roll. She looks on curiously as Michelle cuts the cold butter into the flour and begins to prepare more pie crusts. Katie had made a strict schedule and routine for Michelle to stick to in order to meet the holiday demands, and the next few hours are dedicated to strictly pies. She works steadily as Elvis Presley's smooth voice fills the room with "It's Now or Never."

Nana's doctor has recommended using music as therapy to evoke positive memories and reduce some of the agitation that often comes with her dementia. Katie created a playlist of songs that highlighted Nana's wide range of musical taste. As the morning progresses, one minute she's lost in Beethoven's *Fifth Symphony*, and a few minutes later she's belting out Lynyrd Skynyrd's "Sweet Home Alabama." Lost in the music, it takes her a few seconds before she hears a customer ringing the bell in the bakery.

Michelle removes her oven mitts and is surprised to see Drew through the glass window. For a moment she is frozen. She feels a rush move through her body, and she isn't sure whether to label it as nervousness or excitement. She quickly grabs his boxes and briefly pauses behind the door to compose herself. *Ok … just act casual, like nothing happened. The kiss was nothing but excitement from the news of Katie.* At least that was what she'd been trying to tell herself for the last few weeks.

"Hello, stranger. I was about to put out a missing person's report for you. Where have you been hiding out?" She slides his boxed goods across the counter.

"I was down at the coast for a few weeks fishing with a friend."

"Fishing in November? I thought fishing was for summer."

"November can still be a great time in the sound to catch some pretty nice ones. It's a more peaceful time on the water as well without the summer tourists." He glances around the inn. "Speaking of tourists, how are things here? Seems pretty quiet."

She puts her finger to her lips. "Shhhhh, don't jinx me today. The inn has slowed a bit since peak leaf season, but the bakery is wide open. With Katie out of commission and Mom taking care of the kids, I definitely have my work cut out for me with this holiday rush. Do you have time for a cup of coffee?"

"That would be great. I'm still adjusting to real life after a few weeks off." He follows her through the doors to the kitchen.

"Good morning, Mrs. Richardson." Drew gently pats Nana on the shoulder.

"Nana, it's Drew Jones. You know his grandmother, Rose Holcomb."

"Why yes, dear, how could I forget your boyfriend."

Michelle turns as red as the red velvet cake in the display case. "No, Nana, Drew is not my boyfriend; we're just old friends. Alex is my boyfriend; you'll meet him at Thanksgiving next week."

"Hmm, could have fooled me. Shakespeare once said, 'Love is blind, and lovers cannot see the pretty follies that they themselves commit.' You might be wise to read up on the old bard."

After a moment of silent awkwardness, Michelle clears her throat. "Sorry, dementia does odd things to the brain. Once an English teacher, always one."

Michelle attempts to keep her hands steady as she pours his coffee. "Any cream or sugar?"

"No, black is fine. Never had any fancy condiments in the field or overseas, so you just learn to be grateful for simple coffee." He takes a sip. "How is Katie's recovery coming along?"

"Getting stronger by the day, evidenced by her energy to still be bossing me around."

"Well, that's a good sign for sure. I still can't get over that Billy was a match. What luck, huh?"

"You don't know?"

"Know what?"

"Let's move away from Nana. As you can see, her memory comes and goes, so we haven't even tried to explain this to her."

They step into the dining room, where this morning all the tables sat empty. The fresh pressed linen table cloths are a stark white contrast to the vases of fall foliage adorning each table. Seeing Drew hadn't felt as awkward as she'd thought, but she's glad to have this nugget of conversation to focus on.

"You might want to brace yourself, because it feels like a bit of a daytime soap opera. Billy is actually our half-brother; that's likely why he matched up."

"Wait a minute." Drew begins to cough as the sip of coffee seems to have gone to his lungs. "Billy? Billy who has worked with me all these years is your half-brother. How?" His face portrays his level of confusion.

"Yes, it's a lot to take in. Let me give you the abbreviated version." Drew settles himself into a chair at a corner table with his coffee. Michelle takes a seat across from him. "So my mom became pregnant in high school, and her parents forced her to give up the baby."

Drews face conveys shock. "Linda Richardson, your mother, my third-grade teacher, had a kid that no one knew about?"

Michelle draws in a deep breath and says, "That's right. I told you it would be hard to believe. Mom had always wanted to find him, but she didn't know where to start or how to tell my dad. When it seemed that time was running out to find Katie a donor, she knew she could never live with herself if she didn't at least try to find him. She asked Allie for help, and they were working to find him when Billy showed up as a match."

"I am truly without words. I don't even know what to say. I have so many questions, like how did Billy wind up here, or did he know?"

"He knew. He had researched and found my mom through a private investigator. He moved here to be near family, even if no one knew."

"I can't believe he could keep that from me. I feel like I can't trust who he is now."

"Drew, he's a great guy. Only his wife knew. You have nothing to worry about. He just said that he respected that it was my mom's story to tell. He never wanted to cause any trouble. His adoptive parents were great but older, and have both died. He just wanted a sense of family, even if my mom never knew."

"Wow, is all I can say. That's going to take some time to process."

"You're telling me. My whole family will be adjusting for a while."

"So Steve never even knew about her giving up a child. How did he take it?

"No, he didn't know anything. I'm not sure how he's doing. I think he and Mom are so overjoyed about Katie that they haven't addressed that issue yet."

"You know I think the world of your mom, but I can't imagine getting married and having my wife keep that kind of secret from me."

"Initially I felt the same way, and I was mad at her for keeping that from all of us, especially my dad, but it was a much different time than we can wrap our minds around. My mom was basically told to pretend it never happened. One thing about life, we can't live in the past, we can only live in the now. Right?"

They sit in a moment of silence full of ambiguity, each pondering if they're ready to let go of the past and live in the present.

Her brain scrambles for conversation, a rare occurrence for her, and then she finds it. "We're going to have a huge Thanksgiving celebration this year. With Katie's recovery and welcoming Billy, Lorie, and the kids into the family, we have so much to be grateful for this year."

"I would say so," Drew responds.

"We want as many friends as possible with us to celebrate these blessings. So I officially extend an invitation to you and Grandma Rose."

"Will Alex be there?" He looks at her with anticipation of her answer.

She pauses as she senses a change in his tone that puts her at unease. "Of course. Why wouldn't he be?"

He sits back in his chair. "No reason at all that he wouldn't be there. I just know that Thanksgiving is the busiest time of year to fly and was concerned he might not make it." He pauses for a moment.

She senses a hint of indifference that doesn't seem to match his supposed level of concern.

"His flight leaves Germany early Tuesday before Thanksgiving, so even with delays or issues, he should still have plenty of time to spare."

"We host a huge brunch at the Taproom that morning, but I'll talk with Grandma and see her plans. Since Papa died, she's just not much on holidays. We usually eat leftovers from the Taproom while watching *Home Alone* for the hundredth time."

"Well, not this year. It's going to be a grand feast with so much to celebrate. I love Thanksgiving, and being overseas, I haven't celebrated one in years. It should work out perfectly with your brunch. We're going to have a late afternoon meal here around 4:00. No more excuses, got it?"

"Invitation received. I will let you know soon."

"Can I get you some more coffee?"

He doesn't want to leave, but the clock on the wall catches his eye, and he knows he has to go.

"I'd like to, but I have to get to an appointment." He rises from the table. "Say, I don't have much to offer in the way of baking skills, but how about a reprieve this weekend? I'm headed to Stone Mountain for some trout fishing. Want to join me?"

Michelle feels a strong tug of hesitation. She doesn't need to tempt fate again, but she does want to spend a little more time with Drew before she leaves.

"Didn't you just spend a few weeks fishing? Can't get enough, huh?"

"Freshwater fishing is a whole other world than saltwater, and we're in the prime season for catching some good trout."

"I don't know the first thing about trout, but if it gets me away from this kitchen for a while, then I'm in."

"Okay, I'll pick you up Sunday at 5:00 a.m. sharp."

"Did you say 5:00 a.m.? I thought Sunday was a day of rest."

"Not if you want to catch the big ones."

"Well, can we go later and catch the small ones?"

"I promise, the sunrise alone will be worth the trip."

"What about Grandma Rose? She'll be expecting you at church."

"She gives me a few passes from time to time, so I'll cash one in with her." He also knows that his grandma will be so happy that he's spending time with a woman, friend or not, and she will bless the day away from church.

"Okay, but what do I wear?"

"Just dress in jeans and warm layers. I have some waders for you." He makes a mental note to dig around in the storage shed when he gets home for Suzanne's old ones. He figures when she sees the hint of pink in the camouflage pattern, she'll know they had belonged to her. "I'll have everything you need, including plenty of coffee and food, so you just have to get dressed and show up."

Michelle is brought back into the moment as she hears her dad fussing at Nana Lucy about her high blood sugar reading.

"Sorry, I've got to go explain to my father why I allowed an 80-year-old woman with diabetes to exceed her daily sugar and carb intake for the week in one breakfast."

Drew laughs. "Good luck with that. I have things to get to myself. See you bright and early Sunday."

Michelle waves to him before opening the door to walk into what feels like a raging hornet's nest.

Drew lingers for a moment. Even with her hair swept up under the Dogwood Inn ball cap, and flour from head to toe, she's still the most beautiful woman he has ever seen.

# Chapter 26: Closing the Deal

Drew waits while the receptionist finishes her call. Her desk area is covered in random sticky notes and various stacks of files, all signs that business is good here at Blake Honeycutt's law firm.

"May I help you?" the young receptionist asks.

"I have a 10:00 a.m. appointment with Blake."

"Please have a seat and I'll let him know you're here."

The office is located in the upstairs loft of the yoga studio owned by Blake's wife. The essence of essential oils permeates the air, and the faint sound of ambient music and distant muffled voices can be heard. The large open loft space, which used to hold the stock for the old hardware store, has been nicely renovated to create a modest but comfortable office space.

"Good morning, Drew."

He looks up to see Christina from the Northwestern Bank. Drew rises and shakes her hand. "Good morning."

She smiles and extends her well-manicured hand. They both take a seat and begin to converse about each other's relatives and upcoming holiday plans.

Soon Blake comes out, dressed in his stone washed jeans and camel blazer. It's apparent that he has traded in his New York power business suit to embrace a more laid-back, small-town approach to law.

"Drew, Chrsitina, come on back. Phillip is already in the conference room."

Drew's heart is racing. He never wanted it to come to this, but he has no choice at this juncture. It's either partner with Matthews or lose everything to Jeff and Robert Smith, which in his mind is not an option at all.

Blake leads them back down the narrow hallway and opens the door to reveal a room that whispers of a time period long ago. The room has been expertly decorated in handcrafted furniture from the Revolutionary era, creating a space that feels sacred enough for even Thomas Jefferson himself to have practiced law. Drew takes a seat at the round grand mahogany table that boasts intricate woodwork indicative of the time period.

Blake opens the folder in front of him and removes the contracts. "Drew, there have been a few changes to the contract since we first went over it. After reviewing your situation, Phillip feels that he has a better offer."

Drew crosses his arms and leans into the table. "What kind of changes?"

"Now calm down, Drew. I believe that Mr. Matthews has been very generous, and you'll want to hear him out."

Blake turns to Phillip to continue. Drew begins to flip through the pages, scanning the agreement.

"Drew, after giving this much thought, a loan would only help you temporarily. Even if you can pay that back, with the increased interest in this area, these tax values are just going to increase yearly from here on out. So after working with Blake and an estate specialist I know from Boston, I think we have a long-term solution. Of course, to proceed, you must agree to the proposed buyer."

"Whoa, whoa, buyer? This was not the agreement at all. What's going on here? I thought we had a deal." In seconds, Drew feels his body move from sensations of nervousness to reacting as if he were under full attack. He starts to sweat profusely, and he can now feel the blood racing to his hands and feet.

Blake picks up the phone. "Judy, please bring in the client we discussed."

The room sits in anticipation for minutes until the door opens and in walks Grandma Rose.

Phillip looks at Drew. "Do you approve of this savvy business lady as the owner?"

"Grandma is the buyer? I don't understand."

Grandma Rose takes a seat at the table, and Drew sits quietly while Phillip begins to explain.

"My grandfather left a significant amount of money in his will that was to be used for charitable purposes, and he left that to my discretion. I came here for my own business investment opportunities, but once I saw Carter Falls and all the places where my grandfather spent his early years, I knew this was where he would want his money to be used. He wouldn't want this land turned into an amusement park any more than you do; he'd want this land preserved for future generations to enjoy.

Drew, the heart and soul you've put into revitalizing the mill, these plans are more in line with his vision. If you agree to allow access to the public to certain areas of the property, such as the falls and trails, then Blake here along with my estate friend can help your grandmother create a charitable trust. This action will help you now but also your children and grandchildren."

Drew rises from the table. "This is incredibly generous, but we can't accept it."

"Nathaniel Drew, you sit down right now." Rose rises and gives a stern look to her grandson. "I am not going to let your pride ruin this beautiful gift, especially since this is not about you; it's about me."

"She's right. My grandfather and grandmother had a great life, but deep down, Rose always held a special place in his heart. He would want this for you all."

Drew looks up at Grandma Rose, who nods her head. He picks up the pen and begins to sign. Once the final signature is done, Christina and Blake shake everyone's hands before leaving the room.

"I do have one more personal request I wanted to speak to you about in private," Phillip says.

"Of course. What is it, dear?" Grandma Rose says.

"I'd like to return in the spring with my family and spread my grandfather's ashes near Carter Falls. I think that he needs to be returned to his home to rest at his old stomping grounds." Phillip turns to look at Rose. "According to the stories he shared with me, he spent some very special times here."

Grandma Rose smiles and a single tear escapes her eye. "I think that he would love that."

They walked slowly towards the street, and Drew asks, "Did you know any of this?"

"No, I was as caught off guard as you about the whole deal. Phillip just contacted me yesterday."

"How about John Matthews? Were you aware that he pined for you his whole life."

Rose chuckles. "I wouldn't say he pined away for me. The summer after he graduated from college, he took a trip back to Chatham and tried to convince me not to marry Silas, but I was already committed to your grandfather. Plus, I had no desire to leave Chatham and live in a big city. Years later, I saw John at our class reunion, and he told me that I had made a good decision, because he had been married to his career, and Silas was a better man for me. That's the last contact I ever had with him."

Drew hugs Grandma Rose before she gets into her trusty 1984 Buick Skylark, one of the few splurges she and Papa Silas made in their lives. She always said that a car was just like a man: as long as it's dependable, you keep it for life.

"See, my boy, I told you that you just have faith and put it in God's hands. His timing will always be superior to yours."

Drew breathes a sigh of relief as he looks up at the sky. Maybe God did hear him after all that day on the water. Now on to the next test, to see if the rest of his prayers are about to be answered.

# Chapter 27: Afternoon Tea

M ichelle gently rolls her neck in circles while massaging her shoulders. "I am so glad you asked me to come to yoga with you today. My shoulders and neck were so stiff from looking down, but it feels better already. Candace—"

Allie looks at her. "Ah ... ah ... ah Vira."

"I mean Vira; she really knows her stuff."

"I haven't seen much of you since Halloween, and our time is running out," Allie says with a sad expression.

Allie is right. Michelle has been so busy that she really hasn't had time to think about how close she is to leaving her friend. But now that she does, she isn't sure how she feels about it. She'll miss these impromptu meetups and being more involved with her life.

"I am so ready for Thanksgiving to get here, and I don't think I ever want to eat another pie after looking at them for weeks," Michelle says.

They're greeted by the owner, Emily Bledsoe, one of Chatham's most sincere southern belles. "Hello, ladies, so lovely to see you today." Like Linda, she's a retired teacher who has found her second career in running a small business. A visit to the Revolutionary Tea

Room is like getting to play in a life-size dollhouse. Mrs. Emily walks them by tables of patrons sipping their tea and enjoying leisurely conversations, reminiscent of times gone by. The air is permeated with the delicious aroma of warm teas and fresh baked scones, while the beautiful, handcrafted furniture exemplifies a time when craftsmanship was the standard and not the exception.

"Michelle, so glad you could join us for afternoon tea, and of course Allie is a regular here with us."

Allie smiles. "Yes, it's the one place in town where people don't tend to look for me. But, Mrs. Emily, your blueberry scones are why I can never lose that last bit of weight from the twins."

"Oh tish tosh, you're as lovely as ever; now let's get you seated."

Emily walks them over to a corner table.

"You ladies sit back and relax, and I'll be right out with your tea."

Emily soon returns with a tray of tea, while another waitress brings a three-tiered tray of delights. The top tier holds an assortment of finger sandwiches with various fillings of cucumber and cream cheese and egg salad. The second tier showcases Emily's freshly baked scones, today featuring pumpkin for the season, served warm with clotted cream and jam. The lower tier holds an array of miniature fruit tarts and perfected petit fours decorated with beautiful lavender roses.

Michelle reaches for one of the decadent small pecan tarts and takes a bite.

Allie laughs. "I thought you were sick of pie."

"It's different when you don't have to make them." Michelle finishes her bite. "Plus, they are just so petite and cute."

"So have you heard from Drew? Is he back in town?" Steam escapes as Allie pours tea from the pot into her delicate antique tea cup.

"Actually, I just saw him. He came in to pick up his orders."

"And?" Allie arches her eyebrows.

"And what?"

"Come on, Michelle, what are you going to do?"

"Do about what? It was one kiss, that's all. We were just caught up in a moment. It was no big deal, so there's no decision to make. I have a life across the Atlantic Ocean. My future is not here in Chatham; it's with Alex. That has always been the plan since I agreed to come here."

"Plans can change, you know." Allie tastes her tea before adding more cream.

"Sure they can, but not these. I am solid in my decision."

"Well, say what you want, and I know I have selfish motives, but I think that being back here in Chatham has brought out the best in you." Allie gently lowers her cup to the scalloped-edged saucer. "I've seen parts of you come alive that I thought died with Benjamin."

Michelle pauses, knowing that Allie is right. Over the last few months, she's felt like a butterfly finally emerging from a cocoon of grief and darkness. Every day wasn't just a list of tasks, but she savored the simple things of life. There's something about being back in touch with a place that holds the early stories of her life.

"I have very much enjoyed my time here, and it's been very healing for me. I finally feel like I've truly let Benjamin go and can move on." She hesitates before saying, "But I don't see myself here."

"Okay, but I could write out a very long list of all the things you told me before that you were solid in your decision about, and you later changed your mind."

"I don't think this is on the level of spiral perms or going away to the wrong summer camp. I am not going to throw away a per-fectly great relationship and turn my life upside down over a little flicker of a middle-school flame."

Allie looks as if she wants to say more, but before she can get the words out, Michelle interrupts. "Now, let's talk about you. How is your itinerary shaping up for your trip?"

Allie's entire countenance transforms as she begins to talk about her trip and the work she'll do at the orphanage.

Michelle reaches for Allie's hand. "You see a change in me, and likewise, I see a light in you that I haven't seen since I arrived. You are practically sparkling."

"It feels great to look forward to something and not feel like the complete life has been sucked out of me every day. This trip is so much more than tracing my roots. The work I will do with these children"—Allie stops to compose herself and take a breath—"is the whole reason I went into ministry,"

"I am so happy for you, and your next trip will be to Germany because I only want to hear of your journeys in Africa as a first-hand account, in person."

The sounds of teaspoons clicking and other patrons chattering fade away as Allie goes into detail about her itinerary and all the places she'll visit while on her sabbatical. They savor the afternoon together, sipping tea and laughing just as they had as young girls. Today, the tea is not imaginary, and the dolls they had dressed up and once served are long gone, but the friendship is as sweet as ever.

# Chapter 29: Contemplation

Michelle opens her eyes for what she is sure has to be the hundredth time. She rolls over and glances at her clock, which is now displaying 3:30 a.m. She has tossed and turned all night, so she figures she might as well just give in and get up. Five will be here soon enough.

Her feet are immediately awakened, as the cold air has chilled the floor to near ice-rink conditions. These last few mornings the weather has felt more like deep winter than late fall, which she does not relish. She quickly rummages through a pile of laundry in the corner chair and slips on a sweatshirt and jeans before heading to the kitchen to turn on the coffee to brew.

Even though Drew said he would have coffee waiting, this morning she's going to need this coffee to bridge her to the other coffee. She reaches over and massages her right shoulder area. She would never complain to her family, but these last few weeks had been more grueling than she could have ever imagined.

She flips on the bathroom light and glares at her reflection in the mirror. While some features have changed, certain traits of her physical features are much like high school. She still has long brunette locks and hazel eyes, which seem to have more mossy green flecks dominating this morning. She brushes through her tangles and then pulls her hair several times through the simple elastic hair tie, finally securing into a messy bun. Once again, she gives thanks to the person who created the simple elastic hair tie and finally rid the world of the dreaded plastic-ball-ended hair ties from childhood. Every day, her mom, like most, sent her daughters off to school with hair secured with those tortuous devices. The process of pain and tears that was endured as mothers wrapped and rewrapped those things tighter may have been borderline child abuse. May those things rest in peace at the bottom of the landfill.

It takes the water a few extra minutes to warm up as it courses through the colder than normal pipes. Once it warms, she splashes her face several times in an attempt to wash the exhaustion away. She reaches for a towel and pats her face dry before applying her tinted moisturizer. She has never been one to fuss about her appearance or care much for makeup; she left that to Katie. She brushes a few streaks of light blush on her cheeks and finishes with a neutral lipstick.

She pours her coffee and then burrows herself down into the couch under her favorite quilt. She always feels safe tucked under this special family heirloom. The alternating blocks of red and pink fabric pop against the predominately white background speckled with a hint of pink blossoms. This background creates the perfect canvas to set off the eight-pointed star design.

This timeless work of art had been quilted by her great-grandmother Katherine, who was Katie's namesake. Though she was only a small child at the time, probably around Karry's age, Michelle can still remember the Sunday afternoons spent at her house. In addition to church attendance, Sundays were dedicated to visiting family and catching up on everyone's bodily ailments. While the adults socialized, to stave off boredom, Michelle and

Katie would pretend they were detectives. The most suspenseful part of their adventures was going down into the basement of the house looking for clues to whatever mystery they had made up to solve. They would slowly open the creaky door that led to the basement and tip toe down the stairs, where the quilt frame suspended from the ceiling always held the next masterpiece in progress.

Grandma Katherine and her lifelong circle of friends, Ollie, Velma, Berniece, Frances, and Florence, had made quilts together since long before they each married. They would sit around the quilt rack and sew for hours while sharing each other's happiness and shouldering the burdens. Joys of babies born and sorrows of children lost. Tears of joy as husbands, brothers, and sons returned from war, and tears of despair for those who did not. She had learned that the Bethlehem star pattern, like this quilt, was very popular with pioneers, symbolizing the stars they followed across to the west and their faith in God to guide them. She always thought it an interesting fact that the pattern requires extreme perfection and skill, but at times it has been said that even the most skilled quilt maker would sew a mistake somewhere to reflect that only God was perfect.

Then it happes again. Without warning, there it is, that familiar twinge of sadness. It feels like a wave rising from the pit of her stomach and eventually ending as a lump in her throat. She pulls the quilt tighter in hopes of absorbing by osmosis all the love and strength it holds from those long gone. Her conversation with Allie rattled her a bit. She hadn't admitted it to anyone, not even herself, until this moment, but she isn't ready to leave.

The time has gone by so quickly since she arrived here in September. She remembers how as she had packed to come here; she couldn't wait to get back to Germany, but now as she scans around the room, she knows she will miss this place. Even though she's only been here a few months, she has really settled in and made it her home.

Her mind bounces like a small rubber ball between moments and images. While she certainly wouldn't have wished hardship on her family to get to this moment, she wouldn't have these new memories to cherish. The time spent in the kitchen with Nana Lucy, Katie, and her mom, which seemed so ordinary at the time, now seem precious. She wonders how much longer Nana Lucy will live, but possibly even worse, how long before her mind will be completely gone and she'll remember none of them. Maybe that's the horrible part she wants to miss.

She thinks of her time with Joel, Karry, and Brett and how much more connected she feels to her nephews and niece. She has promised them all summer visits to Germany anytime they want to come, but she'll still miss seeing them every day after school. She knows they will miss her, and not just because she's helped them sneak extra cookies home; this has really been her first time experiencing what it's like to be an aunt. She had only been an aunt in name, but now she has the experience to back the title. She will definitely have to video chat more often with Brett to keep up with all the drama at East Chatham Middle School. After all, she has to know if the secret crush between a certain English teacher and the principal ever amounts to a Shakespearean level romance.

And Allie. It has been so great to not just pick up the phone and call her but to meet her in person and in the same time zone. The imaginary ball slowly stops bouncing and rolls to a stop, and the memory lands on her kiss with Drew on Halloween night. She lingers in this memory, her body warmed as it recalls the feeling of how it felt to have his arms embrace her in that unexpected moment. It felt easy and safe, and she realizes that was the moment when it all shifted. That was the moment when she felt that she was finally home.

A car horn lets out a few quick beeps, and she quickly stands up and brings herself back to the moment at hand. *Stop. What are you doing? Get it together. This is fantasy; get back to reality. It was a happy season, but just a transition. It's time for me to get back to my life.*

She pulls back the curtain; it's pitch dark except for the light coming from Drew's Jeep as it makes its way down the driveway.

# Chapter 30: Fishing for Answers

The Jeep makes a rhythmic hum as they travel towards their destination. They both ride along quietly, sipping their coffee and listening to the radio. The radio station is set to 92.3, the classic rock station, and likely has never been changed since the day he purchased the Jeep. Sunrise is still a while away, but as they approach the park entrance, the moon is bright enough to highlight the distinct granite dome of Stone Mountain.

Drew begins to take items from the back of the of the Jeep. Michelle hands him an old metal box. The corners are rounded from years of bumping into things, and the latch, once shiny and new, is now tarnished with rust.

"Where in the world did you get that?" he asks.

"It's Grandpa's old fishing tackle. I thought we could use some of it."

Drew opens up the box and rummages through the compartments of various sizes. There are rows of colorful lures, some with hooks dulled by use, others still gleaming with the hope of the perfect catch. As he rummages through, the sinkers and bobbers clink softly against each other.

"Afraid those won't do us much good here. Most of this gear is for saltwater fishing."

"How can you tell?" Michelle asks, holding up a hook baited with a small rubber fish.

"The size and weight for one. The heavier lures are meant for rougher waters and heavier fish."

"Seriously, this sounds too complicated. I thought fishing was supposed to reduce your stress. On TV you just drop the little line in the water and BAM you catch a fish."

"Well, three things: One, it's only stressful if you make it that way. Two, it's more complicated than it seems. Three, you've never struck me as a person who believes everything you see on TV."

Michelle shrugs her shoulders and places the tackle box back in the Jeep.

"Here, can you handle this backpack? I'll carry the other gear."

Drew shines a high beam flashlight down the trail, which permeates the predawn darkness. The faint sound of trickling water can be heard as they follow the main road through the park along the banks of the East Prong Roaring River.

"We'll start here. Once the sun comes up and we can see, we'll head over to Garden Creek. Not as many people know about that spot, and I've caught some really nice sized ones there in the past."

Drew removes some things from his backpack that look to Michelle like insects.

"What are those? They look like mosquitoes," Michelle says.

"These are some Mayfair flies that I made while I was down in Swansboro with Sam a few weeks ago."

"You made these? That looks like a lot of work."

"It is, but it's very satisfying to catch a fish off a lure you made yourself."

"I'll just have to take your word on that. You never told me. How did you meet him?"

"Meet who?"

"Sam," she says, raising her eyebrows.

Drew laughs. "Oh, well actually, Sam is a female, short for Samantha."

"Oh, sorry, I just assumed the name, and being a Vietnam vet—"

"It happens all the time, and trust me, she gets a kick out of it. Sam served as a nurse."

"Interesting, females serving in Vietnam—that sure got left out of US history class."

"There were actually quite a few females who served as nurses and other capacities there. A few even lost their lives, like Sam's dear friend Carol Ann."

Michelle looks on as Drew works to set up the fishing gear.

"I met Sam during my time at Camp Lejeune after I returned from Afghanistan. She headed up a fly-fishing group for active duty and vets. And that's where I learned to make these flies. I was hesitant at first. I mean, Papa Silas was so busy with the farm, he didn't have time to take me fishing. But once I got started, it was such a relief to find something to get lost in. It also didn't hurt to spend time hanging out with other Marines who were going through their own struggles."

Drew zones in with a laser beam focus as he threads the line and securely attaches the fly.

"Sam is also my NA sponsor. She's bailed me out of some bad situations, and when I decided to get clean, she was the first person I called. She battled addiction after her time in Vietnam. She also connected me to Dr. Dan, my therapist. They were stationed at the same surgical hospital together."

With a quick flick of the wrist, Drew smoothly casts the line into the water. He hands Michelle the rod and she nervously accepts.

"She sounds like a strong person; I'm so glad you have her in your life."

"She saved my life, and I guess you can say that she's kind of been like a mom to me as well."

"Being with you reminds me that I need to do better. I still take my mom for granted, and you lived almost your whole life with no mom."

"Just had to learn to realize that there was nothing I could do about it but live each day."

He steps in and retrieves the rod from her and repositions her line. "Trout like to hang out under things, so try your line closer to the edge of log."

"I'm not sure you have the patience for this. You should have talked to my dad first; he only took me fishing a few times because all I seemed to catch were trees."

"Well, if you haven't caught a few trees, you haven't been fishing."

A faint light begins to peek from the indigo sky, and slowly like a shade being lifted, the sun emerges. She has certainly been awake many times during sunrise, but she hasn't really stopped and given it her full attention. She never really noticed how much the world comes alive with the sunrise. The sun is like a conductor awakening nature to a symphonic concert each day. The golden rays of the sun gently cue the birds to start singing and dew drops to dance on the evergreens.

This tranquility and stillness is broken by a loud growl.

Drew looks up. "Was that a bear or your stomach?"

She giggles. "My stomach. What did you bring?"

"There's some trail mix in the side pocket. Tank up because we have about an hour to hike to our next spot. I don't need you falling out on me."

They finish their trail mix and pack up the gear and set out. She was a teenager the last time she'd been to Stone Mountain, and she'd never been at this time of year. The trees absent of their leaves allow for an unobstructed view, and the woods seem quieter since the birds and other creatures have fewer places to hide. The squirrels have already nestled up for winter with their stock of nuts, while the birds had flown south.

They come to a gate across the trail, which Drew leads her around, and they begin to follow signs that signal a wild stream designation.

"Have you had any more run-ins with Robert and Jeff?" Michelle inquires.

"Actually, I have really good news about that, but let's get some lines going first. Trout can be a bit skittish, so try to keep your voice low and move slowly down the bank here."

Time seems to slow as the gentle sounds of flowing water create a soothing melody. The air is crisp and cool, and Michelle inhales the earthy scent and allows herself to feel the complete sense of freedom in this vast forest. For this moment, there's nothing in the world but her and Drew.

As the sun moves higher, Drew casts and recasts his lines while filling her in on all that has occurred with Philip Matthews and Grandma Rose.

When he finishes, Michelle replies, "That sounds like something out of a movie, but it has to be a huge relief. So how does it feel to have everything worked out?"

He pauses, keeping his focus on his line in the water because he doesn't know how to answer her. Everything working out in his mind includes her staying, and that part is still a question mark.

"For sure, I wasn't anticipating that blessing, but I'm incredibly grateful. During my time with Sam, I prayed for a solution."

"Prayed? Is that a new-found religion thing?"

Drew quickly turns his head. "Ouch, that was harsh."

"Sorry, I didn't mean it that way; it's just that I haven't sensed much of a spiritual emphasis in your life since I've been back."

"My spiritual practices are very private. God and I have a lot of conversations when I'm near the water." Drew turns his attention back to observing his line for any sense of a nibble.

"So, what else did you pray about?" Michelle asks inquisitively.

"To finally be released of the guilt I've carried all these years."

Michelle's tone softens. "About Benjamin?"

"All of them: Benjamin, Mom, and all the friends I lost in Afghanistan. I had to settle my anger and displeasure with God for taking away so many important people." He pauses and thinks deeply before looking at her and saying, "And for you."

She laughs. "Well, I appreciate it. I need all I can get."

"No ... you ... as in you and me."

Michelle turns to look at him. She's been hoping that this conversation could be avoided, but she knows the subject has to be addressed.

"Drew." She walks over and gently rests her hand on his shoulder. "This time we've spent rekindling our friendship"—she pauses, taking the time to choose her words carefully—"it has been wonderful and unexpected. But it doesn't change the fact that I'm in a very serious relationship, and I am leaving soon."

Drew reels in his line and props his rod up against the large trunk of an oak tree. He opens his backpack and removes a small blanket. He pats his hand on the blanket and says, "Come and sit."

Michelle sits opposite Drew, and he reaches for her hands. "Trust me, I have gone through all of that in my head over and over. If I thought that you were truly happy with Alex, I would never interfere, but I just don't get the sense that you are. Can you tell me otherwise?"

Michelle lowers her gaze and focuses on the frayed edges of the blanket, which are gently being moved by the wind. She picks up a few strands and rubs them between her fingers. "You have spent barely three months with me. You can't think that you know what makes me happy. We are not who we were twenty years ago."

"You're right. The battles of life, the loss, they've changed us in some ways, but in other ways, there are parts of us that will always remain unchanged. I felt that same connection from years ago the first time you walked into the Taproom."

Michelle gives his hand a gentle squeeze. "I am not going to lie to you or pretend that I don't feel anything for you. I am completely overwhelmed and confused by all these emotions. I came here to make peace, to be free, and to move on to the next phase of my life. I never expected to feel …" Her mind is like a snow globe that has been viciously shaken, and she searches and searches but can't find the words.

Drew waits for her to find the word before saying, "To feel?"

"To feel so … complete. After Benjamin's death, I had come to terms with always feeling like something was missing. I guess I always thought he was what was missing from me, and I would never get that sliver of myself back. But being here, I have found what was missing and finally feel whole again." She shifts her gaze back to his. "I'm just not sure if that relates to you, or just being here."

"Either way, isn't that reason enough to ask yourself if Alex and Germany are really what you want? You could move back here and be with your family, and we could have a chance to make a go at this. Who knows, it might not work, but I feel like we're worth the chance. I have so many regrets already in my life that I wasn't going to let you go without telling you how I feel."

Drew tenderly lifts her chin and caresses her face, bringing her gaze back to his. "Michelle, I love you. I have loved you before I even knew what true love was, and that love is still alive in me."

For a moment she is captivated by this idea and begins to lean in closer, until she's hit with a storm of conflicting emotions. She quickly rises from the blanket and walks to the edge of the water, watching as the leaves make their way slowly down the stream.

He moves over to stand behind her. "I'm sorry, I don't mean to upset you or confuse you. I couldn't let you go without making my feelings known. I don't want to wake up an old man asking myself 'what if' one day." He thinks back on his conversation with Sam about no regrets. "Even if I don't like the outcome, I had to know that I at least tried."

Michelle turns to look over her shoulder and gives him a subtle smile. "Like Santiago in *Old Man and the Sea*."

"I guess so, except I was hoping to not only catch my fish but get it safely to land."

"I can't make you any promises."

"The only promise I'm looking for is that you will at least take some time to consider that staying here could be an option."

Before her brain even has time to process his request, she hugs him tightly as her lips whisper a very soft, "I will."

It has been hours since Drew dropped her back off at Nana's, and she hasn't moved from her spot on the couch under the quilt since she got home. During the hour-long hike back to the Jeep, neither Drew nor Michelle spoke a word. In the silence they were each keenly aware that this was either the beginning or the end, and ultimately the decision lay in Michelle's hands. She had found closure here with Benjamin but now found herself in a new dilemma. Why did life have to be so complicated? Too exhausted to walk to her bed, she lay down on the couch. Her mind began to set off what to her was a very exciting chain of thoughts.

What might happen if she stayed? Is it possible that she and Drew could have a future? If she stayed, would the new wear off? Would she eventually feel trapped and resentful of the life she gave up? Wait, what if there was a middle road? What if she just extended her stay, not forever, but just a bit longer to see the bakery through the holidays. Yes, that would buy her some more time, and no one would think anything suspicious, especially Alex.

# Chapter 31: 'Twas the Day before Thanksgiving

A lex finds an open spot and places his luggage into the compartment before taking his seat by the window. He unzips the inside pocket of his brown leather jacket and removes the blue velvet covered box. Prying the box open, he admires the ring again. His jeweler has far exceeded his expectations in creating this vintage inspired engagement ring. The center round stone is set into a stunning platinum setting with three small diamonds above and below it. The sides of the band feature ornate scrolled patterns, which add the perfect touch of elegance.

The female passenger next to him looks over. "Oh my, that's exquisite; she must be a special lady."

"Yes, she is." Alex closes the box and places the ring back in his pocket.

"Well, good luck I'm sure she will say yes, especially with that gorgeous ring."

Alex replies, "Thanks." He slips his noise-canceling head-phones on. This will be a long flight, and he wants to try to get some sleep. A few months ago, he wouldn't have doubted that Michelle would say anything other than yes, but these months apart had been more difficult than he had anticipated. Sure, the time difference was a barrier, but when they did talk, he had felt a distinct distance between them that had never existed before. They had endured many long stretches apart while she was still on active duty, but this was different. He places his pillow against the window, closes his eyes, and reassures himself that once they're together again, all will be well.

The bakery is an absolute mad house this morning. Even though Michelle has been warned that this is their absolute busiest day of the year, she's not prepared for this. It's like flies swarming a jar of honey; as soon as one customer flies out, another two swoop in. Michelle, her mom, and Devin are in constant motion, and of course Katie is there to supervise. She's recovering well and has been given the green light to get out and about more if she wears a mask in large crowds.

Katie looks around. "Where's Nana today?"

"I sent her out with Beth. She's going to ride her around and go have lunch downtown. I was afraid all this chaos would set her off," Linda says as she pipes whipped cream atop the chocolate pies.

Before long, she can't help herself. The instinct takes over, and Katie is in the fray, boxing up cakes and pies.

"Kathryn Marie," her mother sternly yells out, "you may stay only if you sit down."

"Relax, Mom, I'm just boxing up a few things. I'm about to head to the airport with Josh to pick up Alex."

"Please thank Josh again for doing this. I don't know why I thought I could squeeze that in with this madness today," Michelle says, wiping the stray hair back that had fallen from her hat.

"No problem, plus this will give me a chance to drill Alex." She clears her throat. " I mean, get to know him and tell him all of your most embarrassing stories. Let's see, should I start with how old you were before you stopped wetting the bed, or maybe the time you got your pants pulled down in the middle of the school courtyard?" Katie laughs. "Bet you wish I was still sick now."

"Katie!" her mother shouts out again.

"Calm down, Mom, just a little cancer humor. Make sure you have a glass of wine before you meet your future son-in-law tonight. You need to mellow out before you scare him off."

"Well, you'll only have one hour, maybe two if the traffic is heavy. I don't think you can do too much damage to my reputation in that amount of time. Are the kids going with you guys to the airport?" Michelle asks as she gently lowers the 18-layer chocolate cake into the box.

Katie selects two cranberry orange muffins and drops them into a bakery bag and then makes two cups of coffee. "No, the kids are with Brian until tomorrow afternoon. I'll pick them up before I head over here for dinner."

Michelle gives a suspicious look to her mom. " Uh huh, are you sure you and Josh aren't in need of a chaperone tonight?"

Katie grabs the cardboard tray and balances the bag of muffins as she opens the door. "On that note, I'm off. We will see you guys later tonight."

The day whizzes by as customers file in and out. The trusty customers who heeded the advice come to pick up orders they placed months ago, while the last-minute shoppers have to take what's left. Not sure if the pilgrims enjoyed chocolate covered doughnuts for dessert on the first Thanksgiving, but it looks like that's what's happening for a few families this year in Chatham. Once the last customer has left, Linda thanks Beth and Devin for their help and wishes them a Happy Thanksgiving with their families. As they exit the door, she changes the sign from OPEN to CLOSED. "I swear, mark my words, if it's possible, Maxine Johnson will be late to her own funeral. She always picks up her orders at the absolute last minute."

Michelle searches for and finds one last open spot to squeeze one more bowl in the dishwasher before hitting start.

Linda glances at her watch. "We've got a little time before Alex arrives. Let's have that wine now; we'll get the rest of this later. Or better yet, I'll put your father to work. He's picking up a few pizzas from the Taproom on his way home for us all. I'm sure Alex will be starving."

The Taproom. Her mind flashes back to her first day in Chatham, and her first encounter with Drew. This is the first time today she's thought about him. They haven't spoken since he dropped her off on Sunday. As she thinks of tomorrow being the last time to see him, she feels her stomach tighten and a slight wave of nausea hit. These physical cues of unsettledness are increasing, yet she's no closer to making a decision.

Linda pours two glasses of white wine. "Let's go put our feet up in the parlor while we can."

Michelle takes her glass and swirls it before taking a deep inhale. "Ummm this smells like a fresh pear or Granny Smith apple." She takes a sip. "Wow, that's really good."

"I picked this up from Drew the other day. It's called"—she turns the label to read—"Wishes. It's a Riesling; it's their holiday feature this year."

As she takes another sip, Michelle recalls Drew showing her this vat in the winery the day she toured. He had been very hopeful that this batch would be a memorable wine, and now as she tastes it, she can see why he had named it Wishes. It has unquestionably lived up to his expectations.

Linda kicks off her slip-on tennis shoes and props her feet on the ottoman. "So you and Alex fly out next Friday, right? What do you guys plan to do while he's here?"

Michelle is still lost in her memories of her days spent with Drew. Her mind rolls like a mental memory book of their times at Carter Falls and Stone Mountain. She smiles as she thinks about Major and all his silly antics. Sitting here, on the eve of Thanksgiving, September seems like such a long time ago. Fall is quickly slipping away, as are her days here.

"Hello, Earth to Michelle? I said, what are you and Alex planning to do next week?"

"Oh, sorry, Mom, brain fog. I don't know. I haven't thought that far ahead." She's having a hard enough time staying in the present, let alone planning next week. "Alex says that he's just looking forward to spending time and getting to know everyone. Family is very important to him; that's why he's been so supportive of me being here."

"It's been wonderful to have you here. Not just for the help, but I feel like I actually know my daughter again."

Michelle smiles at her mom. "It's been a great time, and believe it or not, I am going to miss this bakery—well, minus the day before Thanksgiving. It's truly remarkable the business that you and Katie have built here. You guys are such a part of the heart of this town."

"We really love it. I mean, don't get me wrong, I certainly have my days of 'What was I thinking?' but I am happy I took the risk." She raises her glass. "Plus it gives me great satisfaction to have proven your father wrong."

Michelle raises her glass. "Cheers to women entrepreneurs and the Dogwood Inn and Bakery, may it be successful for years to come."

She looks at her mom and she can no longer hold in her emotions. Everything she's been holding back for days comes out like a dam bursting.

Linda quickly makes her way over and sits by her on the couch. She scoops her into her arms the way she did when Michelle was a little girl waking from a bad dream. "Oh honey, what's the matter?"

"I'm just so torn. I wish I could live two lives. I never dreamed that this would feel like home again and—" She catches herself.

Linda puts her hands on Michelle's shoulders. "And that you would have feelings for Drew. Your father might be the fireman, but I know flames and sparks when I see them."

"Yes, I have feelings for him, but I don't know if those are real or just drudged up in nostalgia while I've been here. Benjamin and Drew are in my past, and as much as I love it here, my future is not here."

"Michelle, I don't envy your situation, and I can't tell you what to do. Only you can work that out in your heart. However, I can tell you that I missed out on too many years of not knowing my son because I lacked the courage to tell your father. I was so worried about how he would react, and quite frankly, how others would see me, that I let that stand in my way. Regret is a horrible thing to live with. Take your time and do what is best for you."

"Knock, knock! Pizza delivery boy is here." Steve enters the silence-filled room. "Come and get it while it's hot."

"I'll be there in a minute." Michelle sits in the chair and stares out the window. She looks up into the sky at the millions of stars and prays silently for a sign or some kind of guidance. She is envious of Drew in that at least he knows what he wants. She is completely torn between these two paths. As she sits in her turmoil, a wave of guilt comes over her. After all, her big issue seems so petty compared to bigger world problems like world peace and healing sick people.

Tomorrow is Thanksgiving, a day to celebrate the blessings she has before her, and she has so many. Her sister is healing, she's with her family, and she's about to go back to start a new phase of her life. Each a separate blessing, while so many sit hoping for just one tonight. She blots her tears with the corner of her jacket. *Get yourself together. Enough with this fantasy world; it's time to get with reality and do what I came here to do. Put these Chatham ghosts to rest. All of them, for once and for all.*

# Chapter 32: Thanksgiving

Aromas of sage and thyme permeate the air as everyone begins to settle into their seats around the piece milled table. Steve and Josh have brought in extra tables from the fire station to add to each end of the antique dining table to accommodate all the guests. This incredible feast has been prepared as a family affair. Michelle and Katie assisted Linda in the kitchen while Steve and Josh schooled Alex on the wonders of deep frying a turkey.

Linda places the golden turkey in the center of the table, which is overflowing with all the traditional favorites. The center of the table is filled with an eclectic array of serving dishes that hold creamy mashed potatoes, rich gravy, homemade cranberry sauce, cornbread stuffing, fresh baked rolls, and sweet potato casserole with perfectly toasted marshmallows on top. A cornucopia of vegetable dishes of green bean casserole, corn pudding, and perfectly roasted Brussels sprouts are scattered about as well.

Michelle surveys the table, taking in the faces that she soon will miss. Katie is busy filling plates for Karry and Joel, while Josh and Brett carry on a conversation. It seems that the kids are settling in with Katie's new relationship. Michelle watches as Billy and his wife wrestle William into his high chair while baby Stella is being entertained by Nana in her car seat in the corner. Michelle feels a bit let down that she won't get to know her brother and his family better. Allie and Dave and the twins sit across the table, while Alex is seated by her. Drew is seated at the end near her dad, but the chair for Grandma Rose is vacant. She politely declined her invitation, as Drew had predicted.

The buzz of conversation is cut short as Steve gingerly taps his glass. "Happy Thanksgiving, everyone. I know we're all ready to dig in, but I'd like to thank you all for joining our family today as we celebrate an abundance of blessings this year. We give thanks for the blessing of health for Katie and extend our heartfelt gratitude to Billy for his generous donation. May we all give thanks today and be blessed in the year to come."

Glasses are raised and cheers given around the table. Over the next hour, plates are filled and refilled, and the conversations remains steady. The faint sound of sports announcers and the occasional eruption of cheers of fans can be heard from the TV as college football games play in the background. Occasionally, Michelle looks down at Drew, locking eyes with him briefly before turning her attention back to Alex. She knows she has to find time to talk with him, but she doesn't know when she'll have the chance. She even contemplated not telling him goodbye and skipping the entire process, but she knows that's the cowardly thing to do. No more running; she has to face her problems head on.

As Michelle and Katie clear the dinner plates, Linda serves up plates of warm pumpkin pie with fresh whipped cream. Steve is passing around glasses of port when Alex stands up and clears his voice to gain the attention of the crowd.

"If I may, I would like to say something. First, thank you all for making me feel so welcomed here. It's always a bit nerve racking to meet family for the first time, but you guys have been great.

Michelle always tries to explain Southern hospitality, but I understand it firsthand now."

He reaches into his pocket and pulls out the blue velvet box. "Michelle, you have probably wondered what was taking me so long, but I really wanted to do this with your family." He nervously removes the ring from the box and takes her hand. "Will you marry me?"

Michelle looks over at Drew and then shifts her attention to her hand and admires the ring. Everyone in the room seems to be frozen, poised to hear her answer. She swiftly looks at her mom before answering. "Yes, of course I will marry you."

The room is filled with joyous sounds of clapping and well wishes.

"Yuck, are they going to kiss?" Joel says and covers his eyes.

"Oh goody, can I be the flower girl?" Karry says, clapping her hands with eagerness.

As the excitement and wedding chatter settle down, Drew makes his way over to Linda and Steve. "Thank you for the lovely invitation. I'm going to be getting home to check on Grandma. These holidays are still hard on her."

Steve rises and shakes Drew's hand. "Good to see you, Drew. Please give Rose our best. Some losses you just never get over. Your papa was a good soul, one of the best men I have ever known.

"Yes, tell her we missed her," Linda says, hugging Drew just a little tighter than she might otherwise. She couldn't help but notice the look of disappointment on his face as Michelle accepted the proposal.

Michelle quickly springs up. "Let me get the plate I made for her."

They walk through the doors and into the kitchen, and once the door swings to a close, Drew says, "I guess I have my answer. I just wish that you would have told me in private. I wouldn't have come tonight."

"Drew, I am so sorry."

Before closing the door, he turns to her. "If this is what you truly want." He pauses. "Then congratulations."

She watches him until he's almost to the Jeep. She quickly grabs her sweater and catches up to him before he can get in. "I had no idea that Alex would do this today. I was completely caught by surprise."

"I just need to go. The day started off with bad news anyway, so I shouldn't have come," Drew says calmly but firmly.

"What kind of bad news? Did the land deal fall through?"

"I received a call this morning from a Marine buddy of mine." He pauses and looks down. "Sam is dead."

Michelle gasps and raises her hand to cover her mouth. "Oh no, what happened to her?"

"Not sure, likely a heart attack or stroke. She died in her sleep on the *Carol Ann*, and knowing Sam, that's exactly how she would have wanted to go. She lived her whole life on her own terms, so she might as well go that way."

"Drew, I don't know what to say, except I am so sorry. I know how much she meant to you."

"Please don't let me bring you down. Thank you again for the invitation, and I do wish you all the happiness."

Michelle grabs his arm before he can get into the Jeep. "I know you don't understand why I can't stay."

"No, you're right, I don't. But it isn't my decision to make. You've made your final decision, and I have to accept it."

The porch light gives way to the tears slowly welling up in her eyes, and he admires how the starlight highlights her hazel eyes tonight. Since seventh grade, her eyes have always met him the same, whether he was happy, angry, or making stupid decisions. In his life, he had never met anyone outside of his grandma and mother whose eyes seemed to always say, "I love you just as you are." He had spent his whole life trying to prove he was good enough to the world, but to her, he had always been good enough. Unconditional love, likely rarer in this self-absorbed world than the rarest of grapes. He may have to live the rest of his life without her, but he felt lucky to have experienced this kind of love at least once in his life.

Michelle steps in closer. "No matter where I am, I will always hold love for you, and I pray that you will find the happiness that you deserve."

"Same here. That's all I have ever wanted for you, to be happy and loved. I was just holding out hope that I could be the man to do that for you." He glances down and then back at her. "This is supposed to be your night. Now go, be with your family, celebrate."

He reaches over and gives her a gentle kiss on the cheek, feeling the wetness of her tears on his lips.

She watches from the porch as he drives away, and that sinking wave of sadness drops from her throat to her stomach again. Long after he's gone, she sits quietly on the porch, gently swinging and hoping that she has made the right decision. At this moment, it doesn't sit well.

The door opens, and Katie and Allie step out on the porch.

"Hey, everyone is wondering where you took off to," Allie says with a concerned look.

"Everything okay?" Katie inquires.

In the dark recess of the porch, she dries her eyes and replies, "Yes, I'm fine, just overwhelmed with excitement."

"Come inside, we just poured the champagne and are getting ready to toast. My baby sister is finally getting married!" Katie says, rushing through the door.

Allie lingers. "Michelle, it's an engagement, not a marriage. You can still change your mind."

"There is nothing to change. I am marrying Alex because that is what I want to do."

As she enters the dining room, she takes her place by her soon-to-be husband and raises her glass to his. No one questions her tears, as they assume they are all tears of joy. She toasts to her future while silently grieving and reluctantly closing the door to her past.

# BOTTLE IT UP

# Chapter 33: Christmas Eve 2009

The flickering candles in the windows illuminate an intricate pattern of stained glass, each one highlighting a Bible story in the life of Jesus. Tonight, all over the world, Christians will celebrate the birth of a Savior, the one they believe brought hope to the world and eventually suffered death to give mortal men the promise of eternal life. Michelle's eyes shift to the window from the book of Luke that since childhood had been her favorite. The scripture under the image of Jesus with the children huddled around him reads, "Let the little children come to me, and do not hinder them, for the kingdom of heaven belongs to such as these." She has always been comforted as a child at the kindness portrayed in Jesus' face, and with his arms open wide, she felt she would be safe no matter what life brought her way.

On this holy night, as she sits in this space at Calvary Baptist Church, she needs to feel that reassurance more than ever. Her eyes scan down the pew, where her mom and dad looked on intently as they focus on the children's pageant in progress. Karry is dressed as an angel, Joel a wiggly shepherd, and Brett kneels at the manger with his wise man crown and small vase representing the gift of frankincense. Within the walls of this sanctuary everything seems calm and safe. It's Christmas Eve, and everything should be right with the world. But it isn't. Katie's absence is palpable and intense. It has only been two days since they all sat in this very space for her funeral, and everyone is still in a complete state of shock.

Katie had fallen ill the week following Thanksgiving. A few days later, she was in a coma due to sepsis and never regained consciousness.

Though Michelle tries to focus on the Christmas pageant, her mind is anywhere but there. She had barely been home to Germany a week before she was back on a plane to Chatham. Dr. Chamber's words reverberated over and over in her head: "We truly did everything we could; her body was too weak and infection took over. She's gone." One day Katie was alive and full of hope, and now she's just gone. Much like Benjamins's death, it was sudden and surreal. No one expected Katie to die—that is, except Katie, and somehow near the end, she had slipped this letter to Allie.

My dearest Chelle,

As I write this letter, there is no way I can even wrap my mind around the reality that when you read this, I will be dead. I would be lying if I told you that I wasn't scared. I know you have always thought my faith was unwavering, but here I admit that I am scared. After the transplant, everyone was so optimistic, but something in me said to prepare. You know I have always been the planner, so I prepared with the hope that I was once again overreacting. We have always been taught to believe in heaven, and I am holding out hope for all the beauty, rest, and, best of all, that I can get back my pre-pregnancy body! The scripture "to be absent in the body is to be in the presence of Christ" keeps coming up. I can't imagine how wondrous that will be, to be in the presence of Jesus and to see all those who have gone on before us. Yet not being here for my kids is an unbearable pain, and the teacher in me can't help but worry what growing up without a mom will do to them.

You will never know what it has meant to me for you to be here over the last few months. Selfishly I never wanted you to move away, but I also had no concept of the depths of your loss and never wanted you to feel guilty. Just know I missed you terribly. I am grateful for our time of growing closer over the last few months. It's sad in this crazy world that we truly begin to treasure moments and people when we sense the end is near. Watching you with Brett, Karry, and Joel brought me so much happiness. I want you to know that I do find comfort in the fact that they will always have an amazing aunt to confide in when they miss and need their mom. Karry will especially need you. She will need your ear during middle school drama, but please, when it comes to prom dress shopping, take Allie with you. Your fashion sense has never been that great. Also, I expect you to step in and keep Mom and Dad from turning them into spoiled brats!

After my diagnosis, I began journaling. Allie has my journals and will give them to you if you want them. As we have always been the keepers of each other's secrets, I will let you read them and decide what and when to share with the kids. Michelle, I am living proof that we don't know what the future holds. As my last piece of sisterly advice, I will tell you this. No matter the fear or struggle the choice involves, take the risk and choose the path that makes you the happiest. Then live each day to the fullest and never look back. Trust me, you will want to die with as few regrets as possible. I love you all so much, and while my physical body may be gone, my love for you all is eternal.

Until I see you again,

Katie

PS. I am still Mama and Daddy's favorite.

There it is again, that word that everyone seems to warn her about: regret. It seems impossible not to have some kind of regret in life. In fact, it seems that the only way to not experience regret is to not live in the world at all. Wouldn't to some degree you always wonder about a road not taken? Maybe the true quest is to choose the path you would regret not taking the most, and as Katie suggested, never look back.

The last notes of "Silent Night" end, and the smell of hot wax fills the sanctuary as candles are extinguished. She places her candle into the box by the door as Pastor Mark greets her. "Michelle, again I am so sorry for your loss. Katie will be missed by so many, but don't you worry, I will be looking in on your parents and the kids. Call me if you need anything."

"Thanks, Mark." Michelle gives him a hug and quickly slips out the door.

She pulls her coat tighter against the stark December air and follows the narrow path from the church to the cemetery. As she inches her way closer, the smell of fresh dirt lingers in the air, mixing with the sweet smell of evergreen wreaths that adorn many of the graves. The flowers and outpouring from the community has been a sight to behold and a true testament to what Katie meant to so many. Unfortunately, all the kind words and stories of her acts of kindness don't change the difficult fact. Her sister is dead, and she'll never see her again on this side of heaven.

The stars are shining brightly, and Michelle looks at the star-filled sky and wonders what Katie is doing tonight in heaven. Has she seen Benjamin or Grandpa yet? A tear begins to slide down her face and leaves a warm trail. She hears footsteps approaching down the gravel path and turns to find Drew trailing behind her.

"Mind if I join you, or would you prefer to be alone?"

"No, you can stay." She wraps her scarf one more time around her to stave off the wind, which is picking up and growing colder.

"Katie should have earned her angel wings by now, if nothing else just for putting up with me in this lifetime," Michelle says.

Drew smiles. "Her kind and gentle soul will be missed by so many here."

"It's not fair, Drew; it's so unfair. Not that anyone should get cancer, but she was the last person who should. Why not me? I don't have kids that need a mother."

She feels the gentle touch of Drew's hand rest in the small of her back.

"Do you think they celebrate Christmas in heaven? I mean, not like us with commercial stuff, but just marking the birth of Jesus?" A steady stream of tears flow, and Michelle just lets them fall. She has given up trying to stop the flow. Once the gate was opened, it was pointless to try to stop.

Drew wraps his arms around her, and she buries her sobs into his soft coat. He holds her tightly and thinks of all the things he could say, but none of them seem helpful. He wishes so desperately that he could take her pain away. "Michelle, you know that you and I experience God in different ways, but I do believe that she is no longer in pain and at peace."

Michelle lifts her head and gives him a pleading look. "You don't think that once we're gone, we will ever see those we love again?"

He pauses for a moment and thinks about Sam. A few times recently at sunset he has felt her presence so strongly and could have sworn that he even heard her raspy laugh echoing around him. He places the palm of his hand against her cheek. "I do believe that we will see them again, just in our own way."

Michelle reaches into her pocket and grabs a ball of tissues and begins to blot her face. They stand in the cold silence that is heavy with grief yet oddly familiar and comforting to them both.

"I will go and let you have some time to yourself. I just wanted to see you before you headed back to Germany."

She reaches for his hand, and she can feel the warmth of his glove transfer to hers, sending a calming sensation throughout her body. She grabs his other hand and turns to face him. "I'm not going back. I'm here to stay."

Her initial return to Chatham was out of obligation, not choice, but now she's choosing to stay. She had run from the debilitating pain of grief the first time after Benjamin, but this time she will stay and face it head on. Home is more than the geographical location; it is the people around you that make the difference. Her roots are here, and just as the grapevines climb and interlock, so do the lives of people in our communities. Life is indeed like making wine, and she has two choices. She can hold on to the sour grapes of loss in her life, or she can focus on making new blends with what she has left. It has taken a while, but she is finally at peace.

The air temperature shifts to a much warmer feel, and a strong breeze suddenly replaces the pungent scent of evergreens with the sweet smell of gardenias. The trees swaying in the wind draw Michelle's attention along the tree line. There she sees two shadows. Slowly, one of the shadows moves a little more into the light, and this time, unlike before, she recognizes him. Benjamin. There is no doubt: the kindness and gentleness of his eyes is still there. Michelle returns his smile and allows the warm breeze and sweet fragrance to envelope her. Benjamin turns his gaze from Michelle to the shadow near him and extends his hand. The shadow takes his hand, and as they walk away fading deeper into the woods, a familiar voice from long ago whispers softly into the wind:

*"Welcome home."*

She may have had her doubts, but not anymore. As locals had long suspected, there is indeed a heaven, and it looks a lot like Chatham. A place free of suffering, where gardenias bloom year-round and each day teeters perfectly between the edge of summer and the promise of fall.

# Interview With the Author

**Barbie Jo Settle sat down with Melissa Collins Harrell
to get the scoop on her latest novel set in the Yadkin Valley.
Here is a transcript of their conversation from her
viral podcast *Barbie Jo's World*.**

**Barbie Jo**: Melissa, hon, so good to see you back in town.

**Melissa:** It's always great to be back. Thanks for having me on today, and congratulations on your success. Sounds like you've become quite the social media influencer.

**Barbie Jo:** It's just all been a whirlwind, but I am having the time of my life. Now, let's get down to the details. What inspired you to write a book set in our little 'ole hometown?

**Melissa:** Over the last few years, I have been traveling back to the area frequently to write, and I was just amazed at the transformation. When I moved away in the early 1990s to go to college, it used to make me sad to come back and see the decline of a place where I had so many foundational memories. As I write about in the book, so many things declined as textile jobs and tobacco industries shifted. It has truly made my heart happy to see this area so vibrant and full of life again. I try to communicate that through many of the characters but especially Michelle.

**Barbie Jo:** So then, Michelle is really you?

**Melissa:** While it is true that some of my experiences and feelings are shared through her, she is very much still a fictional character. As a writer, all your characters embody a small part of yourself.

**Barbie Jo:** Well, inquiring minds want to know: Were Benjamin and Drew based on your old flames?

**Melissa:** Like I said, as a writer your own experiences do come out, but I will just let people speculate on those old flames. However, I will say that my early experiences with loss did profoundly shape me as a person, therapist, and writer.

**Barbie Jo:** Yes, hon, I remember from your book *Common Threads*, your mama and daddy died so young. Such a shame. Are Linda and Steve like your parents?

**Melissa:** Oh, definitely Steve. Even though my dad was not a firefighter, many of the sayings that he says are spot on for my dad. Linda's tenacity and desire to learn and grow mirrored my own mom.

**Barbie Jo:** And honey, tell us about Nana Lucy. She's a hoot!

**Melissa:** Nana Lucy is a combination of all my grandmothers and aunts in my life. My mother had me young at 17, and so I was blessed to have not just grandmothers and aunts but great-grandmothers and great aunts. They were all such strong forces, and so Nana Lucy is a tribute to them all. She is also who I aspire to be in my older years!

**Barbie Jo:** Did being born to a teen mom feed into your storyline with adoption?

**Melissa:** It was a combination of my personal experience as well as my experiences as a therapist over the years. I was born in 1973, on the cusp of a transitional time where women were given more support and options than to go away and give up their babies. Between the years of 1949 and 1973, millions of women were forced to give up children due to social norms. My mom shared with me as I was older that she was given the option of adoption and quietly offered an abortion. She chose to keep me, but the key word is choice. It's not what choice she made; it's that she got to choose. I know that my life could have been very different if I were just a few years older. I have also worked with so many clients who have been on both sides, looking for children they were forced to give up or looking for the parents that surrendered them. I have always had a soft spot for wanting them to make those connections.

**Barbie Jo:** Girl, I loved those therapy chapters with Drew and Dr. Dan. Those must have been easy for you to write as a therapist. Is that what real therapy is like?

**Melissa:** Therapy can seem intimidating if you have never been, but it's a lot like having a conversation. People think that we tell people what to do, but it's really our job to be a guide and help you find the answers you need. Even in fiction writing I hope to break down barriers to people reaching out for mental wellness support.

**Barbie Jo:** You tackle so many issues in this book: dementia, cancer, PTSD, addiction, grief. Why give your characters so much adversity?

**Melissa:** One thing that is not fictional in this book is the amount of struggles that we as humans face. The problems faced by each character are reflections of real life. We all struggle with something on any given day. My hope is that even through fiction, people can identify with a character and not feel alone and feel hopeful that they can overcome whatever is going on in their life.

**Barbie Jo**: So I did some research, okay, I went onto Amazon, and your previous books were a children's book and a nonfiction book, so why an adult novel?

**Melissa**: Whew, that is a question that I get asked frequently. For me, the stories come and then I write. The story may best be communicated through different genres. I have also been known to like good challenges, and this novel gave me plenty of challenges. Nonfiction is much easier for me, but I do love the challenge of keeping up with characters, their backstories, and the flow of dialogue. I also love the research part. I learned so much about North Carolina history, wine making, fishing, Germany, and so much more on this journey.

**Barbie Jo:** Speaking of characters and their backstories, what made you choose to have such a strong military background in two of your characters?

**Melissa**: There were so many facets that led to this. Even though I currently work in a job focused on military members, this book was well in the works before I started that position. I lived in Goldsboro, North Carolina for over twenty years, and Seymour Johnson Air Force Base is located there. Over half of my work in private practice became working with military families, and I absolutely loved that work. There were just so many challenges that as a civilian I would have never known about had I not had that window into their world. So many young people from rural communities, especially those who have had challenges with school or families, join the military for better opportunities. I wanted to show the benefits and risks of those choices through my characters. And a little secret that most don't know. Unlike my main character, Michelle, I actually did talk with a recruiter in high school and considered the Air Force route to become a doctor. So in some regards, I was writing out my "what if" script.

**Barbie Jo:** No offense, hon, but I had PE class with you, and I don't think either of us would have made it through basic training. Now hon, what is your fascination with cemeteries? Not sure I have ever read about romance blooming in a cemetery—well, maybe Dracula.

**Melissa:** For me cemeteries bring comfort. I see stories. Life, death, and everything in between. I love to stroll through and look at family names and dates and wonder about their lives. As a grief counselor, I find that some people are cemetery people and others are not. I tried to highlight both in the book.

**Barbie Jo:** You talk about not just your hometown but you mention quite a few places in NC; tell us about your reasons for that.

**Melissa:** I know I am biased, but I absolutely adore my home state. We have so many beautiful places to explore and such a rich history. I tried to give a shout out to the places, schools, and people that have been a part of my story and shaped me.

**Barbie Jo:** Well, it is a wonderful book, Melissa. My only complaint is I think you could have given me a few more pages. Now, if you ever want to write a huge best seller, you come interview me about my three ex-husbands. Girl, I have stories and maybe more than a few skeletons in my closet! Speaking of next book, will there be a sequel?

**Melissa:** Let's just say I am sensing some mystery vibes, and what better setting than the Yadkin Valley!

# Recipes from Dogwood Inn and Bakery

**Linda's Lasagna**

8–10 cooked lasagna noodles
1 pound of ground beef
Small onion chopped
Minced garlic
24 ounces of favorite spaghetti sauce
½ cup water
¼ teaspoon nutmeg
1 ½ cups mozzarella cheese
1 ½ cups of shredded parmesan
1 large container of cottage cheese (ricotta can be used)
1 egg
Salt
Pepper
1 tablespoon Italian seasoning

Preheat oven to 350. Spray 9 X13 baking dish

In a large skillet, sauté onion and garlic then add ground beef cooking until well done. Add spaghetti sauce, water, and nutmeg. Cover and simmer on low. Create cheese filling by mixing a container of cottage cheese, ¾ cup parmesan cheese, ¾ cup mozzarella cheese, one beaten egg, salt, pepper and Italian seasoning in a small bowl.

To assemble: Layer three noodles on bottom of the pan, spread half the cheese mixture evenly over noodles, then layer one cup of meat sauce. Repeat with another layer. Arrange remaining noodles on top adding sauce and top with the remaining cheese. Loosely cover with aluminum foil and bake for 30 minutes or until bubbly.

**Nana's Red Velvet Cake**
3 cups cake flour
1 teaspoon baking soda
¼ teaspoon baking powder
½ teaspoon salt
2 tablespoons cocoa powder
½ cup butter softened
½ cup vegetable oil
2 cups sugar
3 large eggs
1 tablespoon vanilla extract
1 teaspoon white vinegar
2 tablespoons red food coloring
1 cup buttermilk at room temp

Icing
½ stick butter softened
1 (8oz) block of cream cheese
1 teaspoon vanilla extract
1 box powdered sugar
1 teaspoon milk (more for a thinner frosting)
½ cup crushed pecans (optional)
1 cup shredded coconut(optional)

Preheat oven to 350. Grease and flour two 9-inch cake pans. Whisk the flour, salt, baking soda, baking powder, and cocoa together in bowl. Set aside. Using a mixer, beat together butter and sugar for about one minute until combined. Slowly add the oil, eggs, vanilla extract, and vinegar. Beat on high for two minutes. With the mixer on low, alternate the dry ingredients and buttermilk and then add the food coloring. Divide batter between the two cake pans and bake for 25–30 mins until the tops of the cakes spring back and a toothpick comes out clean. Cool on wire racks completely before frosting with icing.

### Sunny Italy Dressing

1 cup sugar and enough water to dissolve it
1 (15 oz) bottle of creamy Italian dressing
3 tablespoons red wine vinegar
3 tablespoons of salad delight spices

Mix all ingredients and chill well before serving.

### Meatloaf

1 ½ pounds lean ground beef
½ cup breadcrumbs
1 finely chopped onion
1 beaten egg
1 ½ teaspoon black pepper
½ can tomato paste

Sauce
1 ½ cans tomato paste
½ cup water
3 tablespoons vinegar
2 tablespoons mustard
2 teaspoon Worchester sauce
3 tablespoons brown sugar

Mix the first six ingredients in a bowl by hand. Place in a greased loaf pan. Mix all sauce ingredients together and our sauce over top of the meatloaf. Bake at 350 for 35–45 minutes

## Summer Crush Sangria
½ apple cored and diced up
½ orange sliced with rind on
3–4 tablespoons of brown sugar
¾ cup orange juice
1/3 cup brandy (can use rum)
1 bottle of your favorite dry red wine
1 cup of ice

Place apples, oranges and sugar into the bottom of a large pitcher. Muddle with a wooden spoon for about 45 seconds. Add orange juice and brandy and muddle again for about 30 seconds. Add red wine, stir, then add ice. To serve it up Chatham style, pour into a Mason jar and garnish with an orange slice!

## Revolutionary Tea Room Blueberry Scones
2 cups all-purpose flour
1/3 cup sugar
1 teaspoon baking powder
½ teaspoon salt
¼ teaspoon baking soda
8 tablespoons unsalted butter, frozen
½ cup dried blueberries
½ cup sour cream
1 large egg
1 teaspoon white sugar

Preheat the oven to 400 degrees. Line a baking tray with parchment paper. Mix flour, 1/3 cup sugar, baking powder, salt, and baking soda in a medium bowl. Grate butter into flour mixture on the large holes of a box grater. Use your fingers to work in butter until the mixture resembles coarse crumbs, then toss in dried blueberries. Whisk sour cream and egg together in a small bowl until combined. Stir sour cream mixture into flour mixture using a fork until large dough clumps form. Use your hands to shape the dough into a ball. It will seem dry but keep working at it! Place dough on a lightly floured surface and pat into a circle, about 3/4-inch thick. Sprinkle it with the remaining sugar. Use a sharp knife to cut into 8 equal triangles. Place on the prepared baking tray, about 1-inch apart and bake for around 15 minutes. Cool for 5 minutes. Serve warm or at room temperature.

Printed in the USA
CPSIA information can be obtained
at www.ICGtesting.com
CBHW031156071024
15371CB00067B/716